CASTING
CUPID

CASTING CUPID

A MAIDEN'S BAY
ROMANCE

MARY SHOTWELL

RADIANCE

RADIANCE

An Imprint of Roan & Weatherford Publishing Associates, LLC
Bentonville, Arkansas
www.roanweatherford.com

Copyright © 2023 by Mary Shotwell

Library of Congress Cataloging-in-Publication Data
Names: Shotwell, Mary, author.
Title: Casting Cupid | Maiden's Bay #1
Description: First Edition | Bentonville: Radiance, 2023.
Identifiers: LCCN: 2023946460 | ISBN: 978-1-63373-867-6 (hardcover) |
ISBN: 978-1-63373-868-3 (trade paperback) | ISBN: 978-1-63373-869-0 (eBook)
Subjects: | BISAC: FICTION/Romance/Contemporary |
FICTION/Romance/Action & Adventure | FICTION/Romance/General
LC record available at: https://lccn.loc.gov.2023946460

Radiance hardcover edition October, 2023

Cover & Interior Design by Casey W. Cowan
Editing by Staci Troilo, Lisa Lindsey & Amy Cowan

To the ceiling breakers

ACKNOWLEDGMENTS

ALTHOUGH THE PLOTS and characters are of my own creation, it takes a team to get them into a finished product. Thank you to my agent Amy Brewer for helping me redefine this series and get it in the hands of a great team.

To my publisher Roan & Weatherford, it has been a fun start to this exciting venture, and can't wait to continue with the series. Special thanks to my editors Stacy Troilo and Lisa Lindsey, and cover designer, Casey Cowan.

To my readers, it is your support that I fall back on during times when I doubt myself or get stuck. Knowing I have supportive fans who can't wait to read what's next means the world.

Finally, to Matt, Luke, Evan, and Avery, thank you for listening, making me laugh, and constantly giving me ideas whether you know it or not.

ONE

WORKING AT BEA'S Bouquets in Maiden's Bay, Washington, was not Cynthia Pruitt's dream job. It was a job—she'd give it that. It wasn't that she minded making the floral arrangements or following the meticulous instructions her boss Bea hammered into the slightest of tasks. In fact, being surrounded by some of nature's most beautiful creations brought joy to Cynthia on most days.

But today wasn't one of those days. Today was another day crews were out at sea for their last chance at a big haul before crab fishing season ended. Yet another season she had missed. One more day not on the water meant one more day away from making her dream a reality.

"Cynthia!" Bea stood at the front window, one hand on her hip, the other holding a bouquet of crimson buttercups. "The phone, please."

Cynthia snapped out of her daydreaming of crab pots and saltwater chop and answered the shop's phone. "Bea's Bouquets."

"Hello, Cynthia?"

"Hi, Gwen!" Her teenage—nearly twenty now—niece's soft voice was unmistakable. They had become close since Cynthia moved back to Maiden's Bay after college four years ago and somehow even closer by phone as it was Gwen's turn for college at University of Washington. It was probably easier for Gwen to confide in her aunt over her mother, Jackie, about her love life and happenings. Cynthia was, after all, closer to Gwen in age than she was Jackie.

"Hey Aunt Cee. I was wondering if you could help me out."

"Of course. What can I do for you?"

"I figured since January's almost over, it's probably time for me to get my act together for Valentine's Day, before it gets too crazy."

"You're right." Cynthia glanced at Bea, who by some miracle positioned more deep red buttercups one by one in the already tight window arrangement. "We're quickly approaching our busiest time of the year, so it was wise to call."

"See, they are teaching me something here in Seattle."

Cynthia smiled, the distance of the voice tearing a slight ache in her chest. She had family in town, but it wasn't family. Gwen was the connection between Cynthia and her sister Jackie, and with Gwen gone, the connection virtually vanished.

"Honey, you've always been smart." Cynthia opened the order form on the computer. "I still have your order info from last year. Are you keeping with the same or spicing it up with Nathaniel?"

"The same. I want to make it a tradition. Two years in a row should set that into motion, right? Plus it helps Nathaniel when he knows what I'm getting him. When he doesn't, he has no clue what scale of gift to get me, even though I tell him he doesn't have to get me anything."

"Isn't that sweet," Cynthia jibed. "But are you sure you want to send him flowers?"

Bea snapped her fingers, the threat of a lost sale pushing her eyebrows together in a scowl.

"I know how you feel about Valentine's Day, Aunt Cee. But it's our little thing we have, you know, starting with the single rose on my car, the corsage for Winter Formal, then the graduation bouquet bigger than the cake Mom ordered."

"I know, I know. I'll make sure only the most beautiful are in his when we send it out."

"Thank you." She paused, and Cynthia nearly filled the void before Gwen took the helm. "What about you? Go on any dates lately?"

"I think we're done here."

Gwen laughed. "Okay, okay. Say hello to Bea for me."

"Will do."

Cynthia filled in the order on the computer. Bea approached, hand on hip and mouth pouted, her silver-streaked black hair looking even tighter in its bun. Cynthia tucked loose blond strands behind her ear. Bea had a way to make even the neatest of groomers look disheveled.

"You weren't trying to talk that customer out of buying, were you?"

"First off, Gwen says hi."

"Oh! I can't wait until she's off for summer break. Maybe then I can have the right help here."

Cynthia shook her head. Bea never hesitated threatening to let her go, or gave up on an opportunity to remind her of how easily she could be replaced. Cynthia understood it for the joking it was.

"What makes you think Gwen would work here and not Postal Port? Gwen tends to be a loyal person." She had worked at Postal Port since she could legally work.

Bea shoed her comment away. "That's because Gwen is a go-getter, starting that knitting business all on her own. No doubt she upsells customers at Postal Port unlike someone else I know."

"You're right," Cynthia said. "I don't upsell customers at Postal Port."

Bea let out a short, one-syllable sound known as her laugh. Cynthia winked at her. She loved making her laugh because it took effort and was deeply rewarding, even if short-lived.

"If you must know, Gwen was placing an order for Nathaniel for Valentine's Day. I simply was steering her away from last year's flowers to maybe a noteworthy balloon or chocolates."

"What, so men can't get flowers now?"

"No, that's not what I was saying. I meant to encourage her to change things up from last year."

"Everyone can appreciate a beautiful flower. They are nature's batting lashes, her—"

"Her musical notes on the staff of life." It was one of Bea's go-to speeches.

The bell on the front door jingled, and Cynthia's shoulders dropped in relief. It was distraction enough to walk away from the conversation.

She picked up a water bottle to work on the larger plants in the back. Bea insisted on sprayer versus watering can. They need refreshment, not drowned, she'd say.

She peeked behind her, making sure Bea wasn't watching, and sneaked the headphone buds in her ears. The volume was high enough to drown out the soft music Bea had on repeat throughout the store yet low enough to hear Bea give an order.

She leaned over a pot of dianthus and felt the soil, the soft dirt not quite clumping with her pinch. She sprayed the water bottle near the soil and worked her way up the shelves. She stopped at the sound of a shout.

A figure moved behind the rack. Cynthia pulled out her headphones and pushed the flower pot to the side. A man wiped his eyes and dried his face in his flannel sleeve.

"Oh, my goodness." She hurried to the other side of the rack, nearly tripping on the corner of the metal shelf. "I didn't know anyone was there."

The man held up his hand while he dried his face. "It's okay. I—" He looked up, his deep brown eyes striking hers. "It was my fault." He had a strong, smoothly-shaven jawline and narrow nose. His dark hair was cut in a crew style, longer strands in disarray above his forehead.

Cynthia tucked her blond strands behind her burning ears. "No, the fault is mine." Her voice sounded mousier than usual, probably from the fact all her blood rushed to her head in embarrassment. "I'm the one with the bottle." She jiggled it in her hand, mimicking what her stomach was doing at the moment.

"If I had known the difference between a peace lily and petunia, I wouldn't have put my face in firing range." His playful smile drew her stare to his lips.

Cynthia opted to look at the plant rack, her feet, the ceiling. Anything other than directly at this man who made her heart race.

"Maybe you could help me decide?"

"With…?" Her brain fogged over. He might have explained himself already, but she only caught the question at the end.

"The flowers…." He pointed to the shelf, the sight of the incident in which she was forced to speak with this handsome man.

"Oh, yes. Sorry."

"Good. Do you mind putting down the weapon first?" He pointed to the spray bottle in her hand.

She stared at it to process what he meant, then chuckled. "Sorry. Yeah." She set it down on the shelf. Turn your brain back on and act like a human. She inhaled slowly through her nose, her blood pressure easing up a few nanometers of mercury.

"What is the occasion, and where will they be housed? That usually helps in deciding."

"Well, the occasion is my mother's birthday."

Is he playing her, or is he really just a nice guy?

"I'm hoping she'll keep them in her house. I didn't want to get her cut flowers. It's her sixtieth, so something that will make a bigger statement but will also last more than a week or two."

"You have to travel with these, I assume?"

He certainly wasn't anyone she had seen in Maiden's Bay before. Not that she knew everyone, but certainly she would've remembered seeing him.

He nodded, his smile tightening his cheeks. "Oakside."

"Hmm." She scanned the rack. "With all that in mind then, I'd say…." She walked to the end of the rack and slipped out the pot on the bottom shelf. "Clivia here."

The man stared perplexed at her selection of shiny leaves in a pot of dirt.

"I know they're not in bloom yet, but we're only a week or two away. You'll get lovely bright orange flowers, and the plant is very easy to maintain. The pot should be fine in the seat or trunk of your car."

He examined the pot, touching the green waxy leaves and investigating the info card spiked into the soil.

"Okay. You convinced me."

"If that's all, I can ring you up." The sooner she could end this encounter the better.

"Sure."

She walked toward the front of the store to the counter, feeling the man's stare at her back. The poor guy was just shopping for his mom, as ordinary as any other customer. Why was she so flustered? It was embarrassing what she had done, but not devastating.

Bea stared at the two of them while Cynthia worked the register. Don't come over, Bea. Don't come over. Don't—

"Did you find everything you needed today?" Bea smiled her over-zealous grin she saved for customers.

"Actually," he said, "I was wondering if you gave discounts for being sprayed in the face?"

Cynthia nearly choked.

"What is this?" Bea stared at her.

"It was an accident," Cynthia muttered.

"I'm just joking," he said. "I'm sorry." His face turned serious, and he looked right into Cynthia's eyes before returning to Bea. "She was a great help, and you have a lovely store."

Bea tipped her head in confusion. Or suspicion. "Thank you." Bea lingered, and the man looked back at Cynthia. His eyes widened, and he whispered, almost mouthed, the next words. "Is she still there?"

Cynthia smirked and gave one affirmative nod before handing him the receipt.

"Like I was saying." The man spoke up. "Let me know when those come in. I don't want to miss out." He took a pen from the counter and wrote on the back of the receipt. He slid it over to Cynthia. "You have a good day." He smiled and grabbed his potted plant, then nodded at Bea before exiting the store.

Cynthia looked at the paper. *Coffee?* it read, with a phone number beneath.

Cynthia pursed her lips and faded the smile, folding the paper in half and slipping it into her back pocket.

"What was that all about?" Bea crossed her arms over her chest.

Cynthia cleared her throat. "Nothing." She cleared the counter of soil crumbs, brushing them into her hand, then throwing them in the trash can.

"Sure didn't look like nothing."

Cynthia shook her head. "I'll be back there if you need me." She walked away from the counter, the reminder of that slip of paper in her pocket painting a smile across her face. She didn't dare turn around to show Bea.

The man had written his first name on the back. But she knew his full name from the credit card he had used. Not that she was spying or anything.

She wasn't used to men being so forward. Not that he was overtly forward. In fact he was very polite, but smooth at the same time. Usually they asked for her number. Even then, she was hesitant to text or call back, if she gave her real number in the first place.

Something about the encounter with Liam Reynolds made her think she might make an exception.

TWO

LIAM REYNOLDS HAD never been so delighted to have taken the scenic route from Seattle back to Oakside. Maiden's Bay was not a common stop, but not uncommon. It meant traveling toward shore further north than needed along Highway 101, in the portion known as the Crescent Coast. A handful of small towns dotted a stretch of coastline, each etched into the cliffside like divots in a carton of ice cream left from the rounded scoop.

He knew enough of the town to know the general layout, and that Pearl Avenue served as the main road of shops. If only he had been better prepared for the encounter at Bea's Bouquets.

His hunter green Chevy Tahoe rolled over the last of the curved hills between the shop and Oakside. Unlike Maiden's Bay, Oakside was tucked away from the shore in a leeward sloping valley. Except for a few cliff-side businesses like Oakside Processing and summer homes for the tech elite, there wasn't much visual coastline from the central part of town.

He stretched an arm low over the passenger seat as he slowed to a stop at a red light. The clivia plant's leaves had bounced and swayed with the movement of the truck along the rocky windy coast, but the pot had kept its place on the passenger seat.

Liam could enumerate the differences between Dungeness and Pacific Rock crabs, but heck if he knew indoor vegetation. The woman seemed to be knowledgeable, and something about her made him trust her. Even though she had attacked his face.

Liam smirked, recalling the young employee. Red-faced was an understatement to describe her embarrassment. That's when her eyes met his, gray with the faintest of blue. Who knew gray could sparkle?

He hadn't cared at that point what she recommended. At the register, he could only think about never seeing her again, something that hadn't settled well. Slipping his number to her was unlike him. He wasn't the guy with the slick moves. He was the boring guy in high school who stayed on the sidelines—literally, as second string, he had spent most of his time on the sidelines. Other guys had the sly tricks and sweet talk. It was partly why Sandra left three years ago.

The driver in the car behind him tapped the horn. Liam registered the green light and moved onward, heading southeast. Mom's house was a blip on the grid of established houses. Easy enough to find though, not just because he had grown up in the split-level ranch home, but it sat across from the high school playing fields.

He parked the truck in the driveway behind the silver Audi, which meant Chloe beat him. He carried the pot and knocked on the front door before opening it.

"Hello? It's Liam!"

"In the kitchen!" The smell of bacon traveled with Chloe's words.

"There he is!" Mom stood up from the oak table and kissed Liam's cheek. June Reynolds had looked at least a decade younger than her age up until her husband's death six years ago. Since then, Liam noticed the gray overtaking her thinning hair, as if it had some catching up to do.

"Happy Birthday." He placed the potted flowers on the kitchen table.

"Oh, how lovely." June examined the plant while Liam elbowed his sister in greeting.

"Chloe."

"Liam." She smiled and returned to the griddle on the stove.

"An early dinner of bacon?" he said. "Trying to give her a coronary, too?"

"It's for the cheeseburgers we're having." Chloe rolled her eyes.

"I thought those were Dad's favorite."

"They were, which is why I wanted to make them for Mom's birthday. She said the smell brings back happy memories." Chloe Reynolds stood almost eye-to-eye with Liam, and that was with the flat boots she wore with her skinny jeans and baggy sweater. Heels bumped her up to the tallest of the Reynolds children, with poor Miriam being both the youngest and shortest. Liam hadn't expected to follow in his father's height, anyway, since the Reynolds had adopted him as a toddler.

Liam ruffled Chloe's black hair nestled in a low messy bun. "Got an extra one or two for me?"

Chloe sighed. "I suppose so. If you insist on staying." She nudged him in the right shoulder.

"Ah!" He played up the hit on the old injury.

"Oh, stop it," Chloe said.

He took a seat next to Mom.

"That's okay. You have a seat. I don't need any help." Chloe smirked from the stove.

"We both know how that would turn out. It was killing you having me stand next to you just now."

She swatted her hand at him. It wasn't so much that Chloe liked order as it was wanting things done her way.

"Tell me, Liam, how was the conference?" Mom said. "You gave a talk?"

"It was fine."

"Where'd you go?" Chloe asked.

"Seattle. It wasn't so much a talk as a discussion. I was on a panel giving my expertise on the new quotas for—"

Chloe snored loudly through her nose and closed her eyes.

"I hate you."

She smiled with pleasure. "Where'd you get the leaves?" She pointed to the potted plant.

"Maiden's Bay. I'll have you know that there will be blooming flowers from this heap of leaves in a few weeks. Beautiful orange flowers." He stared at Mom. "So I was told."

"I love them even if they don't bloom." Mom patted his knee.

"Who was she?"

"Excuse me?" Liam turned in his chair to face Chloe.

Chloe held the turner and placed her hand on one hip. "Are you going to tell me you went into a flower shop and found these yourself? You don't know the first thing about flowers."

"Who said I spoke with a woman? Are you saying men can't work at flowers shops and answer questions? That's very sexist of you."

Chloe rolled her eyes. He knew it would get under her skin, considering she was finishing up law school and took pride in carefully crafting arguments.

"Well, was it a girl?" Mom nearly winked in delight.

"She was a nice... young lady, okay? And I didn't approach her."

"Ooh, she approached you, huh?" Chloe lifted her eyebrows.

"She accidently sprayed me in the face with water."

Mom laughed and covered her mouth.

"I like her already," Chloe said. "Are you going to go back? See her again?"

"I don't exactly go to Maiden's Bay much these days. I'm pretty sure I'll run out of excuses to go to the flower shop."

Chloe turned off the stove burner and moved the griddle aside before commencing her lecture. "You keep complaining about how you know everyone in Oakside and don't care to date anyone. Now you meet a woman in Maiden's Bay and refuse to ask her out?"

"I don't complain. And it was barely meeting her. It was no longer an exchange than when you pay at the window at McDonald's."

"Yes, you do complain."

"No, I don't."

"Oh, get on with it, will you?" Mom silenced them. "Are you going to do anything about it?"

"You know, at first I was a little disappointed Miriam wasn't here, but now I'm grateful I only have two nosy Reynolds harassing me."

Mom folded her arms across her chest. "Don't you forget that it's my birthday."

Liam slumped his shoulders. "Fine. I didn't plan on telling you any of this. But I gave her my number."

"Do you do that at every McDonald's window?" Chloe asked.

He grimaced. "Very funny. I wrote it on the back of the receipt and slipped it to her."

"Did you say anything?"

"Did she throw it out?" Mom asked. "Maybe she didn't even see you had written on it."

Liam stood and waved his hands in the air. "Stop, just stop. She saw me write something on the receipt, I slipped it to her, and she looked at it. Happy?"

The two women looked at each other and stewed in silence.

"She's *not* going to call," Chloe said.

"Should've asked for *her* number," Mom said.

Liam groaned. He loved his mother and sisters, but in times like these he missed his father. Barry Reynolds wouldn't have let the conversation get as far as it had. He would've stopped it at Chloe's first question. Then he would've insisted Liam join him out on the back patio at the grill, even in the February cold, to grill the burgers and have a beer. Maybe if Dad had laid off the meats and beer, he wouldn't have had the heart attack. He'd still be here. But then again, he wouldn't have been Dad.

"We'll stop teasing you." Mom gave a hard look at Chloe.

Chloe huffed. "Fine."

Liam caught the sly gleam in Mom's eyes. He knew he should tell her don't start, but it was too good an opportunity to pass up. He nodded. Do it.

"So tell me, Chloe," Mom started, "did I hear right you had a date last week?"

It was annoying, but Liam was happy he had been through the gauntlet first. The look of irritation on Chloe's face brought him enough joy to carry him easily through dinner and even dessert.

There was one thing he hadn't told them—a secret he kept private, guarding it for himself so it couldn't be tainted by Chloe or Mom.

Through the panic and flustering and then acting calm, Liam had the wherewithal to focus his eyes and read the employee's name tag.

Now the waiting for Cynthia to call him began.

THREE

CYNTHIA ENDED THE call on her cell phone. It only took the first few words of his voicemail recording to recognize the friendly voice of Liam Reynolds, and then she panicked. What was she doing calling him? What was she going to say? Hey, it's me, the one who sprayed you in the face the other day.

Luckily she had a lunch date with her friends. Surely they would talk some sense into her, calling a stranger she had just met.

She sat at her four-person table in the breakfast nook, enjoying the view of the water from the house she grew up in. Her parents had clung to the longer table and six chairs those last years through the arguing. Once Dad was gone, she didn't have to feel guilty selling the set. Mom wanted nothing to do with the material things after deciding to move to Spokane.

Cynthia downsized a lot of the furniture and belongings then, especially Dad's tool collection. It made the rooms in the house look larger and feel emptier. When she inherited the keys, the home held mixed memories, from childhood bliss to the torment of her family breaking. The inheritance finalized the severed relationship with her sister Jackie, who never quite moved on from the accident almost two decades ago. At least she had Gwen, even if only through long-distance calls.

Now the house felt hollow, a functional shelter too large for her singledom. Yet she wasn't ready to downsize that part of her life.

Her cell phone rang. Don't be Liam calling back. Who calls back when they see a random number on their phone these days?

Luckily it was Elise. "We still on for lunch?"

"I'm leaving the house now."

"Good because I only have about forty-five minutes before I have to get back to the library. I already have a table."

"I'll be there in a few minutes." Cynthia put the phone in her purse and powdered her face. She wasn't big on daily makeup, but her fashionably smart friend Josie made her feel like she needed to put at least a little effort into her presentation.

She opted for the white hooded down vest over her long-sleeved shirt and took out her ponytail, fluffing her hair out. It might blow around like crazy, but it kept her ears and neck warm. Plus the bright vest brought out the blonde highlights and gave the illusion of at least some color to her fair complexion.

She stepped out into the February air, the late morning sun as distant as the stars behind the veil of clouds. She headed west downhill into town. Like the other Crescent Coast towns, Maiden's Bay sloped downward to the sea. As if the curvature of town around the water didn't seclude enough, the tilt gave an extra kick, the land's way of brushing humans off its shoulder. In Maiden's Bay, there was no other way to go but seaward.

During her morning runs she had to be careful of slick wet spots along the road, but by mid-day anything iced over was no longer. She held her shoulders high near her ears, hands in her pockets as she easily walked the half-mile distance from the house to Pearl Avenue, the main thoroughfare of the coastal community. The town hovered around seventeen hundred residents, but sometimes it felt like twenty when everyone knew everyone else's business. That wasn't always a bad thing.

Tucked between Postal Port and Mariner's Market, Crescent Cafe was her go-to spot for lunch. Well, ever since she had the time and availability to actually cultivate friendships beyond the acquaintances she didn't keep up with from high school.

Elise waved behind the storefront window, the logo sporting a curved croissant as the *C* in its name. The shop swirled coffee and sugar cookie aromas along with cinnamon and butter. For as sweet and luscious as the fragrances of the breakfast and baked goods were, she preferred the freshly made lunch sandwiches. They had a signature turkey melt worth standing in line for. Not that it was ever that crowded.

"No Josie yet?" Cynthia pulled off her hood and unzipped her vest.

"I called her after calling you. She'll be here any minute." Elise rubbed her nose, then tucked her short black strands behind her ears. Cynthia envied such poker-straight hair, just as she envied Josie's tightly coiled tresses. Her hair was somewhere in between, deciding to require either thirty minutes of flat ironing to straighten it or thirty ounces of hair gel to scrunch it into curls.

"There she is. Hey, Josie." Elise nodded to the customer whose brunette curls had obviously been blowing in the February breeze.

Josie loosened her scarf around her face. "Hey there, ladies." If anyone knew the upside of living in a small town, it was her friend Josie. As a morning talk show host for KSMV—the only television station out of southwest Washington for forty miles either direction—and the newly appointed social media manager for the town, Josie was able to convince the most miserly of citizens to follow her lead. Along with her boyfriend Nick Campbell, the fishing captain of *Harpeth Rose*, the two were the power couple of Maiden's Bay.

They placed their orders at the counter and returned to the round table for four. Josie unmasked, slinging the thick scarf over her chair back and setting her gloves on the table.

"Still not used to the winter here?" Cynthia smiled, raising an eyebrow. Winter temps in Maiden's Bay weren't exactly low, with most highs staying above freezing. But the Pacific Ocean played its part in the dampness. Cynthia loved the thick weight of the air in winter, but could understand Josie, originally from South Carolina, taking some time to acclimate.

"I don't know if I should say it's only or already my second winter here. Either way, nope. What I have learned is that I can tolerate just about any weather with the right equipment."

"That is very true," Elise said.

"It'll be nice when we have the fireplace in the new house. I told Nick that's where I'll be for three months."

A waiter brought over Cynthia's tea and the two coffees. They all warmed up their hands over the hot mugs.

"How's the build going?" Cynthia asked.

Josie closed her eyes and shook her head. They were supposed to move into the modest two-story house last fall, but construction was delayed. It had to do with the record amount of rainfall last year and the fact their property lay along one of the steeper lots on the north edge of town.

Either Josie favored the topic of conversation or dreaded it, depending on the day.

"Just remember how great the view is going to be from that living room," Cynthia said.

"We don't have to talk about it." Elise winced as she eyed Cynthia.

"Good." Josie sipped her coffee and shook off the negativity. "I wanted to talk about Valentine's Day anyway."

Ugh. Cynthia would take talk over the unfinished house any day.

"Nothing to report here," Elise said.

"I wondered if you were going to need our services again this year," Cynthia said. At least the holiday was good for business, which made for a happy boss in Bea. "Will you be matchmaking again?" Josie's Corner had a Valentine's special last year, helping to bring a couple together. Bea—after Cynthia's convincing—donated flowers to the lovely couple.

"Yes." Josie shifted in her chair, sitting up taller. "I'm pairing up two people for a getaway."

"Ooh, some place tropical or something?" Elise said. "I may find a plus one if it involves a tropical destination."

"No." Josie smirked. "Actually, here to Maiden's Bay."

Elise gave a thumbs down, and Cynthia nodded in agreement.

"I want this year to be different. I'm not looking for the same old romantic backstory of couples who've been together for a while. I want the prize to be the time together—maybe it's a blind date, or perhaps a trip that brings friends to the next level. Something different and exciting."

"Whoever's picked, are you sure they'd want to be whisked away to the romance capital of Maiden's Bay?" Cynthia hardly got it out without giggling. Admittedly, it was cute to follow Josie and Nick's journey together. But in terms of dating in Maiden's Bay, Cynthia basically had written it off. At least, until recently. Liam wasn't even in Maiden's Bay anyway. It was all foolish.

"I know you're a Negative Nelly with Valentine's Day," Josie said.

"I know, I know. I don't mean to be negative. At least not outwardly. But the flowers, and the chocolate, and then pushing two people together with high expectations doesn't make anyone fall in love."

"I think you'd feel differently if you were dating someone," Elise said.

Cynthia gave Elise big eyes. *I knew I shouldn't have told you about him.*

The waiter arrived with their food. The hot turkey melt in front of Cynthia made it more imperative to end the uncomfortable conversation. She sneaked a fry as Josie and Elise received their plates.

"Elise... do you know something I don't?" Josie said.

Cynthia shook her head, pursing her lips together. Don't say it.

"Just tell her! She's going to find out eventually."

"Only because you'll blab about it," Cynthia said.

"You knew what you were doing when you told me." Elise addressed Josie. "She met a guy at work—a customer. He gave her his number." Elise swayed her shoulders up and down like a schoolgirl chiming, You can't catch me.

"A guy from Oakside that I know absolutely nothing about. Except for the fact he has a mother."

"One that he remembered on her birthday," Elise said. "That means something."

He did seem genuinely kind, not to mention his good looks, in that initial encounter. Is it possible to gauge a person's nature in five minutes?

Cynthia waved off the thought of him. "It would never work out."

Josie perked up. "Because of the distance?"

"That and the fact that I'm going to try out for greenhorn on

Nick's crew." At the age of twenty-five, it was well beyond time she made steps toward her dream of running her own boat. Sure, she had years of boating experience under her belt—she had Dad to thank for that. But she couldn't captain a crew without ever having been part of a crew, and being a greenhorn on *Harpeth Rose*—the largest, most successful crabbing vessel to come out of Maiden's Bay—was her foot on the ladder. The very bottom rung. "If that goes as planned, dating isn't exactly an option."

"There are so many things wrong with what you just said." Josie folded her arms over her chest.

"Here we go." Cynthia braced for impact.

"For one, Oakside is *not* that far away. Two, you know I can talk to Nick about the position. I'm sure he'd meet with you to discuss it."

Perhaps addressing the second would push conversation away from the first point. "I know that, but I don't want any favors. I want to earn my place like everyone else. I actually think it'll be good for me to try out next week."

"Have you told Jackie?" Elise furled her eyebrows.

"No. We're not exactly on speaking terms right now."

"She's your sister, Cynthia. I honestly don't get what the beef is between you two." Josie bit into her sandwich. "More importantly, did you tell Bea yet?"

"No." The turkey melt suddenly lost its luster. "I'm not exactly looking forward to it."

"I can imagine." Josie sipped her coffee and put her hand up, a thought ready to spill out. "Third—"

"There are still more in your list of problems with what I said?"

"Yes. Third, who says you can't date once you're part of a crew? Hello, you're looking at the girlfriend of that crew's captain."

To be honest, Cynthia wanted the position so badly that she was willing to sacrifice a social life to dedicate her time and effort to the crew. But she couldn't argue Josie's point.

"Tell you what." Josie dabbed the napkin on the corner of her mouth. "We can talk about the ins and outs of fishing life later."

Cynthia relaxed, happy to oblige. Her stomach grumbled. She was once again feeling optimistic about the signature lunch and took a bite.

Josie leaned in, eyebrows raised. "Now tell me all about this guy from Oakside."

FOUR

Friday, January 26

FROM THE BACK windows of Oakside Processing, the darkening clouds over the horizon muddled the delineation between sky and Pacific Ocean. Liam Reynolds stood on the second-story platform and rubbed his right shoulder, the eternal ache in the joint since his accident three years ago alerting him to the oncoming rain.

He had never believed in such rubbish before the accident. When Liam played on the high school football team, Billy Jorgenson had torn his ACL junior year during a bad tackle against Bishop, and swore up and down his knee hurt before incoming storms.

Perhaps Liam still didn't fully believe in it now. But he was certain of two things—it was going to rain, and Nick Campbell had better arrive soon or else it was going to be a hell of a wet time docking and unloading.

Just as the anxiety mounted, the dot in the distance grew enough to catch its distinctive silhouette. The long arm of the crab pot crane. The square navigation bridge. All atop the ninety-seven-foot, rusted, clunky vessel that was *Harpeth Rose.* As it neared, the white foam of its wake on either side splashed with the wind.

"We've got incoming," he shouted below, the sprawling first floor housing thirty or so employees for the day shift. Thirty-two to be exact. He knew, not only because his job as manager required it, but because he made sure to have eight extra on-hand for Nick's expected return.

Throughout the limited weeks of Dungeness crab fishing, depending on where the catch led *Harpeth Rose,* Nick unloaded either directly at Oakside or at Maiden's Bay with Liam sending a truck for pick-up. He knew Nick well enough though to know this last haul would be here.

The employees divided into their stations, with a third stepping outside for docking and unloading, a third at the sorting tables and packaging stations, and the rest ready to haul off the product to vendors and restaurants.

It took thirty minutes for *Harpeth Rose* to arrive and safely dock. Liam put on a yellow rain slicker, just in case his shoulder forecasted the time of rain better than the weather anchor, and walked out the back of the building onto the dock.

Nick Campbell and his younger brother Ben were chatting with an employee filling out the docking paperwork.

"Nothing like staying out until the very last day." Liam interrupted and shook Nick's rough hand. Nick gave him a brief hug and pat on the back. Although Nick had a few more inches in height, Liam had the breadth in muscle. His football days were long in the past, but as Mom always said, he was built to play football. His muscular build and broad shoulders, injured or not, made him not mind the five-foot-ten stature.

"They kept coming up hot the past few days, so there was no reason to stop."

"Never mind the impending dark wall of clouds." Ben shook his head, rolling his eyes. He wore his uniform, a long-sleeved shirt and vest with black sweatpants tucked into brown boots. It was hard to believe Ben stayed dry in sweatpants, but it drove Nick nuts, which may have been worth it to Ben. Plus he had a full beard, a staple to help with warmth on the water.

"The season keeps shortening, but we brought back more this season than the last three," Nick said. "It was worth risking the weather."

"Easy for you to say," Ben said. "Not like you have a kid relying on you to, you know, stay alive."

"Oh, it's only going to rain. Nothing we haven't handled before."

"Will you two ever change?" Liam chuckled. Nick, the oldest of the three Campbell men, inherited *Harpeth Rose* after their father died.

When their mother Carol retired as mayor and remarried, she handed down Campy's Bait and Bar to them as well, with the youngest sibling Joel managing. With the brothers' constant bickering, it was amazing either entity kept afloat. "Come on inside, I'll fix you some coffee."

Nick and Ben exchanged glances and nodded.

"I got it covered," Ben said.

Nick followed Liam into the building. As far as factories went, Oakside Processing not only had one of the best views from where it sat along the coast a mile and a half southwest of the town of Oakside, but it was aesthetically pleasing. The new design followed that of an innovative office building, with reflective glass windows and sleek black lines rather than the original rectangular blaring white building that had sat within the town's eyesight. The architectural design made it easier to gain the town's and county's approval for the new build, along with its somewhat isolated location and expanded job opportunities.

Once inside, there was no question what the building served as—a processing plant for fish and crab. The smell permeated from the large main floor into the front office space and entranceway. It wasn't necessarily bad since it processed the freshest fish and crab anyone could encounter outside of being on the boat catching it. But it was persistent.

Liam adored the smell. It reminded him of being out on Sea Prairie, working his way up from greenhorn to deckhand. Those were some of the hardest, scariest, and best times of his life, even if they were short-lived. Not all dreams were meant to last forever.

"Here you go." He gave Nick a mug of hot coffee in his office upstairs overlooking the main floor. "Glad you had a good harvest this season."

"Me, too," Nick said. "Especially with it being Ronald's last."

"Ronny's out?" Liam sat in his chair behind the desk.

"I take it you don't watch Josie's Corner? Or follow her posts on the Maiden's Bay Facebook page?"

"You mean to tell me your girlfriend talks about the state of your fishing crew on her show?"

"Not usually as a topic of importance, no. But she worries about me going out more these days, and losing Ronny doesn't help. She's talked about how she feels on her show."

"That doesn't bother you?"

"Not when her viewers are on my side." Nick grinned.

"Put another name on your side," Liam said. "I don't blame Ronny for retiring. He's had a good long run. One of the hardest workers I know. You got a replacement?" Losing someone that high up in the crew was tough. Bringing someone from the outside could jeopardize the entire dynamic.

"I'm bumping up."

"Wise move."

"I figured everyone has been in their position for… coming on four years at the shortest? They have all mastered their current positions and know what to expect in a step up. They've earned the promotion."

"I hear ya. It's tough work, and four years as a team is a great achievement."

"Yep." Nick sighed, taking off his tattered purple Washington Huskies cap and rustling his hair. "Bumping up means I'm going to need a greenhorn. We've been getting by without one up until now. In fact, the men didn't care to split the take with a greenhorn and were happy covering duties. But with Ronny out, we can't keep it up."

"That's a lot of menial work for the rest to pick up in addition to their own duties."

"Agreed." Nick eyed him, mouth curling into a grin. "We could use someone with knowledge and respect for the position."

Liam cocked his head to the side. Surely he didn't mean him? "If you're trying to get me on board, you know that's not a possibility." He patted his shoulder. Outside of Sea Prairie crew and those who remember reading about the accident, no one else knew the extent of Liam's injury. It wasn't something he shared in passing conversation, or deep conversation, not that he had many of those lately. But Nick knew Liam's limitations. Liam could never repay Nick for how he turned his life around for the better. "You helped me get here, remember?"

"I helped you get an entry-level position. You worked up to management on your own." He folded his arms as if he had won an argument.

"I'll take the praise." Liam lightened. "Still, this is the closest I can get to the water without working on a boat." It took him over a year to come to terms with that reality. If coming to terms was what he could call it. Every now and then his body ached for the water more than it ached from the injury.

Nick leaned back. "I understand that. But I could use your help."

"How so?"

"I have my eye on someone, but have reservations about choosing without properly vetting."

"Of course."

"So, I'm holding a sort of, well…. Let's call it a 'casting call,' if you will, for the position. I really want to see what this person is made of, but I'm giving a few others a shot as well. Keeping the options open. That's why Josie's been talking about the crew on her show. She helped spread the word in the community and beyond, and I now have five contenders. I could use you to help me provide some competition to the applicants—motivate them to really do their best. Plus I'd value your input. You know what it takes."

"Provide competition? As in, you want me to be a fake competitor for your tryouts for greenhorn?" Out loud it sounded hilarious. On the other hand, perhaps it was genius on Nick's part. It took more than desire to work well on a fishing vessel. It took heart, dedication, skill, and the right fit with the rest of the crew. Liam did have the expertise.

"It's just over a week away. I'd put you up with the other applicants at Constance's Inn in Maiden's Bay for the week. Think of it as a sort of vacation."

"A week away? I don't know."

"Come on. Crab season is over. Even with your routine arrivals next week, I'm sure you could find someone to cover. You're not the only manager."

"I know, but… can I think it over?"

"Sure. I'll just need to know soon since we're setting up rooms with Constance."

"I'll let you know in a day or two."

"Great." Nick stood. "I'd better get on down there. There's no knowing what's happening with Ben in charge."

"I don't know. I think he's been a bit more responsible since becoming a dad."

"Maybe so. Just don't tell him that."

Liam held the door for Nick as they walked out of the office onto the platform. Nick walked down the metal stairs while Liam looked out onto the floor below. Each station bustled with life, the fresh crab forming speckled red queues at the sorting tables.

Nick was right that next week would be slower without the seasonal influx from crab fishing. But playing the part of a want-to-be greenhorn? Deceiving people didn't sit well. It wasn't exactly like it would be a vacation either if he had to participate in any of the tasks. Who knew if he could realistically fool anyone with his shoulder's limited ability. He hadn't even tried to do that work in over two years. The last time he did—urging Stan Boris to give him a shot on a short salmon run two years ago—he left defeated and deflated. Unfortunately, word of an unfit crewman within the industry traveled as readily as the sea breeze.

But Nick was his friend. A trusted friend. One who came to his aide when he needed a friend the most. He wouldn't have had this job if it weren't for Nick. What harm could it do to help him out, especially when it involved making sure the right crew member was chosen to be on Nic's boat?

Besides, being in the quaint seaside town of Maiden's Bay for a week couldn't hurt.

Especially since he'd be a whole lot closer to Cynthia.

FIVE

Sunday, February 7

"IT'S THE BUSIEST time all year!" Bea flung her hands in the air. "How can you leave me right before Valentine's Day?"

"Between Darrell and Joanna, my hours are covered, and you should be fine. It's only one week, and there's no guarantee I'll be selected."

Bea worked in silence, the ferocity of her cutting increasing with each stem.

"I'm sorry, but it's my dream." Cynthia had held off telling Bea for this very reason. Most people found it hard to understand why anyone would want to spend their working hours at sea on a fishing vessel. Ever since stepping onto Dad's boat for the first time, she knew. It was in her bones that she belonged out there.

Perhaps waiting until the very day of leaving was not the best choice. But if she told Bea sooner, she would've heard the pushback every day she set foot in the store. The woman was a fierce, tough boss who didn't accept anything less than perfection. Bea attributed it to her Chehalis ancestry. Whether that part of her bloodline or not, Cynthia couldn't deny it was in Bea's genes, and she simply couldn't respect her more for her work ethic. If anyone had prepared her for working with a crew of men on a hundred-foot fishing vessel in some of the worst seas, it was Bea.

"You've told me you wanted to run your own business since you were a little girl, and here you are. You pursued that dream. I want to work my way up and eventually be a captain of my own boat."

"Impossible." Bea shook her head.

Cynthia greatly respected Bea, who overcame seemingly countless obstacles to get to where she was today. However, even Cynthia's tolerance for naysaying had its limits.

"Are you going to tell me I can't because I'm a woman?" It was the usual go-to for the doubters in her life, Jackie being one of them. Although Jackie did have other reasons for objecting. But Cynthia only cared about the opinions of actual crew members—those who knew what was required to succeed. No one else's mattered. If she hadn't grown up reading about women like Linda Greenlaw, the first female captain in sword-fishing on the East Coast, she probably would've thought it impossible, too.

"No, I'd never say you couldn't do something because of your womanhood. Chehalis women held roles just as important as men. Some of the best leaders were women, and I have no desire to destroy your dream based on silliness."

"Okay, good, because I'm not sure how I would've taken that coming from you."

Bea nodded with a humph, seemingly satisfied to have made her statement. "I say it's impossible because you're so old."

Cynthia gasped, and Bea broke a smile. "You're just messing with me, now." Cynthia chuckled. Although Bea was upset, she was not *that* upset.

"It's never too late to pursue your dream." It came out sounding robotic, a parent's scripted line fed to a child. But it couldn't be true for every dream, hers included. Not like someone could dream of being an NFL quarterback and start working for it at fifty years old. Some dreams had doors that shut without opening windows.

"You pursue," Bea said. "You'll always have a place here."

"Thank you, Bea. It means a lot."

"Unless I close because I can't fulfill orders for Valentine's Day."

"I will miss you." Cynthia held her hand out for a shake, and Bea shooed it away in offense.

"Come here." Bea hugged her loosely, but Cynthia appreciated the meaning.

"Remember, now—it's only for a week. For now, at least. I'll still be in town."

"Go, go. Don't draw this out." Bea held the front door open, and Cynthia stepped out onto the sidewalk of Pearl Avenue, rolling her suitcase. It was strange to pack for a trip to her hometown. The family house would be blocks away up the hill. Still, it felt like leaving the familiar behind for something different.

The last three days of rain were long and plentiful, so the current—albeit partial—sunshine did not go unappreciated. She headed north along the main avenue through town. Traffic was lighter than usual for a Monday, which didn't mean much when a traffic jam consisted of a line of five or six cars stopped on red at the main intersection. The break in the rain left the possibility for locals to tack on an extra day to the weekend or take a day trip.

She crossed Pearl onto Ocean Street—O Street as the locals called it. The avenues, roughly running north-south, followed the curvature of the shoreline, while the streets jutted out of the semicircular west coast to the hilltop like spokes of a wheel. Whether by chance or on purpose, street names ran alphabetical, from H Street—Hawkes—to P, otherwise known as Pearl, that formed the main road through downtown. Pearl was the only avenue on the curved grid that acted as both an avenue and a street, arcing travelers through downtown, then branching farther northward to Highway 101.

Cynthia began the slight ascent on O Street to Constance's Inn. She had been by the tall building just as much as any in downtown Maiden's Bay. She often visited Elise at the library across the street, and occasionally visited Dad's grave at the cemetery up the hill. She even worked with Constance when Josie had convinced her to update parts of the inn during her ongoing Revitalize Maiden's Bay campaign. Fresh flowers were apparently one of the changes, and it stuck because she or her coworkers prepared them every two weeks, yet she never herself stepped inside.

The inn's blue-gray exterior matched the ocean on an overcast day like today. The inside could not have been more different than out, the floral wallpaper smattering the room in yellow. Mini lampshades in the shape of kegs hung on the central chandelier. To the right sat a worn dark leather couch and a magazine rack, and directly ahead on a wooden plank held by an upright anchor, between two armchairs, were the bi-weekly flowers she helped prepare.

No matter the shock of color, the entranceway was tidy and clean. The neutral beige carpet was perhaps a recent update judging by its plushness.

"Why, hello. Cynthia, right?"

"Yes." Cynthia set down her luggage and approached the counter. "We met a few times at Bea's. I wasn't sure if you'd remember me."

"Of course I remember. I thought, what a delightful young woman. Such dainty yet sturdy hands."

Cynthia blushed. "I see you've incorporated the flowers nicely."

"Oh, thank you. I also have them on the tables in the breakfast room back there. Breakfast is six AM to nine AM, since I brought it up."

Cynthia smiled. Constance was one of those people who had gray-streaked white hair and wrinkles galore, yet didn't seem to add a wrinkle or white strand beyond that. As if at some point in her life she woke up like that and stayed that way for twenty years.

"If I can have you sign in here." She opened a book headlined with today's date, and Cynthia signed her name.

"Don't worry, I have electronic records. I just like the old-fashioned record-keeping ways, too. Doesn't hurt to do both. My accountant loves me, let me tell you."

Constance looked over the remaining room keys hanging behind her. "Let's see, you're part of Nick Campbell's group." She grabbed a key. "Your group is split between the second and third floors. How about the second floor? There's a shared bathroom at the end of the hallway. The good news is you get to have your own room with two twins. Room 2."

Cynthia accepted the key and hesitated. "Do any of the others in the group get their own room?"

"Oh, no. The rest are men. They're sharing, one double and one triple in a room. In fact, my other rooms are completely booked, and I had to turn a nice couple down this week." She stopped and covered her mouth. "I don't mean that in any negative way. The room is fully paid for, so it's no loss on my part. I feel a little guilty when I have to tell a potential customer no."

"I understand." Cynthia didn't like telling customers no either, but not so much because she wanted them to walk out of Bea's happy. No, she didn't like it because they usually complained to Bea for being out of stock or not foreseeing the demand on rare, out-of-season flora.

"I'm wondering if...."

"What is it, dear?"

Cynthia had thought such a situation might occur. Women assimilated into crews more and more, but the overall likelihood another woman was trying out was still drastically low. "You know, if I'm going to be on a fishing boat for days, sometimes weeks at a time, I'll be sharing sleeping quarters. I might as well start now."

Constance let out a note with her surprised expression. "You want to pair up with one of the others?"

"Sure. They can decide, I guess, who gets what room."

"I'm only waiting on one to arrive yet."

"Perfect. Send him to Room 2."

"Are you sure?"

Considering Constance clung to old ways, perhaps she was uncomfortable pairing opposite sex strangers to a room. "As long as you're okay with it."

Constance pursed her lips. "When you run an establishment like this for decades, you see everything. You know what I say? Be who you are."

"That's what you say, huh?"

"Mmhmm. That, and never pass up free food. Both things will bring you joy." She nodded in satisfaction with her life lesson. "As long as you are comfortable and appreciate this place in all its dilapidated quirky charm, it's my pleasure to accommodate you."

"Thank you. I like it here already." Cynthia rolled her suitcase to the staircase and walked up the steps, the plush carpet soft under her shoes.

Room 2 was near the stairwell, the shared bathroom at the opposite end of the hallway. The lack of bathroom should have left space for the bedroom to sprawl out, but the twin beds stood no further than two feet apart. Seashells dotted the duvets like identification posters at the tourist shop. The walls were painted seafoam green with deep mahogany trim at the baseboards and around the two west-facing windows. Unfortunately the second floor wasn't high enough to have a view of the ocean, but rather the wall of the apartment building next door.

It didn't matter the accommodations. This was temporary, and the goal was to secure a spot on *Harpeth Rose*, whose quarters would probably make this room look like paradise.

Cynthia pulled the thin curtains closed over the windows and checked her watch. All candidates were to meet at five PM at the dock outside Campy's Bait and Bar in less than an hour. Whoever her roommate was, it looked like he was going to be late. She didn't know Nick Campbell extremely well, but enough to know he did not like late.

No matter. If the competition wanted to be late, shame on them.

The fewer the obstacles in the way of her dreams, the better.

SIX

NICK CAMPBELL DID *not* like tardiness. Which was why Liam Reynolds left Oakside, Washington with an extra hour to reach Maiden's Bay.

He drove his decade-old Chevy Tahoe north on Highway 101. He had taken care of it enough so it didn't look that old, and it did the job well enough. At least he didn't have a plant on the front seat to mind over.

It was hard to imagine any road could be more beautiful. Weaving along the coast, at moments it felt like the SUV would disappear off the rocky crags, just as the next bend revealed a sandy beach. There were pockets of towns—not even towns, more like niche communities—nestled within the curves of coastline.

Not many stops existed for gas or eating, the latter of which Liam regretfully did not plan for. His stomach rumbled as he checked out the time. Even though he left early, he worried whether he'd have time to check in at the inn before the meet-up at the dock.

After Nick's visit, Liam had looked over his calendar. Outside of a long weekend here and there, the last time he had gone on vacation was over three years ago. Back when he was dating Sandra. She loved to travel and spring spontaneous getaways on him. It was partly why he had fallen for her. But eventually he saw she needed that spontaneity all the time. She couldn't settle down in one place. She couldn't just be with him, in a room, enjoying the mundane aspects of life.

Static intermittently played into the song on the radio, shaking

Sandra out of his mind like erasing an Etch-A-Sketch. The station broadcast from thirty miles south of Oakside muddled in this area. He had driven the highway enough to know that meant he was halfway to Maiden's Bay.

He had been through Maiden's Bay a number of times, but only ever briefly—an hour or so to eat at a café or stretch his legs at the sandy postage stamp of a beach at the park on the north side. Nick had been at him to visit and meet his girlfriend Josie over dinner, but managing the plant kept Liam busy enough. Making the trip to see someone else's girlfriend wasn't at the top of his agenda.

Nick was a good friend, though. And when Nick Campbell asked for help, there was no denying it. Liam kept convincing himself he did this for Nick, but in all honesty, his last visit to Maiden's Bay tipped the decision in the northward direction.

Which was silly, because he had only met Cynthia once. There was something about her, a kindness in her smile, a softness in her eyes.

That was two weeks ago, and she hadn't called. Did he really expect her to call? He probably scared her, for goodness' sake.

One day his cell rang. It was a Maiden's Bay area number, with no voicemail left. He wanted to call back, but worried maybe it was her, and she had hung up because she didn't feel comfortable about it and he didn't want to push it. Again, not the slick move guy.

The Tahoe climbed the final hill before the town limits. The glass top of the lighthouse pierced the horizon. At the crest, the full black-banned white siren stood proud over the seaside town, flanking it to the north, while bluffs secured its southern border, as if the town claimed a slice of the ocean for itself.

Liam descended into town, the highway curving him away from shore. He exited and weaved his way down the leaning ramp of the bay's land to the flatter streets of downtown. Pearl Avenue was about all he knew of the town. Campy's Bait and Bar served as downtown central, right at the dock in the middle of the bay's coastline. Bea's Bouquets and the café were south of Campy's, and the park beach north. As much as it was a central hub of Maiden's Bay, Liam had never been inside Campy's Bait and Bar. Yet another thing Nick pestered him about.

As he passed Bea's, he scanned the windows, looking for signs of anyone inside. The front door swung open, an employee holding the door for a customer. His heart ticked, then dropped. Tall with long dark hair and bangs. Not Cynthia.

He turned off Pearl Avenue onto Ocean Street. A beautiful, ornate Victorian house appeared to his right up ahead, a lovely property for a bed and breakfast. He checked the map app on his phone, confirming his destination laid not to his right but his left. He turned into the alleyway parking between two nondescript buildings with about forty-five minutes to spare.

He slung his duffel bag over his left shoulder. After the accident, he resigned to using his left arm more, and by now didn't think twice.

Although only sixty five miles or so north of Oakside, the town felt cooler and damper. The ocean was much more accessible, too, providing a low din of crashing waves beneath the light clatter of the charming downtown.

The sign above the door read, "Maiden's Slumber Inn," with a woman figure staring out to sea, the lighthouse a beacon in the gray sky. He walked through the entrance to the front desk and set down his bag. Two guests stood in the narrow hallway ahead past the lobby, hovering around a coffee pot. The kitschy chandelier and framed maps on the wall—some the major fishing and crabbing grounds off Washington, others seemingly random areas—gave the lobby a touristy seafood restaurant vibe.

He rang the bell on the desk, and an elderly lady appeared from an office room.

"Is this Constance's?"

"Sure is. I know the sign says otherwise. I didn't want to change the name officially, since it's a historic landmark and all." She shrugged. "I'm Constance. Sorry I didn't hear the door. Hearing isn't what it used to be, but welcome."

"Hi." He smiled, matching her warm greeting. Her light skin folded and creased as much as the Pacific coastline he had driven. He suspected she had many stories locked away beneath the white hair, waiting for the right time to be shared. "I'm here with the Nick Campbell group."

"Oh, yes. Good. You're the last to arrive." She opened her eyes wider. "No offense by that."

He chuckled. "None taken." He took the wallet out from the back pocket of his jeans and showed his ID. "I drove in from Oakside. Not sure how many others travelled further."

"Not much." She looked up quickly. "That is, I don't suppose." She pointed to a page on an open ledger. "If you can sign here."

"Sure."

"Breakfast is in the back, six to nine."

She returned his ID. "You'll be on the second floor. The shared bathroom is at the other end of the hall." She handed him the key. "Room 2, with another of the group. I hope that's okay."

"Yeah. Nick informed me we'd share rooms."

"Good, because I had it differently before changing it. She insisted."

"She?"

Constance smirked and nodded. "Is there a problem?"

He hadn't really pictured a woman participant. Why wouldn't there be? There were plenty of women working on fishing vessels nowadays. Okay, not plenty, but definitely more than a decade or two ago. Certainly way more than in his father's time. How embarrassing to have reacted so stupefied by the possibility. "No problem. In fact, good for her. If she's fine rooming with me, I'm fine rooming with her."

"All right then. Enjoy your stay, and let me know if you need anything else."

He left the desk with a nod and carried his bag up the stairway, a narrow set of steps with fresh beige carpeting, the new smell faintly present. He knocked on the door of Room 2 and readied the key, but it swung open in front of him.

He stood, mouth open, words—heck, air—not coming out. How was he to breathe when his eyes met the sparkling grays of the very woman he met two weeks ago in the flower shop?

SEVEN

"IT'S YOU."

"It's me." Cynthia was as shocked as the man looked, standing at the door to Room 2. He held a stuffed duffel bag and wore work boots, jeans, and a blue flannel under a navy Columbia jacket. Crew cut. Brown eyes. The eyes and face she had accidentally sprayed with water at the store two weeks ago. The Oakside Guy.

Liam.

"You're… here."

"Yep, I'm here." Cynthia mirrored the man, frozen in the doorway. Did he track her down? It was possible he had gone to Bea's and asked about her, but Bea wouldn't divulge her whereabouts to a stranger.

"As much fun as this is, I have somewhere to be." Harsh maybe, but honest. What was she to say? *Why are you here? Should I call the cops? Did I nearly call a stalker the other day?* Still, she wished she had a way to check how she looked.

He rubbed the back of his neck. "Are you, uh, here for the greenhorn position?"

He knew about the tryouts? "Yes."

"Me, too. I guess we're roommates." The words flowed out slowly like syrup.

"What?"

He jiggled the key in the air and nodded toward the room. "The tryouts for Nick?"

"You're also trying out?" This wasn't real. She had fallen asleep waiting for the meetup. That was it. Just a silly dream. Except digging her nails into the palm of her hand wasn't waking her up.

"Yes." His body relaxed with a sigh. "May I?" He stepped inside, brushing past her, his scent woodsy and fresh. He scanned the room.

She'd be rooming with someone. The arrangement was determined thirty minutes ago, and long suspected beforehand. Why was it so hard to wrap her head around the fact that he was her roommate?

"I see you've claimed the bed by the windows."

"First come, first serve I suppose." Her shock manifested into quips, which she had no control over. "Unless there's some reason you need to be by the window?"

"No. You keep it. I'll be fine here." He set his bag on the bed nearest the door and took off his jacket. It would've been odd—not as odd as the reality he stood here right now in this room—if he needed the window. Seemed like it wouldn't make sense to want to work on a ship. Fat chance natural light reached the bunks, or even the galley at that.

"I have to admit." He sat at the edge of the bed. "I'm surprised to see you."

Good. That meant no stalking, and this was all just a weird, once-in-a-lifetime coincidence.

The surprise was definitely mutual. Was his surprise specific to her, or generally speaking because she was a woman? "I can promise you, this"—she waved her hands in the air in his general direction—"is not something I predicted."

He nodded in what seemed like a wave of relief.

"With that said, is it outlandish to believe I'd want to be a greenhorn?"

"No, I just—you work at the flower shop. I didn't know you were into fishing."

She folded her arms. "It's Maiden's Bay. How can anyone *not* be into fishing?" Her sincerity only slightly outweighed her sarcasm. For as much as it was the town's backbone, the desire didn't apply to everyone. All anyone had to do was ask Jackie.

"Fair enough." He smiled and ran his hand through his crew cut, the deep brown locks on top loose but cleanly shaped.

Her fingertips pressed on her skin, the phantom sensation of running her fingers through his hair too palpable. She whipped herself out of the stare, nearly gasping at her silly behavior.

"You know, I can room somewhere else if that would be more comfortable for you."

Damn it, he caught her staring, hadn't he? She probably just weirded him out by her stare, wondering if he got the short straw in roommates.

Yes, clearly it would *be more comfortable for me.* But she couldn't say it aloud. She didn't want to be that person. The picky one complaining about her roommate and making everyone's lives more difficult in order to be accommodated. If particular now, how would she be perceived in tryouts?

Suck it up, Cynthia.

"I've already gone over this with Constance. But I have a feeling there will be a lot of sticking up for myself and all of womankind this week. If I'm going to be part of a crew, I should act the part. I know I'll be in tight quarters on that vessel. If I can't get along with you, or whoever else is partaking in this week's activities, then I may as well go back to arranging flowers." The words served herself as much as they did Liam.

"Not to diminish what talent you may have as a crew member, but you are pretty good with a spray bottle." He bit his lip, and soft wrinkles crinkled around his eyes.

Okay, so he managed to make her smile. He had a talent for it.

"It seems like we keep getting off on the wrong foot." He stood and stretched out his hand. "I'm Liam Reynolds."

Cynthia shook his hand. "I know. I mean, I saw on the receipt. I'm Cynthia Pruitt."

"Pleasure to meet you officially."

"Same." Pleasure wasn't the appropriate word. Awkward? Untimely?

"So you did read it. The receipt?"

She nodded, not wanting to give him the satisfaction of words spoken, while hoping he hadn't noticed a random call from her area code.

"Can I get something out of the way?" He rubbed his chin as if he missed a long-lost beard.

He's going to ask about the call.

"We'll be rooming together, so best get on with it, I suppose."
Don't ask about the call.

"Did you—did you end up calling me?"

He asked.

"I want to apologize for being so forward with you at the store. It's not like me to give out my number like that. I guess I was feeling confident at the time, but then I doubted I did the right thing and probably scared you."

"It's okay," she managed. "You don't have to apologize. We can just forget about it." *Please forget about it.*

"What I meant to say in all that is that I missed a call from Maiden's Bay a few days ago. Any chance it was you who had made the call?"

Cynthia's cell phone alarm beeped—the fifteen minute warning she gave herself to get over to the dock for the first meeting. Perfect timing, considering she didn't want to explain she indeed called him, then lost the courage to follow through with it. It was ridiculous, calling a man she had met for no more than five minutes. But the fact he stayed in her head for two weeks and made her skin flush and body act like it had no idea how to function normally at the moment said something. It was the wrong time in her life for it to say anything, let alone something.

"We'd better get going for the debriefing," she said.

"Debriefing. That sounds so official."

"I do hope you're not one of those goof-off, class-clown types that won't take this seriously." Never mind that was her type back in high school. She moved on from slackers.

She fumbled with her purse, struggling to remember what she was doing with it in the first place. She pulled out her license, a credit card, and some cash, and stuffed them in the zippered pocket of her rain jacket.

"No, not at all. I was just trying to lighten—"

"Good, because I take this really seriously. I've wanted this opportunity for a long time, and I'm not going to squander it over achieving some laughs."

"I understand."

"I'm going to leave now. Nick doesn't like tardiness."

"I'll walk with you."

"You don't have to do that."

"I know I don't have to. We're going to the same place. It kinda makes sense, right?"

Cynthia conceded, and Liam followed her out of the room. She locked the door behind them, hoping her anxiety over his presence had remained on the other side of the door.

"You know Nick?" Liam asked.

"Yes. Not closely, but enough." She placed the key with the other items in her jacket.

"That should give you an edge, I'd say, over the other applicants."

"Including you?" She smirked. *There* was her fighting spirit. Her years of experience operating boats and navigating the channel a hundred times over would be invaluable. But she didn't come without weaknesses as well, and wasn't sure what to expect of the competition. Liam was physically built and looked strong. Definitely an asset when dealing with swinging crab pots over the deck.

"I'm sorry to disappoint you, but I know Nick a little, as well." They walked down the stairs to the first floor.

"Oh." Of course he knew Nick. He intended to try out. The only coincidence in all of this was that she did, too. Nothing to get weird about. "I guess it makes sense. Hard to want to be a part of a crew when you don't know the captain at all."

"There's truth to that."

"You sound like you may have experience."

"I—"

"There they are!" Constance refilled the brochures on the welcome desk. "Everything okay with the room?"

"Yes, thank you." Cynthia continued to the door.

Liam helped himself to a piece of candy out of the dish on the desk. "Hope the meeting isn't too long."

"I have some snack foods if you'd like to bring along a brown bag for yourself." Constance moved away from the desk, and Liam held up his hand.

"I appreciate it, but we'd better get going. The room is perfect." He winked at Constance, then hurried behind Cynthia, exiting onto O Street.

Cynthia sucked down the chilled air, her nerves alight, stretching goosebumps across her arms, yet heating her core. The fact Liam merrily ate candy meant he stayed cool and calm, which was irritating because she was anything but. The thought of food right before her first meeting of tryouts was nauseating. Did he not care about the position? Or was he so confident in himself he didn't worry?

"What's that building over there?" Liam pointed across the street, the blue Victorian house with faded white trim a notable property amongst the more cosmopolitan downtown. If any part of Maiden's Bay could be called cosmopolitan. It was the sort of building that begged to be an inn, although somehow the three-story painted brick suited Maiden's Slumber Inn just fine.

"That's the library, and soon-to-be Maritime Museum."

"I had heard about that—the museum. I wonder if it's going to bring in a lot of tourists."

"I think that's part of the point." Her friend Josie had advocated for the museum to be located in Maiden's Bay, and came up with the idea of merging it with the library. After all, the library housed many of the documents and artifacts that could be displayed. "Although I worry about Maiden's Bay becoming solely a tourist town. Two souvenir shops on Pearl are enough."

"I can't see that happening. It's far enough away from the Seattle crowd, and I don't think the fishing industry will ever leave this area."

"That's true." The conversation had been a pleasant distraction from the tryouts, even if it only lasted thirty seconds.

Liam tapped her arm, slowing down her brisk pace. "Do you know where we're going?"

"Yeah, just down Pearl here." She pointed past the two-story ship-lapped cube of Campy's Bait and Bar on the west side of the main street. "This isn't too far a walk for you, is it? Perhaps I should've wandered around town more." It wouldn't exactly be sabotaging her competition. Merely tiring him out.

Liam chuckled. "Can't get rid of me that easily."

They crossed the street, heading toward Campy's.

"Have you been to the dock before?" Cynthia asked.

"Surprisingly no. Nick comes to Oakside more than the other way around."

What would Nick be doing in Oakside to know Liam? Oakside was primarily known as the nearest catch drop-off. No doubt Nick frequented there.

Cynthia stopped in front of Campy's, Liam nearly walking straight into her. "Do you work at the processing plant? In Oakside?"

Liam's confident smirk vanished—only for a second—before he gained his composure. "I do."

"That's how you know Nick. No wonder why you want to go up for greenhorn." It fell into place. "You see Nick and his crew and *Harpeth Rose* docking with her catch." Saying it out loud pulled at her stomach, harboring a pang of jealousy. He probably did have more knowledge than her, so she had better keep her eye out for him. But like her, he looked to be mid-twenties. Maybe near thirty. They were both probably at a disadvantage on mere age alone.

"That is how I know Nick." He stuffed his hands in the pockets of his jacket. "And you are right about him."

"How so?"

"He doesn't like tardiness, so we'd better go."

EIGHT

LIAM FOLLOWED CYNTHIA down the planks of the dock behind Campy's Bait and Bar. The wooden structure laid out like a T jutting out into the bay, with parallel arms on both sides providing moorings for a hodgepodge of vessel types—sailboats, outboard motor boats, pontoons. A wooden ticket booth positioned close to the back of Campy's sold passage for whale watching tours, sunset cruises, and fishing day trips.

He actually had been to the dock via boat when refueling Sea Prairie those years ago, but left that information out with Cynthia. Technically he stayed on the vessel, so it wasn't really a lie. So why did he feel bad?

Perhaps if it were a complete stranger, it wouldn't have been so hard. This was the woman he suddenly acted courageous with two weeks ago, giving her his number. In three years he hadn't met anyone he wanted to date, yet a brief stumble into the store was all it took. What were the odds she was trying out? Not only that, but the odds he was roomed with her and not any of these other people?

Was it a stroke of luck? Was that how he should view this? He had tried to come up with excuses to visit the flower shop for the week, and now he needed none. She'd be right there with him. His heart fluttered and nerves rattled, a mixture of excitement and nausea. It was one thing to hope for a date with someone. Quite another being thrown together in a hotel room.

In the twenty minutes they shared today, she had shown him so much of herself, whether she knew it or not. She was determined for sure. And intelligent. She already accurately guessed he worked at the plant. Would he be able to keep up the charade?

A crowd gathered ahead on the end of the dock at the top of the T. The rusted stern behind Nick Campbell displayed the chipped white letters spelling out *Harpeth Rose*.

Nick stood with his brother Ben, facing landward. Two other men stood in front of them, and Cynthia took a place beside one of them.

Liam nodded in response to Nick's nod.

"Cynthia, Liam," Nick said. "This is Sean." The rail-thin, pale young man tugged at the rim of his baseball cap in greeting. Liam wondered if he ever had the need to shave yet with such a young face.

"And Miguel." Miguel was even lankier and a few inches taller than Sean. Unlike Sean, he had a shadow of facial hair over his bronze skin. He and Sean couldn't have been older than nineteen, twenty.

"Here come the others."

Two guys, chatting and walking closely together, quieted down as they approached the group.

"Just introducing everyone." Nick waved them forward to line up.

"Greg," the huskier man said. Liam pictured he'd be safe as quarterback with someone built like Greg as guard. His voice was deep, and he carried a jolly smile, his teeth white against his brown skin.

The last man was Theo, the shortest of the group of strangers, with jet black, spiky hair under his hood. He said nothing, but waved briefly.

It was blaringly obvious Cynthia stood out in the group. Liam could only imagine how she felt sizing up her competition. Hopefully she knew brawn and youth weren't, in fact, prerequisites for the position. Muscles weren't always better on the boat. The strongest of men could break when out at sea. He'd seen teenagers who had grown up in fishing families shun the profession after a day on the boat.

"As you all know by now, I'm Nick Campbell, and this is my brother Ben." Ben pulled a hand out of his baggy sweatpants pocket and waved.

"It has been over four years since we've hired a new member for our team," Nick said. "Greenhorn is the traditional starting position for anyone who wants a season, a year, a career on a fishing vessel. We're hoping it's the latter. Based on your applications, you've indicated you're in this for the long haul. You've all expressed your reasons for wanting a position on *Harpeth Rose*. But it's not enough to want it. We need to know you are smart, capable, and able to blend in with our crew."

"Crew is family," Ben said. "Are family? Not sure what is right there." He shrugged. "Sure, we have our fun at times, but we take the job seriously."

"Do we now?" Nick leered.

"Seriously? The one time I'm dead serious you have to pull this?"

Nick grumbled. "Go ahead."

"Thank you." Ben straightened his vest. "It's one of the most dangerous jobs in the world, and we need to be able to trust each other to not only survive, but to succeed."

"You all are the top six applicants for the position," Nick said.

"Seven…." Ben nudged Nick in the arm, and everyone looked down the line. An elderly man stood slumped at the end. He pendulated front to back, catching himself with his foot before swaying again. His face was knobby and weathered, as much as Liam could see under the hat.

"Gus, what are you doing here?" Ben asked.

"I saw you all from Campy's out the window. Figured I'd check out what's going on. Don't want to miss anything."

At first Liam thought the man was drunk, but his words came out too controlled.

"This is not for you, Gus." Nick shook his head. "You want to go back to being a greenhorn again?"

"Did they even have that position in the 1800s?" Ben said out of the side of his mouth.

"I was the best greenhorn that crew ever saw," Gus said, pointing a wrinkly finger.

"Come on, man." Ben took Gus by the arm. "Let's get you inside."

"Excuse us for a minute." Nick joined Ben and led Gus away, who didn't go without at least a verbal fight.

Cynthia leaned in close, the scent of honey and mint from her hair catching the breeze. "Gus used to date Constance."

"Really?" Picturing someone like Gus with Constance proved difficult. Constance seemed refined and mature, while Gus appeared brash and aloof.

Cynthia nodded, sadness in her eyes. "I don't know the details. He seemed happy while it lasted, but when it ended it was back to spending his evenings at Campy's again."

"Poor guy." Breakups weren't easy. Did they get any easier at Gus's age?

"I see where you stand," Cynthia said.

"What is that supposed to mean?" Her eyebrows stood at the edge of anger, just like they had when she questioned him at the inn about his—misunderstood—disbelief she was trying out. While he did not long to be on the other side of it when full blown, it took effort not to notice just how damn cute she looked.

"Maybe it's poor Constance. Why assume she was in the wrong?"

"I didn't—" He huffed. "I'm just saying it's sad to see when someone wears their heartache. If that's how he's outwardly acting, imagine what he's feeling on the inside."

"Oh." Cynthia backed away. He felt her eyes on him as Nick and Ben returned. Those beautiful gray ones that almost hurt to look at straight on.

"Sorry about that," Nick said. "Now where were we?"

"Wrapping it up." Ben spun his finger in the air.

"Okay, let's get to it. We couldn't make such an important decision based solely on paper, so you've been invited here to try out. We appreciate you coming out to do this." Nick locked eyes with Liam for a split second before moving on. "You're taking time away from your lives, your families, when there is no guarantee we will end up hiring one of you. But if you're truly out for this job, you'll get used to such things."

Ben tapped his watch.

Nick rolled his eyes. "For the next five days, you will be given tasks to perform, tasks that will train you and test your abilities for the various skills you will need to be a successful crew member. Often these tasks will be performed by yourself, or with another from the group. There is no elimination except self-elimination. Unless you are asked to leave due to jeopardizing your safety or the safety of others, it is up to you if you stay the course or leave. Your first task will be given to you tomorrow morning, seven AM. We will reconvene here. Thank you for coming out, and we will see you in the morning."

Liam hadn't realized how tense he was until he sighed at the group's dismissal. He wasn't even trying out for real.

"That was intense." He scurried to catch up to Cynthia, who had made her way to the side of Campy's Bait and Bar.

"What did you think of the others?" Cynthia asked. "Theo seems quiet, so that could mean he's the toughest competition."

"Because he's quiet? There's no way to tell yet."

"Liam." Nick stood near the front door of Campy's Bait and Bar. "A word?"

"Sure." Liam gave a stiff smile to Cynthia, who looked ready to tear his head off for being individually called out.

Nick held the door open, the first floor the "Bait" portion of the establishment. Faint music bled through the ceiling from the bar upstairs, mixed with the occasional chair—or whale by the heaviness of it—sliding across the floor. The walls and flooring of the tackle shop were dark like navy steel, drawing the eye to the rows of rods and reels. Nick led Liam to the back office, weaving between the displays of outerwear and footwear in the back.

The cyan office walls adorned posters of fish and crab species, as if Liam had stepped into a marine scientist's lab. A heavyset man in his forties stood up from his chair behind the desk, patting down the cowlick on the back of his head.

"This is Ryan," Nick said.

Liam shook his hand, Ryan's grip firm.

"Mind if we take a few minutes here?" Nick pointed to the door.

"No problem. I have inventory to check on anyway." Ryan left, and Nick took his seat.

Liam took the chair in front of the desk.

"Ryan is a fairly new manager."

"Working out?"

"So far. Joel has his hands full with the bar, and Ben and I can't be at the store or the dock enough to run either one."

"You guys manage the dock, too?"

"Not since we put Gus in charge. Although you've seen the guy tonight. Who knows how long we can rely on him?"

Liam recalled the elderly man crashing their meeting. A broken heart and the prospect of losing his job? "He's had it pretty rough lately, I've heard."

"Yeah." Nick shrugged. "Which is why we keep him working. I don't know if I have the heart to let him go. Or the replacement." He rolled the chair forward and leaned his elbows on the desk. "Anyway, you all settled? Drive up was okay?"

"No worries. Constance seems like a hoot."

"She really is. The inn is a landmark, but Constance is the true touch of history."

"I have to admit, I was a little surprised when I met my roommate."

"Cynthia?"

Liam registered how Nick guessed correctly. uickly. "You knew?"

"No." Nick shuffled in the chair and adjusted his hat. "I just assumed by your surprise. When you were out, there still weren't many women on board. Still aren't."

"That's true, but I do understand it's a little different now. In fact, I think she's pretty determined and focused. So far I'm impressed. But I promise to assess everyone as equally and fairly as I possibly can." It was the reason Nick had asked him here in the first place. Not to get more than friendly with a prospective crew member. Being reminded again couldn't hurt.

"Yeah, about that." He leaned back in the chair.

"I think I know what you're going to say." Liam leaned closer, elbows on the desk. "You want me to go along with the tasks." Considering Nick hadn't addressed him any differently than the other candidates, he supposed it to be the case, and he was prepared to do what he could.

"That's what I wanted to talk to you about."

"Go ahead." Liam half-expected a lecture on safety with his history of injury.

"I'd like you to at least try to look as if you're making an effort for the position. But I know your limitations and respect that."

He wasn't completely incapable, but knew Nick was looking out for him. "Thank you." He touched his shoulder, then quickly pulled back his hand. His shoulder had a knack for aching whenever it was being talked about.

"As I said out there, I'm going to be dividing up the group. I'd like for you to really keep an eye out for Cynthia."

Liam sat up straighter. Nick had said her name. Again. "It's her, isn't it? You said there was someone in particular you were hoping to test out."

"Please keep it to yourself. But yes. Therefore I may have you around her more than the others."

"I see." Uneasiness trickled down his spine. On the one hand, he wanted to assess all the candidates in order to help Nick find the best. Being around one over the others didn't allow for fairness. On the other, it meant more time with Cynthia. Something he wanted after five minutes with her two weeks ago. However, the more time around Cynthia, the more chances she had at cracking the truth out of him.

"Thanks again for doing this though. What made you decide to give it a go?"

His heart jumped as he composed the reasonable answer. "You asked for help. You helped me get started at Oakside Processing. I'm happy to return the favor."

Nick nodded and stood, prompting Liam to get going. "Are you sure that's the only reason?"

Liam swallowed, a dry lump in his throat. Was it written all over his face? Was Nick joking with him or serious? How could he have possibly known about Cynthia before this? Did she tell Nick?

Stop being paranoid. She barely knows Nick. Why would she tell him about that one customer she sprayed weeks ago? He settled his muddied thoughts. "Helping you, yes, plus it's fun to be a tourist every now and then."

Nick smiled and led him out of the office. He knew nothing of Liam and Cynthia's encounter before today. Liam needed to stay focused and keep his roaming thoughts at bay.

"All right," Nick said. "If you need me for anything, you have my cell. Otherwise, I'll see you tomorrow morning, sailor."

"Tomorrow morning, Captain."

NINE

THE EARLY MORNING hours were designed for running, according to Cynthia Pruitt. Preferably right before the edge of the sun crested above the horizon, when dark shadows morphed into familiar objects.

The western edge of town lay at the sea, while the eastern outskirts spread up the gradually steeper hills closing off the valley, affording Maiden's Bay an unusually late sunrise. Still, 5:45 AM was early for anyone to be about, let alone out for a run.

She had started running east from Constance's, warming up her calves by attacking uphill. She passed the parklike surrounds of the cemetery, slowing at the statue of St. Nicholas in a boat. The black plaque below listed the names of sailors lost at sea. It hadn't needed updating in five years, and hopefully wouldn't for another fifty.

She curved to the south, breezing through the neighborhoods of houses, their bottom corners slicing into the hillside and top floors fighting for views of the ocean.

She turned down Arbor Avenue without a thought, down to the cul-de-sac and back. Passing her sister's house was routine, glancing to see if anyone would happen to be on the porch early in the morning. There never was during her run. What would she even do if Jackie had been out? They hadn't spoken since Dad's funeral—one week after the funeral, to be precise—when the house was willed to Cynthia. Jackie already had a house with her husband, a home in which Gwen grew up in. The fact was it wasn't about Dad's death or the house. Jackie's anger ran deeper.

Cynthia looped back north beyond downtown and cut over to the coast, enjoying the downhill reprieve before her other ritual. Running the lighthouse stairs wasn't an option for everyone in Maiden's Bay. Luckily she had an in.

She eased by Campy's and the dock, beyond the handful of houseboats dotting the coast, before arriving at Maiden's Bay Municipal Park. The acreage of trees marked the north end of the bay and provided shade over walking trails, picnic tables, and the finest stretch of sandy beach in the bay. Cynthia loved how it protected her from the wind rolling off the Pacific, before the raw exposure on the lighthouse peninsula.

The brief roadway from the park to Lone Lady was paved and wide enough for one-way traffic. Below the road lay large rocks and boulders, providing tidal pools for all sorts of marine life with suckers and tentacles. The waves crashed during rough weather, sending foam sky high.

A few parking lines had been painted decades ago when the lighthouse still required a keeper. They faded and crumbled from the ice and storms, a piece of history washed away.

The lighthouse itself stood well maintained. Cynthia sprinted up the front steps to the red door, the lock left open. Mr. Ludlow, the keeper—although technically he volunteered his maintenance services these days—was out sick last week. The open lock signaled his likely return.

"Hello!"

She always announced, even if Mr. Ludlow couldn't hear an air horn through the wind at the top. The task looked daunting when she stood at the bottom, with over two hundred steps winding around to the landing at the top.

Cynthia paced herself but pushed for good timing. Not her fastest, but it had been a while.

"Good morning, Cynthia." Mr. Ludlow stood outside the doorway to the gallery. He waved and returned to staring at the sea.

"Morning! Good to see you back."

"Good to be back."

Sometimes Cynthia sat out on the gallery with him, talking to the bearded eighty-year-old man who had more stories to tell than years to his life. Retired from the Marines and still volunteering in the local Coast Guard Auxiliary unit, he had seen it all and then some, but usually kept quiet on those matters. He mostly liked to talk about his grandchildren, the infamous Campbell brothers. He had a soft spot for Joel, the youngest of the siblings. Cynthia didn't socialize much with Joel, but felt like she knew him better than Joel's friends probably did.

This morning though, Cynthia had somewhere to be. "Have a good one!"

Mr. Ludlow tapped two fingers on the rim of his hat. "As always."

She turned around and attacked the spiral staircase downward. The breeze was welcomed when she left the lighthouse behind.

The traffic was so little in town she didn't hesitate to run on the road itself. She finished with a sprint down Pearl Avenue, as far as J Street on the southern end.

She stretched briefly and turned back north, walking for a cool down. Second Mate Thrift looked lifeless without its clothing racks out on the sidewalk. Shipyard Souvenirs sat between Two Schoops— with its logo of upside-down schooner sails as ice cream cones—and Postal Port, like a black hole with its flashy lights not yet warmed up for the day. Downtown really was her favorite part of the area.

She paused at Bea's Bouquets. Bea had outdone herself with the Valentine's display, with an enormous overflowing bouquet of delicate sweet peas in white, blush, and periwinkle atop a white table flanked by white seats. Working with Bea taught her to appreciate beauty in the simplistic.

A car pulled into the back of Mariner's Market across the street, most likely an employee getting a move on with the bakery items. Crescent Cafe next door was the only lit storefront on the street.

She took it all in, soaking in the sights, sounds, and aromas as if it was the first day of her new life.

Her watch read 6:19 AM. She broke back into a run up O Street to Constance's.

"Good morning." Constance waved from the hallway leading to the breakfast room. "Can I get you anything this morning?"

Cynthia wiped the sweat from her brow onto her sleeve. "I'll take a bottle of water. And a coffee to go, if that's okay."

"It sure is. That's what I'm here for." Constance grabbed a water bottle out of the mini fridge and poured a cup of coffee.

Cynthia had no clue if Liam was a morning person, but something about him told her no. "Actually, can you make that two coffees to go?"

Constance obliged, double-checking the lids on the hot brew and giving her a carrier to help.

Cynthia reached Room 2 upstairs and unlocked the door, knocking before entering. Her gut was right. Liam was out cold in his bed, lying on his stomach with arms sprawled out.

She set the drinks down on the desk, taking off the lid of hers to cool off. She grabbed her clothes and bath items and showered down the hall. The water pressure was low, but nothing she wasn't used to living in Maiden's Bay. She had always assumed it had something to do with the town arranged on a slope, but had no idea if that was anywhere near correct.

She dressed and bypassed makeup, opting for moisturizer and a swipe of lip gloss, then returned to the room. Liam still lay in bed, turned over on his back. She let the door close a little louder. His body flinched at the smack.

"I don't know if you set your alarm at all, but it's almost time to meet with Nick." Cynthia secured her items in her bag and cradled the coffee. Even though she had warmed up substantially during the run, the body heat wore off faster in the cold of winter. Heat was half the reason she drank coffee.

"I got you some coffee. I don't know if you drink it, but I also got some cream and sugar if you'd like."

Liam wiped his face in his hands. "Thank you." He reached out with his arm, hand floating in the air.

"Oh, here." She handed him the coffee. "We're going to have to go soon if you want to be on time."

"Nope." He stood up, wearing only blue plaid boxers. His abs and sculpted quads tensed, and Cynthia turned around, as if him standing in boxers was more revealing than lying down in them.

"What do you mean nope?" she mustered.

"I mean I don't want to be on time."

She wrinkled her eyebrows. Who was this guy? "Okay, then I guess I'll go by myself."

"I mean to say that I don't want to be on time. I want to be early."

"Oh, okay."

"So let's go."

Cynthia turned around, and Liam had picked up jeans off the floor, wearing them again, and a pullover under his Columbia jacket.

Wasn't he going to use the bathroom? Or brush his teeth? Or wash his face? Fishing crew, she thought. Didn't matter what she thought he ought to do. Just accept it.

They exited the room, and she locked the door.

"Give me a second and I'll be down." Liam wandered off down the hall.

"Okay." Thank goodness. Hopefully he was doing all of those things, but then again, they needed to get going if they wanted to be prompt.

She went downstairs, and Constance once again smiled at her. "Did you sleep well? I noticed you were up early. I just hope everything was all right."

"Yeah, no problem." Other than not being able to sleep. She had said she was fine rooming with a stranger—a guy stranger—yet it was extremely awkward knowing Liam was a few feet away. Was it better or worse she knew him? Not really know him know him, but knew him enough. She had called him before chickening out, after all.

Maybe it was just her nerves about today. Yep. It had nothing to do with the fact an attractive, charming man slept in a bed next to hers.

Liam ran down the stairs, hair wet and matted down. The freshening up suited him, the floral scent of Constance's provided soap no longer perfumy but softened somehow, alluring. For a second she pictured cozying up on his shoulder, nuzzling his neck.

"Ready?" His eyes opened wide, eyebrows high.

Cynthia nodded. Those pesky images needed to stay out of her head. This was an important week, after all. She waved bye to Constance before heading out the door, walking away from the irrational thoughts.

"You were up early." Liam zipped up his jacket and stuffed his free hand in his denim pocket.

"I didn't know you realized."

"I'm a bit of a light sleeper."

"Is that so?" Liar. "I went for a run."

"In this weather?"

"Why not? It helps me stay in shape, good for endurance, which I'll need on the boat, plus I'd better get used to being wet in freezing temps if I want to be greenhorn."

"Once again, you preach the truth."

They reached the end of O Street and took a right on Pearl.

Liam had looked muscular, but it wasn't until seeing him without his shirt on this morning that Cynthia realized he was very in shape. Which was bad news for her. Perhaps in more ways than one.

She refocused, shaking off the thought. "How about you? You run?"

"I'm more of a strength training person ever since…. Well, I get bored with cardio."

"Maybe you haven't found the right activity. Or should pair up with a buddy."

"Maybe I will," he said. "Can you think of anyone?" His deep brown eyes softened with his smile.

The heat returned to Cynthia's core as if she was still running.

They finished the walk to the dock in silence, arriving first. The other four men were swiftly behind, eyes weary and mouths quiet.

"Thank you all for being on time this morning." Nick stood beside a blue cooler, Ben yawning into his fist beside him. "Let's get right to it."

"Let's," Ben said.

"Part of being a greenhorn, or any crew member for that matter, means knowing your equipment. Here's your task for today." He swung open the lid of the cooler.

Cynthia leaned closer, catching a mess of metal.

"You'll work in pairs. Each pair will receive a cooler like this one containing a number of different-sized hooks. It's your task to sort them, as quickly as possible, into five bins."

Nick shut the cooler. "Cynthia, Liam, you'll have this one. Sean, Greg, follow me. Theo, Miguel, follow Ben. When you're through, report back to me. I'll be in the office." He pointed to Campy's Bait and Bar.

"And break!" Ben clapped. Nick nudged him with an elbow.

Cynthia looked at Liam, who shrugged his shoulders. "Not quite what I expected," he said.

Cynthia wouldn't have guessed sorting hooks either, but figured there would be psychological tests—like how long you can handle the same task for hours on end. This definitely checked off that box.

"Shall we?" she said.

"We shall."

They sat on the wooden planks, and Cynthia laid out the five plastic bins in a row.

"Did that feel like we're on a reality show or something?"

"A little bit." Cynthia held back a chuckle. Nick had looked dead serious, and for such a menial task. But she studied the position enough to know that greenhorns weren't to question their assignments. They had to listen first. The learning would come with time.

"I was hoping we'd be on the boat today." She put on the thick gloves and scooped a handful of hooks, which strung together like the game with monkeys and a barrel.

"I wasn't." Liam placed his scoop on the inside of the turned-over cooler lid.

"Why not?"

"What? Oh." Liam cleared his throat. "I meant that... maybe it's best we do some tasks on land, get the hang of it, before setting foot on a boat."

"Hm. Maybe." Cynthia winced and took off the glove on her right hand.

"You okay?"

"The hook went straight through the glove."

Liam grabbed her hand, his skin rough and strong on hers. His hand shook, as if he had just gotten off a thrilling roller coaster. Was he nervous around her? Scared? He seemed so calm this morning and yesterday evening.

She slipped her hand away. "I'm fine." She sucked at the pierce in her skin and replaced the glove.

"They look thick, but they're not hook-proof. Just be careful, okay?" Liam spread out the hooks on the white lid.

Her hooks against the wood of the dock were a tangled mess. "Surprisingly, working at Bea's toughened up my hands a bit."

"Oh, really?"

"Plenty of thorns and prickles and needles. Plants can be violent."

"I guess I never thought about that." He used his index finger to slide the hooks into their respective piles. "You may want to work with me here. Hard to see what's what against the wood. And with the lip of the lid, you won't lose any hooks with the rocking—if we were on a boat."

It was Cynthia's nature to argue when someone, especially a man, was telling her how to do something she was perfectly capable of doing. But he had a point. Or several. Plus she'd better get used to being told what to do and not overanalyzing it.

Reluctantly, she scooped her hooks and moved next to Liam, dumping them in the middle of the lid. He already outsmarted her. Could Nick see that from Campy's?

"Sounds like you've done this before."

Liam's hand froze, and he looked her straight in the eyes. "I have done this before. Not a freezer full of hooks, of course."

He was being nice and helpful, but Cynthia's stomach turned. How did he know what he was doing? The other men had looked annoyed until Nick and Ben whisked them off to who knew where. Liam went straight to task with no complaints.

"I know we don't exactly know each other at this point," she said.

Liam paused, looking up from the cooler lid. "I have a feeling there's a 'but' in there."

"But why do I get the feeling you're hiding something from me?"

Liam returned to sorting, moving faster. "You're right. There's something I haven't told you."

"You've tried out for this before? You secretly practice sorting hooks in your spare time?"

His answer was not one she had expected, but rather one that tore at her confidence and her chances to achieve her dream.

"I've been a greenhorn before."

T E N

PERHAPS IT WASN'T the best thing, being honest with Cynthia. To say she took his confession of being a former greenhorn lightly would have been as big a lie as the one he still kept from her.

The rest of the afternoon, Cynthia had worked in silence, the tasks ranging from tying knots to untangling nets. He had tried sparking conversation, but after she walked away from him after the third attempt, he let it go.

It was understandable. She really wanted the position, and to hear her competition had more experience threw her off. But the last thing he wanted to do was discourage her. In fact, he wished she had spoken with him because he had many tips that could help her out.

She would learn it all in time. Just not from him.

He had a twinge of additional guilt, thinking he ruined his chance at romance with her. That's not what the week was about. He just needed his heart to get the memo from his head.

Nick and Ben led Miguel, Sean, Greg, and Theo to the dock. Nick waved Liam and Cynthia over. "Good job, everyone. I know today's tasks weren't fun, but fishing requires a lot of maintenance, repetition, and patience. That's what today was about, in case you question what we're doing here. Get some rest, and tomorrow you'll get your hands dirty."

Ben collected all the work gloves, and the four other contenders left. Liam turned to Cynthia, his best chance at conversation with Nick around.

"I could certainly use some food after that." Liam glanced at Cynthia, who still wasn't looking at him. "Care to join me for a bite?"

Maybe he had been wrong. Maybe she didn't care about giving Liam the cold shoulder in front of Nick.

"I'm going to head back to Constance's." She said it without eye contact.

Nick looked at Liam, eyes questioning. He eyed Cynthia, and she turned up the charisma with a smile for Liam. "Thank you though. I'll see you back at the room?"

"Sure." Liam held off the smirk. His plan worked, even though she declined dinner. At least she had spoken to him.

"Something I need to know about?" Nick asked.

"Nah. Long day." He touched his chest. "For me, not for Cynthia. Well, you'd have to ask her if she thought it was a long day."

"All right." Nick buried his confusion. "Get a good rest for tomorrow."

"Will do."

Liam walked along Pearl Avenue toward the pink neon cursive letters of Campy's Bait and Bar. Campy's looked to be the only place in the immediate downtown to eat past two PM. Although he did set out on this journey—at least partially—to get to know more of Maiden's Bay, he wasn't exactly in the mood to roam around. He hadn't been lying to Cynthia on at least one thing—his stomach felt hollow.

The tasks today had been menial, but that didn't mean they weren't tiring. It had been years since he had to do anything remotely like them. He forgot how much of fishing lied outside the strenuous, physical aspects. The tiny taste of it today had him thinking....

Was he really not capable of being a greenhorn? Had enough time gone by and progress made with his shoulder that he could actually perform duties on a crew?

He hiked up the outer stairs to the second floor deck, a wraparound porch that had lived through the constant barrage from the salt air. Inside, the restaurant was dark despite the numerous windows, the side walls lined with booths and free-standing tables and chairs in between. In the middle of the room stood the bar like an island, with a foosball and pool table behind it. Double doors led to the back deck, offering what would've been the best seating to view the dock and bay were it not for the chilly February air.

The atmosphere carried a light scent of tobacco, as if he had stepped into an antique cigar box that hadn't been full in ages. Chatty patrons fought the Eighties rock music blaring from the jukebox for air space. The sole flatscreen TV played The Weather Channel on mute.

A waitress caught his attention. He pointed to the bar, and she nodded in approval. He weaved through the tables to the middle and unzipped his jacket. A group somewhere behind him to his left burst into a short round of laughter. Liam glanced over and caught the stare of one of the men. It took him a second to process the thin youthful face of Sean.

If Liam wanted any company over dinner, it was Cynthia. But it seemed rude not to at least say hello, on top of suspicious if he spent all his time with Cynthia or by himself.

"Hey, there." Liam stepped up to the booth, jacket in one hand, the other hand stuffed in a pocket. The whole group was there—Greg, Miguel, and Theo, nursing beers. Liam questioned if some were old enough to drink legally, but that responsibility fell on the owner.

"Guess I missed the memo."

"Or you got it," Greg said. "You're here."

"True."

"Grab a chair." Miguel pointed to an empty table, and Liam swung a chair to the end of the booth.

"If this was day one, can't wait to see what the last day has to offer us." It was a joke, but Liam did worry about the intensity of the tasks as the week would progress. Nick knew Liam's history, but was he expected to go full-out to perpetuate the charade? Or perhaps the better question—could Liam actually do it?

"Yeah," Sean said. "Real ball-buster."

"Why do you think we're here drinking?" Miguel smirked.

Something didn't feel right, but maybe it was just Liam being the odd man out. Unlike his—mostly quiet—time with Cynthia, he hadn't seen the guys since the morning. Where had Nick sent them for their tasks? He considered asking, but didn't want to step on toes.

"Do you all know each other?" It certainly looked it, with the banter and closeness in the booth. Especially how close Greg and Theo sat.

No one said a word. The men stared at each other. Eventually Sean stopped sipping down beer and spoke up. "I guess it doesn't hurt to tell the truth." He stared down the other three.

"You're right. Might as well tell him." Miguel turned to Liam. "We're all from here. So yes, we know each other."

"You're friends, but are competing for the same spot on Nick's boat?"

"Sure." Miguel shortened his answer by drinking.

"What he means is…." Sean widened his stare at Miguel. Something moved under the table—was it Sean's foot?—and Miguel yelped. "We *are* friends. Greg and Theo are a bit more than that, though"

"Oh, okay."

Now that Sean had said it, Greg took Theo's hand in his on the table.

"How about you?" The bass of Greg's voice cut through the background racket with the strength of Thor's hammer. "We haven't seen you around here, so where are you from?"

"Oakside." His mind reeled with the information that all four of the other contestants were locals and knew each other. Surely there were going to be candidates from other towns, maybe even from Seattle or Portland. Why else have everyone stay at Constance's?

"If you're locals," he said, "then you also know Cynthia."

"Not a whole lot," Miguel said. "I've seen her around and know she works at Bea's, and I only know that because of Theo's mom."

"My mom and Bea are cousins." It was the first time Liam heard Theo speak. He had to strain to distinguish the gentle voice over the music and chatter. "Why do you ask about Cynthia?" Something in his soft tone implied he knew Liam's true feelings.

"Just wondered."

The room grew hotter, the collar of his shirt tight around his neck.

"I went to high school with her," Sean said. "She was a senior when I was a freshman, so I didn't really have much interaction."

"Well, maybe next time you should invite her to come with you." As long as none of you worked on a boat before. He was amused with the thought, but also understood why she was so upset over it. "Doesn't seem quite fair to leave her out."

They again played the staring game with each other.

"Yeah, sure," Sean said. "No problem. We would've invited you both if we had seen you this afternoon."

The others nodded in agreement. It felt like a hollow assurance and the end of the conversation at the same time.

"I'm going to get a drink and something to eat at the bar." Liam stood, swinging the chair back to its table. "I'll catch up with you guys tomorrow."

"Tomorrow," Sean said.

Liam sighed on his way to the bar, tension releasing from his shoulders and jaw. There definitely was something odd going on. Maybe Nick would know the situation. Maybe it came down to preferring a local, or maybe Josie's media reach didn't extend far beyond the community.

Liam sat down on a stool at the bar, slinging his jacket over the high back.

"Not eating with your friends?" The bartender threw down a drink napkin. Liam was taken aback for a moment, not quite knowing how to process the young face of Joel Campbell. He was a fresh-faced amalgamation of his older brothers, with the same chiseled nose as Nick's and eyes as friendly as Ben's.

"Them? No. I got the feeling they have their own thing going on. Fifth wheel and all."

"Feelings hurt?"

Liam chuckled. "No."

"Okay. I was gonna say I got a drink for that."

"What else do you have a drink for?"

"Oh, you know. Boss fired you. City turned off your power. Family left you. Just about anything."

"No drinks for happy moments?" He reached for a menu down the bar.

"Isn't that the default here in Maiden's Bay?"

Liam shrugged at the half-joke. "I haven't spent more than a day here until now. I guess I'll let you know after this week."

"I'm a little offended it'll take you that long to find happiness here." The Campbell brother smiled. "How about you tell me what you want to drink."

"I'll take whatever stout you have on tap."

Liam perused the menu, a laminated rap sheet of generic seafood fare—fish and chips, fried shrimp, seafood gumbo, and chowder, depending on the day of course. The bartender returned with his drink.

"So how was day one?"

"Excuse me?"

"The greenhorn tryouts."

"How'd you know I was here for that?"

"You said you've never been in Maiden's Bay for long. But for those of us that are, we know everything. Word spreads fast." The man laughed, his cheeks plumping up the otherwise thin face. "Don't be weirded out. I saw you out there with Cynthia this morning." He pointed to the window in the corner overlooking a portion of the dock.

"Plus, Gus here tried to join you." He pointed out the man hunched over at the end of the bar, the one Cynthia said had dated Constance and Nick said managed the dock.

"All right, you got me." Liam swallowed the cold ale.

"You got a name?"

"Liam."

"Joel." He stretched out a hand to shake, and Liam obliged.

"I figured as much. You're like a hybrid of your brothers."

"Hopefully the better bits of the two." He chuckled. "I figured I'd better meet the man who caught the eye of Cynthia Pruitt."

Liam choked on the last bit of chilled stout in his throat. "What?"

"I've known Cynthia for years. Indirectly, I guess you could say. My grandfather manages Lone Lady. You know, the lighthouse?" He pointed to the northern corner, the black-banded tower visible if Liam leaned over the bar.

"Why's it called that?"

"You know how the name Maiden's Bay came about, right?"

"I heard it had something to do with sailors leaving their women, never to return."

"The tale is that women never had a chance to marry, leaving them maidens. But honestly there were many wives who lost their husbands, as well."

"I guess it's better than calling it Widow's Bay."

Joel nodded. "True. Anyway, the lighthouse, with it's one black band, is said to be the Lone Lady, a finger through the sky that held on to the promise of marriage only to remain alone forever."

"If that doesn't paint a picture of happiness." Liam sipped.

"Now it's a place where teenagers graffiti their initials in the hopes of keeping devoted to each other as much as Lone Lady. It's also where my grandfather spends his mornings. Grandpa Ludlow isn't in the best of health these days. Cynthia visits him on her morning run and chats with him. He tells me all about it. Highlight of his day. I guess my point is, she's a good person, so don't screw it up."

"What he means to say is, don't be like me," Gus yelled thickly from his corner.

Liam's mind whirred with questions, processing Joel's information. "What makes you think there is anything going on?"

"I told you. I saw the two of you out there this morning."

"So? She barely spoke two words to me. In fact, she didn't even look at me for most of the day."

Joel grinned. "Exactly."

ELEVEN

THE MOST PERSISTENT feeling Cynthia had all yesterday afternoon—and night for that matter—was irritation. Not because she pricked her gloved fingers on a number of sharp hooks, or that her hands cramped from tying knots for two hours.

Because of Liam Reynolds.

How could she have possibly considered calling him? The man clearly had kept a secret from her. It's not like they were best buds, but still she roomed with the man, and he hadn't told her he had been a greenhorn before.

No wonder why he stood cool and calm at the briefing Sunday evening. She would be, too, if she had worked the position for any amount of time.

The worst part was, she knew she could learn a lot from him. But could she set aside her pride to ask him for help? He had seamlessly moved through the exercises yesterday. She hadn't wanted to even look at him she was so… irritated. Every now and then she'd glance over to see how he tackled a problem, picking up what she could at a distance.

Now she stood next to the other four candidates away from Liam, willing herself to focus on Nick's words.

"As a greenhorn you'll be gutting and chopping tons of fish. You'll have to be quick, yes, but you'll have to be able to stomach it as well."

Like yesterday, she swigged down coffee for breakfast. The lack of sleep began to take its toll, her focus drifting with the heaviness of her eyelids.

If only Liam had retired early last night. Instead he came in at who knows what hour. He hadn't technically awakened her because she couldn't sleep, knowing he was out there doing his I've-been-a-greenhorn-before things without her. Or maybe after a few drinks he chatted it up with other locals.

She rubbed her temples, both to push out thoughts of Liam and to shield her eyes from the rare sunshine appearing in early February. She cursed not wearing sunglasses, but at least she was smart enough to dress in layers.

"Unlike yesterday," Nick continued, "you're not going to be doing this on land."

She perked up. Could it be as soon as day two to step aboard *Harpeth Rose?*

"We're going to divide you into two teams on these smaller watercraft." They stood next to a twenty foot fiberglass boat named *Rust Bucket.* Ben waved from the next boat over, a shinier, sexier wooden boat named *Cool Calypso.*

Cynthia was a mixed bag of emotions. Still not *Harpeth Rose,* but at least she'd be on the water today.

"Let's have Greg, Liam, and—"

Not me. Please not me.

"Cynthia, come with me. The rest, off with Ben."

She wasn't going to catch a break. Not only was she with Liam, but she missed out on the nicer boat.

"Is there a problem, Cynthia?" Nick asked.

Her body had betrayed her, shoulders slumped in disappointment. She straightened. "No, Captain. I'm ready."

She stepped aboard *Rust Bucket,* more of a recreational vehicle than fishing vessel, with a short sunbathing deck on the bow, and bench seats behind the driver's console. She pulled her hair back in a low ponytail, anticipating the breeze when moving.

Nick stood at the wheel. "Everyone go ahead and get comfortable while I take us out in open water."

Cynthia sat closest to Nick, four large coolers taking up most of the deck's leg room in the back, with two more in front of the console. Liam sat on one of the coolers up front, and Greg sat nearest the stern, thick arms folded over his broad chest.

Cynthia watched Nick closely as he took them out of the No Wake zone of the calmer dock into the broader area of the bay. *Rust Bucket* wasn't much different than what she and Dad had taken out, so it would be easier to handle than the larger fishing vessels.

But clearing the bay into the south-flowing California Current to the open ocean took maneuvering with any vessel. She preferred staying away from Lone Lady's rocky shoals of the north and leaning closer to Shipwreck Alley to the south. The same thinking likely caused the number of shipwrecks in Maiden's Bay's past. The unpredictable current made it dangerous to steer clear of the rocks. Often in winter the wind blew toward the shore, and older ships had to battle it out to stay clear of the abrupt shallowness of the bay floor, which constantly changed. Not to mention the wreckage of past ships. Sometimes the remnants of an eroded hull would peek its head out of the water on the rare calm day. Dad once peeled her off the wheel because she nearly sliced into the decaying wood of a wreck. Every day she went out that summer, she practiced boating in and out of the bay.

She paid no mind to *Rust Bucket's* actual course. Rather, she watched Nick. His movements came as second nature, as if the boat was an extension of himself. He swiped flawlessly past the few trawlers and netters and right over the steep shelf to the open Pacific Ocean. She had never seen anything like it.

Nick cut the engine. "Okay, here we are."

She looked for Ben's boat, squinting behind and around them. She had been so focused on watching the professional maneuvering she didn't pay attention to the other team. They were nowhere to be seen.

"Everyone bring it in," Nick said. "I know it's cramped on here."

The deeper water was not as choppy as the bay, but without the forward push of the engine or an anchor down, *Rust Bucket* swayed side to side. Cynthia stayed put while Liam sat across from her. Greg wobbled when he stood and stepped forward. He gripped the rail, weaving through the coolers closer to Nick.

Nick handed each one in the trio gloves and a knife. "Under your seat, Cynthia, are bibs and galoshes. I highly recommend wearing them." Cynthia did not hesitate, putting on the heavy waterproof overalls and passing a set to the others.

"In these five coolers are nearly three hundred pounds of fish to gut," Nick said. "If you will, Liam, grab the one you were sitting on."

Liam brought over the cooler from the front.

"This one is empty." Nick opened it. "Put your chopped fish in here. Once you've emptied out a cooler, use that one as the bucket, and so on. Everyone got it?"

"Is there a certain way you want us to gut?" Cynthia asked.

"We're not preparing a meal here," Nick said. "Chop them up as we would for bait. If you're in doubt, watch Liam."

It took every modicum of power in Cynthia not to roll her eyes.

Nick moved to the bow, sitting on the remaining cooler up front and propping his feet on the sunning deck. He adjusted his UW hat off his head and placed it further down over his eyes.

"Is he taking a nap?" Greg furled his eyebrows.

Cynthia shrugged. Dad had often done the same thing once she got them to open water. It was a challenge for him to keep his eyes open with the lulling of the waves.

But right now, there was too much to do to worry about Nick.

She put on the gloves and grabbed the first fish. She turned over the empty cooler's lid onto another and set the fish down, slicing the four-pounder into bits.

"Good thinking," Liam said.

She continued working, avoiding his gaze. No sense in seeing his smugness for having taught her something yesterday.

Liam handed a fish to Greg and slapped down one for himself. "We're going to be here a while." He didn't look at her, but Cynthia knew he was talking to her. "Plus, we room together. Don't you think it would be better if we got along?"

"We get along already. Quietly."

"Look, I'm sorry if I upset you yesterday. I didn't tell you the truth about me, not that we exactly shared our life stories or much of anything to each other. But now you know. Can we move on, please?"

"At least you told Nick you were a greenhorn before." She looked at Greg, readying for his surprise. He covered a burp out his mouth with his sleeve.

"Then again, of course you would. Why wouldn't you want to brag about that on your application?" She threw the pieces into the empty cooler and grabbed another. "What I don't get is, if you've already been a greenhorn, why do you still have to try out? Must not have been a good one."

"I'm not feeling so hot." Greg slipped off the bib suspenders, unzipped his vest, and fanned his shirt. It wasn't more than forty degrees, closer to thirty with the windchill out in open water, but beads of sweat rolled down Greg's face.

Cynthia grabbed Nick's rambler from the dash. "Have a sip of water." The rocking was heavy, but she had grown up with it. Seasickness wasn't so bad on the bigger vessels in this sea state, but *Harpeth Rose* could see swells in the tens of feet in inclement weather.

"Whether I was good or not, who's to say?" Liam said.

Cynthia stopped her movement, taking in his expression. His face looked withered, as if he had been wallowing in grief the past hour. She must've struck a nerve, but didn't know whether to feel good or bad about it.

"I suffered an injury. A bad one. Nearly took out my shoulder for good." He tapped his right shoulder. "I couldn't continue."

Okay, she felt bad. "I'm sorry. I didn't know."

"I know."

She sighed. "And now? You seem to be doing all right. You want to work your way up?"

"Something like that."

It was an odd reply, but she didn't press it. She had been hard on him. Why? She barely knew him. If anything, she treated strangers with kindness until they gave her reason to doubt them. Had he really given her a reason to be harsh? Just because he had been a greenhorn before. She hadn't known the whole story and was quick to judge. Perhaps it was easier to be mad at him than to think of what could happen if she wasn't. Don't be silly, Cynthia.

Liam had dreams and obstacles just like anyone else. And he was right. Why make the week any tougher than it already was?

"What do you think Nick will do with all of this fish?" She hoped the question lightened the mood.

Liam stared ahead, thinking. "Campy's special?"

Greg got up from his seat and bent over the starboard side, heaving.

Liam winced. "Guess he didn't like that idea."

Cynthia wanted to laugh, but seasickness was one of the worst feelings in the world. Her first overnight trip with Dad nearly landed her in the hospital from dehydration, unable to keep anything down the first thirty-six hours. But, as the old sailors' tales went, she developed her sea legs—and stomach. Seasickness hardly hit her again, and when it did, she knew the tricks that helped ward it off.

She set down her knife and took off her gloves, rushing to his side. She poured some water from the rambler over his neck.

He stood back up.

"Rinse your mouth. You'd be better standing for a while, holding onto something. Fix your eyes on an object, maybe back there on land or one of the trawlers. It helps."

Greg took another sip from the rambler. "Thanks."

"Of course." She smiled. "It can strike even the toughest of people."

"Come on up here, Greg." Nick waved him to the bow. Greg handed Nick his rambler back.

"You can keep that." Nick's tone reflected his repulsion.

Cynthia met Liam's eyes. His mouth broke into a crooked smile and she chuckled.

"Keep going, you two," Nick yelled back.

Cynthia grabbed another fish and stepped up her speed.

"You feeling okay?" he asked.

"Me? I can do this all day."

"Honestly," Liam whispered, the light lap of chop on the sides of the boat providing little noise outside the occasional seabird cawing. "I think that was the whole purpose of this exercise."

Cynthia thought the same thing. Just about anyone could chop fish. Sure, it stunk. Although the fresher the fish the more the smell appealed to her. She loved visiting fish markets up the west coast. The smell of the salt and sea and life sucked her in.

But this wasn't super fresh fish. And the boat bobbed back and forth, making it dangerous to hold a knife, let alone wield it.

Still, she loved every second. Even with Liam around.

TWELVE

NICK HEADED *RUST Bucket* back to shore around four in the afternoon, as the sun hid behind low clouds and loomed over the horizon. They had been out for the better part of a day, but Liam wasn't ready to set foot on land.

He remembered that feeling, before the accident. First there was excitement during departure—that this would be the trip to bring back that jackpot catch. After a few days of setting, retrieving, eating microwaved gruel, and spending downtime in restless sleep, the mere thought of a hot shower set his body aching for home. Once there, as the routine went back to normal and a hot cooked meal wasn't special anymore, he longed for the water again.

That was three years ago. It wasn't supposed to be now. He wasn't supposed to have enjoyed being on the water, smelling fish, getting his hands dirty outside of the processing plant. The less exciting, monotony of the plant. If he wasn't helping Nick, Liam wouldn't have stepped foot on *Rust Bucket*. He had purposely moved slower than Cynthia, not wanting to aggravate the injury. Never had he imagined it wouldn't be aggravated. But his shoulder felt great.

What did that mean? Did it mean he actually could join a crew again as greenhorn? Had he ruled out his passion too soon in life? No one had ever said he would never be able to work on a fishing vessel again. Only that it wasn't likely.

The fact he was even considering it a possibility brought him something he hadn't felt in a long time. Joy.

But what about Cynthia? She had spent several hours bent over, cutting old fish, determined to earn her spot. Could he take that away from her for his own benefit? Did he even have a chance to outshine her? And what about Nick? Liam agreed to this to help Nick find a crew member. Is it wrong to suggest himself as an option?

Ben Campbell was waiting at the dock when *Rust Bucket* arrived, *Cool Calypso* secure and the crew long gone. Had Nick kept them out much longer than Ben?

"You head on back, Greg," Nick said. "Try to get some rest and eventually something in your stomach. You'll feel a lot better for it."

Greg nodded, walking up the dock without a word of goodbye.

"What's with him?" Ben grabbed a cooler off Cynthia.

"Sick," Nick said. "Can you handle the rest of this? I want to talk to the rest of my group here."

Ben nodded. "We need to talk about Gus. He just about guided a tour boat straight into a pylon."

Nick sighed. "Let's talk later." He gestured for Liam and Cynthia to follow him toward Campy's Bait and Bar.

"Hey, Nick!"

"Yeah?" Nick turned back, and Ben held a lid of one cooler.

"What am I supposed to do with the fish?"

Nick shrugged. "It's my gift to you." He continued up the planks.

Ben mumbled to himself behind them.

Liam looked at Cynthia, who held back a smile.

"Brothers," Liam whispered.

Cynthia's smile faded, and focus returned. Had he done something to upset her? They got along better this afternoon, hadn't they? It shouldn't matter now. Not if he was actually going to pursue this. He needed to talk to Nick first. If Nick wasn't open to it, then no point in fretting over all the what-ifs.

Nick led Liam and Cynthia to the back office on the first floor of Campy's and stopped at the doorway. "Cynthia, have a seat. Liam, I'll be with you in a few minutes."

Liam nodded and kept his distance from the door. He roamed

around somewhere in the galoshes section, pondering the difference between men's and women's styles, when Cynthia exited the office.

"Liam." Nick waved him over.

Cynthia briefly waved to Liam. "I'll see you back at the inn."

"Okay." So, he wasn't hallucinating about today. She was talking to him, and nicely.

He stepped into the office, and Nick shut the door.

"What was that all about?" Liam sat in front of the desk as Nick swung around behind.

"I really only wanted to talk to you," Nick said. "I thought if she saw I kept you back again she'd be onto us. So I asked her back, too, and made up some small talk."

"I'm impressed with the attention to detail you put in a lie."

Nick shook his head. "It's for a good cause. Anyway, what are your thoughts on Cynthia today?"

Liam relaxed, sitting back in the chair. "She's cut out for it. I was impressed, not just with her ability and determination. But how she jumped to Greg's aid." All true, but if he was going to vie for the position himself, should he really be talking her up?

"I'm not looking for an onboard nurse."

"I know that. You know what I mean. She saw a man down and handled it. Like any crew member should do and would want done for them."

Nick nodded.

Liam sighed, hand scratching his forehead.

"What?"

"Don't you think you're being tough on her?" After his onboard illness, Greg lazed about with Nick the rest of the time. Cynthia followed her orders and continued working, but Nick could've stopped her after two coolers. Surely at three.

"Tough? She chose this, like everyone else on *Harpeth Rose*. Their motivations may all differ, but it's still a choice. She was out for a few hours today. That's only the tip of what she'll have to endure. We're out for days, sometimes weeks at a time. And if the crabbing grounds are hot, we don't slow down. She'll be chopping and baiting long hours. You know all this, Liam."

"I know…." Is this really the life he wanted back for himself?

Nick smiled.

"What?" Liam shuffled, uncomfortable with the slyness of the grin.

"You like her, don't you?"

"I told you, I think she's cut out for it. I was impressed today."

"No, I mean you *like* her."

"I don't—" Liam rubbed his neck. "It's complicated. More so after today."

"You don't have to be embarrassed. You're not really her competition, for goodness sakes."

Nick saying it out loud was a punch to the gut. There was no sense in trying to hide it from Nick—both his new career hope, and that he did like Cynthia, but he was still sorting out the reasons other than her being a walking enigma. "It's hard to start a relationship on a lie. I had to at least tell her I had been a greenhorn."

"How'd she take that?"

"Not so well."

"I wouldn't think so. I had heard she was fiercely determined, but she's made it clear these past two days she's really competitive."

"That's putting it nicely."

"It's a good thing. As long as it doesn't get in her own way."

Liam nodded and stared at his feet.

Nick folded his arms across his chest. "Why do I get the feeling there's something else?"

Tryouts lasted a few more days. If he had the slightest inkling to do this, he had to say so. "I'm thinking I want to try out for your crew. For real."

Nick's eyebrows nearly hit the rim of his hat. "Are you serious? You mean, be out there at sea again?"

"I know it sounds crazy. But being out there on the water today— it's been years since I let myself go there. I don't want to seem ungrateful for the opportunity you gave me at the plant, but the more I'm away from it looking in, the more I realize that's not what I want to do forever."

"And fishing is? Are you sure you're up for that?" Nick put up a hand. "Don't get me wrong. I know you know what the lifestyle is like. You've lived it. Any crew would be lucky to have you with your work ethic and knowledge of the job. I mean, physically, do you think you are able? I don't want you to be more confident than you should be and reinjure yourself."

Liam stood, pacing the room before leaning on the back of the chair. "You think I want that?"

"It's not just the risk you are putting yourself in. I wouldn't want you, or Cynthia, or anyone else out there if they couldn't handle it, whether it's physical, or emotional, or psychological. You saw Greg today. Getting sick on the water is not necessarily a deal-breaker. But how he handles it from now on will show his true worth as a crew member. Will he quit? Or will he learn from it? And will it endanger the rest of the crew?"

"You're preaching to the choir," Liam said. "I know."

"But it's hard to be objective when it's someone you care about."

Liam bit his lip. He knew Nick was referring to him, but it held true for Liam's perception of Cynthia. How could he objectively assess her with how he's been feeling about her? Add to it becoming her real competition.

"All I'm saying is give me a chance—the same chance you're giving everyone else. I'll step down as your help with assessing the others, of course. Treat me as you would treat them."

Nick sighed. "This is a big ask."

"I wouldn't ask if I wasn't serious."

"I know." Nick stood and faced a framed picture of him and his brothers in front of the building. They had eyes full of optimism and baby faces of teenagers, before the responsibilities of adulthood. "Okay. You try out with the rest of them. But if at any point you change your mind, or put yourself in harm's way or anyone else unnecessarily, promise me you'll back out."

Liam placed his palm on his chest. "Promise. I appreciate it, Nick."

"Well, you should at least make it through tomorrow. It's only half a day because I needed to ask something of you. It's the reason I called you in here in the first place."

"Sure, anything." Liam's cell rang. "It's the plant."

"Go ahead." Nick shooed him away.

Liam stepped out of the office onto the main floor. "This is Liam."

"Liam, it's Colin." Colin was one of the other two floor managers who luckily helped cover Liam's previously scheduled days this week.

"What's going on, Colin? I said not to call unless there's some kind of emergency."

"That's why I'm calling. The water ozone generator is down."

"You're kidding me. How long?" Ozonated water was an essential part of processing in almost every step, from washing the take to forming the ice used in the shipping packages.

"Thirty minutes. I called when we tried all our options here. The distributor's rep can't come out for another day."

"A day!" Every minute down meant workers without work. Lost production. Jeopardizing freshness and sanitary conditions. "I'll be over there. I don't know if I can fix it, but I'll have to try."

Liam hung up and returned to Nick's office. One phone call was all it took to wipe away his fantasy of being back on a fishing vessel. Who was he kidding? He was gone what, two days, and the plant was in dire straits. How would he be able to leave? He had a job that he excelled at, with employees who needed him. Leaving seemed impossible.

But he couldn't shake his curiosity.

"What was it you were going to ask me?" Maybe it was something he could do from Oakside. Maybe he could dart back, solve the issue, and come back tomorrow.

"Josie's been highlighting people pursuing their own happiness throughout the month as part of a segment on the morning show. She's been on my back about having applicants from these tryouts on the program. She especially wants Cynthia to get a woman's perspective. Why she wants to change jobs, especially to one like this, blah, blah, blah."

"You want me to convince Cynthia to do the show?"

"No, that's already a go. Cynthia and Josie are good friends. Josie would like one of the guys to go on as well. I've already asked the others."

"Let me guess. They all said no?"

"Bingo."

"Oh, come on Nick."

"I wouldn't ask if I had other options. Please. It's really important to Josie, and I want to see her happy. We're trying to move into a new house, which of course has been delayed time and again. I don't know if she's getting restless or what."

"So I'd be doing this for your relationship?"

He let out a deep breath. "Sort of."

"I can't, Nick. I just got a call that a generator is down at the plant, and they can't seem to get anyone out there until tomorrow."

"A generator?" He straightened in his chair.

"Water ozone generator."

He tapped the desk with his index finger. "I have someone who could look at it."

"Yeah?"

"He helps out with *Harpeth Rose* and maintenance here at the store. He's kind of the go-to mechanic around town."

"Can he be out there before tomorrow?"

"Let me check." Nick picked up the phone and dialed. Judging by the banter, he was talking to Ben. Nick held up his hand to Liam to stay put and thanked Ben.

"Ben's sending him over. You should have a running generator within a few hours."

"Thank you for that."

"Happy to help."

Liam sighed, chuckling at the circumstance. "Fine. I'll do it."

"Do what?"

"You know what I mean. The show. I can't say no to it now after what you just did."

Nick nodded and smiled. "Like I said. Happy to help."

THIRTEEN

CYNTHIA CLOSED HER eyes as the shampoo rinsed out of her hair. She opted for a jasmine and coconut shampoo, courtesy of Constance to every guest. The bubbly lather's fragrance rid her of the I-chopped-fish-all-day smell. Just because she enjoyed the smell of marine life on her didn't mean the rest of the world did.

She toweled off her hair, wrapped the towel around her torso, and hurried to Room 2. It felt amazing to put on yoga pants and her gray oversized hoodie. It once had a white logo of The Spokane Spatula, a favorite restaurant of Mom's when Cynthia visited, but it long ago faded with the frayed hem and hood strings.

The ring of the phone startled her. Hopefully it wasn't Bea. Tomorrow morning had been one of her scheduled shifts that Darrell would cover. If he backed out, she was out of options. Not something Bea particularly liked to hear.

"Hello?"

"Hello, it's Constance. I hope I'm not disturbing you."

Cynthia relaxed. "Not at all. Is everything okay?" Liam had not returned yet from Nick's office. Nick certainly hadn't spoken to her for this long. Could something have happened to him? Why her mind went straight to Liam was a question she'd put off for another time.

"Oh, yes. As of a matter of fact, I have something I'd like to give you. I think you may enjoy it after the day you've had." Either Constance assumed the type of day, knowing Nick Campbell, or word spread through town. Both options were highly probable. *"I had a guest check*

out early, and he gave me two vouchers for dinner at The Codfather." The name may have been silly, but the restaurant near the top of the hill ranked the fanciest in all of Maiden's Bay.

Cynthia assessed her yoga pants and hoodie. "I appreciate you thinking of me. But I'm sure you have other guests, especially out-of-towners that would love the experience."

Constance's silence oozed disappointment enough. "Are you sure? They cover everything, including wine. I thought you could get to know that roommate of yours, since you are strangers forced to be around each other. You could show him the town on the way. I'm sure he would love that. From what Liam has told me, he hasn't seen much of Maiden's Bay."

"Really, I love that you thought of me." From the sounds of it, Constance wasn't thinking of her—more like her and Liam. Their footing improved today, but dinner at Maiden's Bay's finest was a giant leap on the social comfort ladder.

"Maybe next time someone leaves something, give me a call?" Cynthia turned around. Had the door to the room clicked? Or was she hearing things?

"Oh, fine. You're probably right. I'll find a visitor who hasn't been. You enjoy your evening."

"Thank you, Constance."

She hadn't known Constance as much as Josie or Nick, but the more she got to know her the more she believed all of the pleasant opinions of those who did. She was genuinely kind and honest. With a bit of a kick.

Of course it hadn't been Bea calling. Thank goodness. That was all she needed after a day of fish chopping. Bea would've called her cell phone, anyway. Which was... *where* at the moment? She checked the bed and desk and inside her purse, and she shot up, happy her brain was working. The bathroom.

She slid on the free thin white slippers and walked down the hallway, the plush bounce of the carpet cushioning her feet. She opened the door and steam hit her. Through it stood a muscular man.

Cynthia turned away when she processed bare skin and the man's surprise. "I'm so sorry. I had just been in here and didn't realize anyone had—I didn't mean—I left my phone."

With her eyes closed and one hand on the doorknob, she pointed to the sink.

"It's okay, Cynthia."

She opened one eye. Broad shoulders and sculpted pecs. Lean nose and strong jaw. Eyes the color of walnut.

Liam.

He clenched a towel around his waist with one hand.

Cynthia's face and neck burned. Heck, she probably radiated light from her humiliation.

His other hand held out the phone. "Cynthia?"

"Oh, right. Thank you. I'll, uh… see you around." She had done enough seeing him already. "I'm going to the room now."

"Okay." He smiled. "I'm going to finish up now."

"Sounds good. I mean, do whatever you want." She turned away, shaking her head during the—how did the hallway get so long?—walk back to Room 2.

She wanted to pull the hood over her head and hide in the bed. First she had put her foot in her mouth, insulting Liam before realizing he had been injured. Now she walked in on him in the bathroom. *What's next, Cynthia?*

The longer it took Liam to return, the worse she felt. "Just get it out of the way. Move on from it." She collapsed onto the pillow. "And now I'm talking to myself. Yep, he really had drawn the short straw on roommates."

All she could see when she closed her eyes was wet skin, pecs expanding and contracting with his breath, water rolling down his abs to where the towel wrapped low around his waist.

A knock at the door sprang her upright.

"It's just me." Liam entered, a smile across his face as wide as his sculpted chest.

She glanced down at his clothed torso, then back to his face. She quickly diverted her stare to the desk, half not knowing where to look, half convinced he'd see her thoughts through her eyes. He's just your roommate. Plenty of roommates walk in on each other.

"Well, *that* was interesting."

"I'm—" She opened her mouth to say something. The door wasn't locked. *I didn't hear the water running. I didn't know you returned. I am an idiot.*

But he went on. "Fortune is smiling on me today."

Not exactly how she'd put it.

"First the generator went out at the plant."

Cynthia scowled. "That doesn't sound like fortune smiling."

"Ah! But then Nick helped me and it all worked out. And now...." He flashed two rectangular pieces of paper in his hand.

"What are those?"

"I must've left an impression on Constance because she came looking for me and stopped me in the hallway. Gave me not one, but *two* dinner vouchers for tonight."

Cynthia shook her head. Constance had seemed intent on the two of them going to dinner. She failed with Cynthia, but then there was Liam. Well played, Constance.

"Why are you shaking your head?"

"She offered me those also."

"Oh." He sat on the bed and slipped on his shoes. "You didn't accept them? Is it not a good restaurant?"

"No. Actually, it's the best in Maiden's Bay. The best for seafood."

He spread his arms out, palms up to the sky in confusion. "Again, why would you pass this up? Haven't you ever heard that it's never a good idea to pass up free food?"

"Constance gave you her advice, too, I see."

"It's good advice."

Cynthia crossed her legs and folded her arms. "I've been before. Plus I'm already in my comfy clothes."

"You weren't on your way to shower?"

"I already—" She caught what he meant, and her skin singed like a stovetop burner. "I'm so sorry about that. I wasn't paying attention."

"It's okay. I guess I've lived by myself for so long I didn't even think to lock the door."

"You shouldn't have to think that."

"Really, it's okay." He touched her knee gently, kindness in his eyes. It calmed her, but as the awareness of his touch lingered, her senses heightened, quickening her breath and pulse.

He withdrew his hand, as if realizing the tension within herself.

"You're honestly going to turn down a free dinner because of your wardrobe choices?" He stood up, a look of childhood glee on his face. "As you see here, I am wearing the finest khaki cargo pants. I don't know if you've heard, but I've been told many times that these have gone out of fashion well before I purchased them."

"I would've said something, but I didn't want to be that person." It was said in jest, but she honestly liked his outdoorsy-and-don't-care style. Not like Mitchell, her last boyfriend, who'd been afraid to hold a fish, let alone gut it. Boyfriend wasn't even the right word. Three dates was hardly a committed relationship. Ironically, for all the rugged outdoorsmen Maiden's Bay and all of western Washington had to offer, she ended up dating the guys who cared more about their hair than the environment.

"Of course, no outdated outfit is complete without your standard checkered flannel shirt and—hold on." He swiped the navy vest hanging over the desk chair. "Wait for it." He put it on over the cobalt flannel and zipped it up. "Not only will I be toasty warm, but if the power goes out and they lose heat in the building I'll be all set to chop firewood."

"How versatile." Cynthia couldn't help but laugh.

"You shall also be warm and cozy in your current ensemble. You'll be ready to rock the warrior pose in those yoga pants, useful if you need to... poke someone in the eye?" He shrugged. "I'm not exactly sure what use the warrior pose serves."

"They would never let me in like this."

"Nonsense. Why would they turn down paying customers?"

She stood and slipped her phone in her purse. "Because we wouldn't be paying customers."

"True. I guess we're prepaid customers. Even so, come on. If they kick us out, then shame on them. Unless you've eaten already." He raised his eyebrows.

That was it. He gave her an out, right there in front of her. Of course it would be a lie, and she'd have to be sneaky about actually getting a meal at some point before he'd return. That was what logical Cynthia said to convince herself. More convincing was Liam standing in front of her, his eager face shaking his eyebrows up and down like a kid at summer camp waiting to hear whether or not he can jump in the lake.

"No."

"No?"

"I didn't eat yet." She swung her purse on her shoulder. "Let's go."

"Really?"

"Yes, really. Before I change my mind." She stepped out into the hallway, and Liam locked the door to Room 2 behind them. "By the way, how do you know warrior pose—any yoga pose—for that matter?"

They trotted down the steps to the lobby. "Are you saying guys like me don't do yoga?"

"No, I—I just meant that it looks like, with your... physique... your—" She touched her shoulders and flexed. Just stop, Cynthia.

"Wow, I'm gonna stop you there."

"Thank you."

"That was painful to watch."

Cynthia laughed, hand covering her eyes.

"Honestly no, I don't do yoga. But I did try once. My sisters dragged me along. People claim it's a good thing to add to the mix for strength training."

"It didn't take?"

"Not at all."

"Enjoy you two." Constance winked from behind the counter.

Liam waved as they walked by. "What was that all about?"

"She want sus to bond or something. Get to know each other."

He held the door open for Cynthia, and she walked through. "Then we best not disappoint her."

FOURTEEN

LIAM HUFFED AS they hiked up Third Street, the vest starting to feel like a bad choice. The road shot up the hill, which inclined steeply after the first three blocks or so. "You sure you don't want me to drive?"

"I thought you liked strength training." Cynthia's hair, slicked back in a wet ponytail, swung side to side with each march of her feet upward.

"Let's be clear." He held up a finger. "I may *do* strength training, but I never said *like.*"

"I get it," Cynthia said. "I love running. And I hate it."

They turned right, leveling off onto what felt like the highest road in Maiden's Bay, then left onto a narrow road opening to a parking lot. The Codfather sat etched into the hillside, a wide wooden staircase rising from the parking lot to the front door.

Liam stopped at the top of the stairs, turning around to face west. The low sun cast shadows on downtown Maiden's Bay, yet amber hues still bounced off the glass fronts of the houses in the hillside neighborhoods. The ocean in all its vastness looked so small and distant below.

"It definitely has a view." He gestured for Cynthia to go in first.

The dusk's haze was blinding compared to the dim lighting of the restaurant. A man in a white shirt with black vest and pants greeted them. Soft jazz music played overhead, and light chatter with clinking silverware and glasses danced around the room.

The host sized them up, taking in Liam's cargo pants all the way down to his boots. He cleared his throat. "Tickets?"

"Oh, right." Liam pulled the tickets out of his vest's inner pocket.

The man scrutinized the print on the passes. "Right this way."

He led them to the left, the main dining space filled with round tables for two and the occasional table for four in the corners. A woman snapped her fingers at the host. "Table 15."

He pointed his thumb behind him, perplexed.

"Yes, Gerald." The woman waved him off.

Liam and Cynthia turned around and followed Gerald to the other side of the restaurant. They passed three tables along the front window to the last one in the corner.

Liam leaned down to whisper in Cynthia's ear. "Maybe they're trying to keep us hidden."

Her mouth curled down in a wince, eyes scanning the restaurant.

Liam caught the sparkle of pearls and diamonds accenting cocktail dresses. Most of the men wore suits and ties, and one couple sat in tuxedos.

"I knew we were underdressed." Cynthia tugged her hoodie strings.

He touched the middle of her back. "You look lovely." Fancy dresses and fine jewelry had their place on the rare occasion, but he much preferred a more relaxed look. A woman who felt comfortable in her own skin was sexier than anything she could wear.

"Here you are." Gerald pulled out the chair for Cynthia and handed over a single menu card. "The waiter will be around for your drink order. Enjoy."

After the hike up, Liam was parched. He drank half the glass of water from his table setting. It was embarrassing how much he was out of breath. Perhaps he should look into cardio more.

"Wait a second." Cynthia dropped the menu card. She examined the two candles and clipped red roses in the petite square vase between them. The white linen tablecloth was strewn with shiny red confetti in the shape of hearts. "I can't believe this. I can't *believe* I forgot."

"What is it?"

She closed her eyes and leaned back into the chair. "This is their Valentine's dinner."

"Valentine's? That's not for several days." Was that right? Such holidays were so hard to remember. He had no reason to remember the past three years, anyway.

"I know. But they're always booked, so they started having their special dinner two nights in a row, then three. Apparently it's for the whole week now. I wondered why the host asked for tickets. I thought, how could he know we had vouchers? Because everyone does for the Valentine's dinner. I mean, come on—the candles, red roses, heart confetti. All that's missing is someone walking around playing a violin."

He examined the menu, four courses, in which he had three options to choose from for each. "I think you're right."

The woman who had snapped at Gerald appeared at the table. "Hello. I'm Rowan and will be taking care of you this evening. Would you care for champagne?"

"I thought the meal only came with wine." Cynthia pointed at the menu's fine print.

"On the house." Rowan smiled, waiting to pour.

"Then by all means." Liam raised his glass and waited for Cynthia to decide. "I'm rolling with Constance's advice on this one."

"I thought that only applied to food."

He shrugged. "I figure we made it this far."

She lifted the glass and accepted the champagne. She read his surprise and returned his shrug. "When else am I going to sip champagne in yoga pants?"

Liam smiled. Cynthia didn't strike him as the type to be spontaneous, but she was quickly proving him wrong.

They placed their salad and appetizer orders, and Rowan left the bottle of champagne on the table.

Cynthia stared out the window, sipping the dry bubbles.

"I'm sorry," Liam said.

"For what?"

"I kind of cajoled you into coming, and I don't want to ruin Valentine's for you if you had plans with someone else." He had wondered about her dating status since sharing his number in the flower shop, but hadn't the perfect opportunity to bring it up until now.

She waved it off. "No, I didn't. Or don't, I should say."

It had been a relief that she relaxed her anger with him today. For her to have agreed to dinner at this place was euphoric. He watched her lips as she spoke, clinging to her words.

"Valentine's Day is so cheesy to me. It's all about being over-the-top and buying into these physical things we think the other person would read as romantic." She finally caught his eyes, the setting sun and candles vying to light her smooth, narrow face, cheekbones glowing without makeup. "I know I can sound harsh." She straightened the napkin on her lap, like a nervous habit. "Flowers and chocolate don't make a relationship is what I'm saying."

"You don't have to justify that with me. Trust me."

"Sounds like you have a story to tell."

He had wanted her to call these past two weeks and found himself disappointed she hadn't. That was before he knew she wanted the fishing life. Now that he knew, and she was here in front of him, asking him to open up, did he want to go there?

He shrugged. "Depends on whether I have an audience."

She placed her elbows on the table, leaning in. "Do tell."

The fire in her eyes struck him with fear—fear that if he continued there was no going back. Maybe it was too late. He was already smitten.

"Well, the last girlfriend I had was all about decadence. She wanted extravagance, trips to whisk her away, flashy things. At first, she made things exciting because of it. But then—"

"It got expensive."

"That was a side effect, yes. But it was more about her not being able to be happy as 'us.' She couldn't spend a quiet night on the couch, or lie in bed skipping breakfast on a Sunday." He flustered at the thought of sharing a bed with Cynthia. They were already sharing a hotel room, which was rough enough, knowing she was merely feet away. He swallowed the imagery. "We always had to be doing something, out somewhere, or getting stuff."

"I think that would drive me mad."

"It does after a while. You start thinking that you're not enough to keep this person happy. That you have to always be giving more than just yourself."

"That's awful. I'm sorry to make you talk about it."

"You didn't make me do anything." He wanted her to know all of him. "Don't be sorry. It was over three years ago, so I'd like to think I've moved on."

They sipped their drinks, the pause in the conversation growing awkward. The arrival of their salads filled the void that quickly expanded. He hardly knew anything about this woman, this beautiful woman in a gray hoodie with her matching gray eyes.

"You're not into Valentine's Day, so let's change the subject. How'd you get to working at Bea's, then trying out for greenhorn on Nick's boat? Those are two very different life choices."

She covered her lips as she finished chewing, the first timidity he'd seen since sitting down. He could watch her do that all day. Or chop fish, for all he cared.

"Bea's sister and my father were in hospice care, just up the road, at the same time."

"Oh my goodness. Is your father—?"

"Passed away, a year and a half ago."

"I'm sorry. My dad passed away, too. Six years ago. Heart attack."

"Sorry to you, as well. Dad suffered a stroke, which was sudden. I'm assuming the heart attack was unexpected?"

Liam nodded.

"Well, he survived the stroke, but the slow decline afterward…. It was inevitable."

"Did it at least give you a chance to come to terms with it, as much as you could?"

"It did. Sometimes I think seeing him fade away was tougher than if it were abrupt." She touched the corner of her eye. "I'm sorry, this conversation has turned for the worse."

"It's okay. Not at all." He smiled. "You were saying Bea was there at hospice?"

"Yes. I got to know Bea—well, it's hard to really *know* Bea, but knew her enough—from seeing her there during our visits. Her sister passed away shortly after my dad. About a month later, she had an opening. I'd spent those last two years out of college helping my dad until he was moved to hospice. I wasn't going to say no to an opportunity like that."

"You... you keep surprising me."

She tilted her head, eyes suspicious. "What does that mean?"

"When I met you at Bea's, you were this—dare I say—embarrassed woman—"

"I sprayed you. In the face. It *was* embarrassing."

He chuckled. "Then I see you out there." He pointed to the window, the tip of the sun waving adieu to the shade of night. "You're confident, and passionate, and eager to learn and listen."

"Am I?"

"Well, maybe not from me at first."

She sat back, letting go of the candlelight that revealed the flush of her cheeks.

"You obviously have a natural knack for it," he said. Which didn't help his chances. But no thinking of that right now. Not tonight.

"Thank you. I owe it all to my dad. My mom didn't want him to take me out on the water, let alone teach me boating or fishing. But Dad took the time, and he was a great teacher."

"Where's your Mom now?"

"She moved to Spokane after she and Dad divorced."

"So you don't have any family here now in Maiden's Bay?"

"I do, actually. My sister and her husband are here, and my niece, although she's away at college. We don't exactly get along all that well, Jackie and I. She wasn't happy Dad left me the house."

"Sorry to hear that. My sisters and I go through the usual sibling bickering, but it's good to have family." Even if they nag you when it comes to relationships.

She stared at the table.

"I'm sorry. I didn't mean to make you feel bad about it."

"No, I get it. If I could mend the rift between me and Jackie,

I would. She doesn't agree with my life choices. It's hard to change someone's mind when they've thought one way for so long."

"As in, your choice in career?"

She nodded. "Or how my father encouraged me to pursue it. We haven't spoken since he left me the house."

Although she opened up, he hadn't expected the evening to turn to such a somber one. *Way to go, Liam.*

"What about you? Why try again after, how long?"

"Three and a half years or so. If I'm being honest...." Was he ever going to be totally honest with her? It wasn't in his nature to lie, and for so long, to someone he grew to care about. "I'd resigned to managing the process plant forever. I hadn't even had time off until now, if you can believe it. "

"That says a lot though, about your work ethic and dedication."

"Or that maybe I was just stuck in a monotony that didn't leave me happy."

"Fishing makes you happy?"

Did it? It was the million dollar question of the week. Was he ready to give up all that security, risking it for life on the water again?

"It did while I was in it. Part of me hoped it would in coming back." The other part hoped he'd hate it, to whole-heartedly accept his lot in life. "I had to know for sure. More than just knowing in my head. I had to know everything else. And I got a hint of that joy again yesterday. I had thought for so long that my injury limited my abilities, and ultimately the possibility of being happy. I'm starting to see that I've been wrong."

"I think it's you who are surprising me."

He smiled, bewildered.

"When we met at the inn, I thought you were going to be the cool student in class. You know, the one who manages to ace everything without putting forth the effort. After what you told me... I think it's amazing that you're putting yourself out there again." She tilted her head slightly, a smile growing. "It's almost a shame you have some tough competition."

He held up his champagne glass. "May the best person win."

She obliged, clinking glasses.

It had been a whirlwind of a week already. The possibility of switching jobs, this beautiful woman in front of him as his main threat in achieving his goal, and then there was the fact he was asked by Nick to monitor her progress in the first place. He couldn't tell if the champagne made it worse or helped to blur it out.

He took down another gulp. "You said your father left you a house. Is it here in Maiden's Bay?"

"Yes. In fact...." She stood, gazing out the window. "You can see a bit of the roof and chimney from here."

He stood, leaning over the table. Her arm touched his shoulder, pushing him closer to the window as she leaned out of the way.

"Right there." She pointed out a slate roof and brick chimney, nearly halfway down the hillside.

He pointed. "That one?" He turned, his mouth near her cheek. Her hair smelled of coconut over the smoke of the candle.

She turned toward him, her lips in touchable distance. Soft warm breaths tickled his mouth. Every piece of him wanted to kiss her right then. Except for that voice, the one reminding him of his deceit in all of this, that she was competition and could end his dream of joining a crew as quickly as it had returned.

A woman approached the table, playing the violin. No. It was too much.

They parted, sitting down while the violinist played with a smile.

Cynthia's eyes grew wide and she mouthed, *I told you.*

The woman swayed with the notes until the music hit a crescendo into the finale. It took every ounce of composure to not look at Cynthia, who covered her mouth.

"That was lovely," Liam said.

"Beautiful." Cynthia bit her lip. The woman smiled and bowed, then walked off to the other side of the restaurant.

Liam and Cynthia laughed, Cynthia wiping her eyes, cheeks round and red.

"You called it," Liam said.

"I didn't think she was ever going to stop."

Liam caught his breath, staring at the gorgeous human being in front of him.

He hadn't wanted her to stop. He didn't want the conversation to stop. He certainly didn't want the night to stop.

But that voice reminded him it had to stop.

FIFTEEN

CYNTHIA SWATTED THE ringing in the room. *No. Too early. That can't be the alarm.*

She sat up in bed, wiping her eyes and shutting up her phone. They hadn't exactly stayed out late last night by any means. But the two glasses of champagne may have been one too many, and the decadent chocolate cake after already being full made her feel sluggish like a bear in hibernation. The morning run wasn't going to happen.

The bed next to her was empty. She hadn't heard Liam leave the room at all, but then again, it was the deepest sleep she had in a while. She changed into a long-sleeved shirt, pocketed pants, and a pullover. The bathroom at the end of the hall was empty—after confirming with a knock—so she splashed water on her face and brushed her teeth. She had given in to the dinner, then champagne, then his curiosity. Not everything was revealed, but she hadn't had a more serious conversation with someone in ages.

Her phone buzzed as she entered the room. *I didn't hit snooze, did I?* She cleared the head fog enough to see Elise was calling.

"Morning, Cynthia."

"You're calling early." Cynthia sat on the bed. "I thought we agreed to a communication hiatus during tryouts."

"We did, but that doesn't hold when you go out on a date."

"What are you talking about?"

"Are you telling me you didn't have a romantic dinner with a—how did she put it—a solid hottie?"

"How did—what—?" Of *course* someone there last night knew Elise. She was a librarian who could roll off names with overdue accounts and how much they owed. And this was Maiden's Bay. "It wasn't like that. Constance had tickets, and he's also trying out." She sat on the bed, wondering how much to tell her. How could she not tell her?

"Elise… it's him. The Oakside guy."

"What do you mean it's him?"

"The guy I was out with last night is the guy from Oakside. He's also my roommate, and trying out." The more words that spewed out of her mouth, the crazier it all sounded.

"What are you going to do?"

She shook her head. It was the million dollar question. "I'm focusing on getting this position."

"I sense a but. From what I hear, it's a cute butt."

Cynthia shook off Elise's homophone humor. "Look, I would love to divulge with you the physical perfection of a man that he is, but he's my competition. It's hard enough to focus on what I need to do when he's here." Cynthia heard footsteps in the hallway. "I think he's coming."

"I want to hear everything once this week is through."

"Okay, okay."

Liam knocked before entering.

"Look, I gotta go."

"We'll catch up Mon—"

Cynthia hung up and straightened herself.

"Everything okay?" Liam asked.

"Yeah. Just a friend wishing the best for me." Elise's idea of best had more to do with Liam than the greenhorn job.

"Figured it was my turn to get coffee."

"Thank you." She cradled the cup and took in the aroma, as if the scented air had magical powers to cure her grogginess. He was already dressed and ready for the day.

"You got up early."

"Yeah, I couldn't—" He scratched the back of his head. "I wanted to get a good start. I guess rooming with an early riser motivated me to get out there."

"Glad I could help." She winced as she stretched her hamstrings and quads.

"You okay?"

"I'll be fine. Just a little sore from my last run. Usually worse the second day."

"I thought you ran frequently?"

"I do. I don't think anyone's supposed to really know this, but I know the lighthouse keeper, and he lets me run the stairs in the morning. Just once, up and down. But he had someone filling in for him the past week, so I didn't get my usual steps in. Monday was the first time since he's been back."

"That seems like it would be quite a workout."

"Two hundred six steps."

"I'm getting tired and dizzy thinking about it."

She smiled and drank the coffee while exiting the room. Coffee after toothpaste made for a bitter mixture in her mouth.

They stood side by side outside the door to Room 2. There was something in the air, something pulling her to say something, to acknowledge last night. She had a good time, and they were both so tired by the time they returned that—at least she—went to bed right away. But Elise was wrong. It wasn't a date. It was an impromptu meal with her temporary roommate. Temporary was all this could be.

Liam walked toward the steps, and the moment passed. What was she going to say anyway? It probably would've sounded stupid and just left her feeling awkward. They were roommates and competitors. He was here for the week, and then they'd move on with their lives. *Temporary.*

They walked downstairs, Cynthia's muscles arguing with her brain until they reached the lobby.

"How was dinner?" Constance sported an apron and held an empty coffee pot. "I didn't get to catch up with you two when you returned last night."

"It was delicious," Liam said. "Thank you again for the tickets."

"Yes, thank you," Cynthia said. Sneaky Constance.

"I'm so glad you enjoyed it. I remember last year's Valentine's Day dinner was absolutely wonderful. I probably won't get to do it this year."

Cynthia looked at Liam, who frowned. Poor Gus. Poor Constance. They had broken up just after the New Year, so it had to feel pretty fresh. Apparently it did for Gus, judging by his constant presence at Campy's Bait and Bar.

"We're heading out." Liam waved. "See you this evening."

"Okay. Enjoy your day. Another sunny—well, cloudy one, but that's better than rain, right?"

Cynthia nodded and followed Liam out the door. The temperature was slightly cooler than yesterday, the sun nowhere to be seen within the quilt of thick clouds overhead. She zipped the pullover all the way up, shielding her mouth and chin from the finicky breeze. The wind couldn't make up its mind on which way to blow, the few dead leaves left in mid-winter twirling in the air.

"What do you think he'll have us do this morning?" Liam asked.

"Not sure. All I know is that we don't have any tasks this afternoon." Was that something everyone knew, or only her? She had Josie's interview on deck. At first, she didn't care to participate, but for one, it was for Josie, and two, if she didn't get greenhorn with Nick, maybe someone else watching would care to have her on board. The latter required logistics she wasn't willing to think about yet.

The four other greenhorn contenders trickled in, and everyone walked further down the dock. Nick, Ben, and three others waited next to *Harpeth Rose*.

"Any idea what's going on?" Liam said out of the side of his mouth.

"Maybe we're actually setting foot on *Harpeth Rose* today." Just saying the name out loud sent tingles down her spine. "I know Billie there is part of Nick's crew." It was essentially a week-long job interview, after all, so she had done her homework.

"Good morning. Welcome to day three of tryouts."

Ben perked up. "The final day."

"No, it's not," Nick said.

"Oh. *Almost* the final day."

Nick gritted his teeth. "No, it's not."

"How much longer is this gonna go on?" Ben whispered loud enough to hear.

"It's for the week, a week is not three—never mind. We'll talk about this later."

Ben tipped his head back, sulking.

"The good news is that we'll just be out for the morning. The not-so-good news, depending on your stomach and affinity for tight quarters, is that we'll be running a drill on *Harpeth Rose*."

Cynthia practically squealed. Setting foot on *Harpeth Rose*'s deck was such a dream come true, it made the tryouts worth it, even if she didn't make greenhorn.

"Don't worry, Greg," Nick said. "We'll keep her in the bay since we have to be back mid-day. Should be better conditions."

Greg's face turned sour. If only she had Dramamine on her, Cynthia would give him one. Or five. If he strived to be a greenhorn, though, he'd better get his sea legs—and stomach—sooner rather than later.

"Since she's a much larger vessel than what we worked on yesterday, I brought some extra help. This here is Fred." The older forty-something man waved and winked at Sean. Of course. Sean had a familiarity from the first time she saw him, and now she placed it. Crewman Fred's son. Great. Might as well cut the week short and crown Sean the victor.

"My deckhand, Billie," Nick continued, "and most everyone knows Joel."

"Interesting," Liam said. "Didn't know he fished, too."

"Do you know Joel?" This time she was the one side-speaking. Too many surprises this morning.

"Know is a stretch. I know he knows you."

How did he know that? She did know the town's bartender and youngest of the Campbell brothers, mainly through his lighthouse keeper grandfather. What could he have possibly told Liam in the short time he'd been around?

"Now that we got that out of the way." Ben motioned to get on with it.

"Today you'll be learning the ins and outs of *Harpeth Rose.* Mainly the ins. We've set up a race in the form of a scavenger hunt. After we get her out in the cape, you'll be sent to your first location. One of us will be waiting at each checkpoint to give you the next location. Pass through all five locations, and hit topside. The first one to throw the grappling hook overboard is the winner."

"What do they win?" Ben asked.

"There's no physical prize. The prize of learning the ship and where everything is."

"That's exciting."

"It's an exercise." Nick turned to the contestants. "When one of your crewmates sends you for something, getting lost or delayed is not an option. Time is of the essence out at sea. I urge you to pay attention to the layout as much as possible because it's important."

Cynthia's skin tingled as they boarded *Harpeth Rose.* The nearly one hundred foot fishing vessel was not the prettiest of boats. Its hull was a dull metal gray, with dings and dents throughout. The newest part was the crab pot crane, the shiny black arm lying parallel to the deck, looking like the weight of it would sink *Harpeth Rose* at any second.

Nick ordered his crew to their positions, the men sprawling out, working to bring up the ropes off the dock and acting as lookouts in maneuvering the harbor.

This was it. This was what she had dreamed about for so long, seeing the bow cut through the water on its return, or leaving a foamy white wake on its departure. She'd worry for days while it was out at sea, as if her own family were out there. Jackie would get a real kick out of knowing that, after all the family had gone through.

But it wasn't so much about the crew. It was the boat itself—what it represented. It served as a giant symbol of opportunity, albeit a metallic mess, but wasn't that appropriate? Women could work fishing crews these days, but it still wasn't easy for them to belong. She'd have to prove herself more so than the men, just like *Harpeth Rose* had to prove her worthiness season after season.

They had cleared the dock, and Nick brought the vessel out to the middle of the bay, safe enough from both the rocks by Lone Lady and Shipwreck Alley. "Crew to your checkpoints. Everyone else gather round!" Nick waved the competitors over to the wheelhouse near the stern. "You'll start with different locations, but will go in the same order." He handed each a slip of paper. "You may begin."

Cynthia unfolded her paper. Galley. She ran to the nearest stairs and stepped down into the belly of *Harpeth Rose*. The galley should be one of the easiest locations to spot, considering it would be one of the larger open areas. She turned right, down the companionway, and into a wider room. A tight booth sat in the corner, and a fridge, microwave, and stovetop were nestled amongst ramshackle cabinets.

Ben sat down in the booth, and she stared him down for the next spot. "Bunks."

That was harder to guess. Although the galley was in a larger space below, it probably wasn't the case for the bunks. They'd be pretty tight.

"What are you waiting for?" Ben asked.

"I'm thinking." It wouldn't be pleasant to smell the galley when trying to sleep. She followed her gut and moved in the opposite direction of the galley. She passed a door and kept moving forward. Greg and Sean brushed by her, all three having to give way to each other in the narrow passage.

She pulled back a curtain and discovered a set of six bunks, three beds stacked vertically at a time. No one waited around with the next clue. She moved on, turning into the corridor and nearly slamming into Liam.

"Sorry."

"No, it's okay," he said. "Tight quarters."

They shimmied by each other, her feet stepping on his. Her arms brushed his chiseled chest, and she froze, Liam's handsome eyes and strong jaw just inches away.

"There's no one over there, by the way." Cynthia nodded toward the bunks.

Harpeth Rose swayed, and Liam leaned his arms on the wall, boxing her in. "There isn't?"

She had watched his lips as he spoke. "No." Her hand begged to reach out and touch his cheek, a shadow of beard forming over the last two days. Could he feel her heart racing?

Another rock, and Liam caught her by the shoulder. Cynthia placed her hand gently on his elbow.

"Guess I'll head back that way," Liam said.

She moved left as Liam moved to his right, pressing them closer. She couldn't move. *Don't close your eyes.* If she closed them, then she'd give in. Her lips would pull to his, and it would be over.

"I had a good time last night," he said.

Now he decides to talk about it? She had a race to win. But damn if he wasn't ruggedly sexy and smelling magnificent in the salty air.

"That's sly of you. But I've got a contest to win."

"What do you mean?" He smirked. "You didn't have a good time?"

"I'll tell you *after* I win." Cynthia darted out, shaking out the thought of Liam so close to her, trying to remember where she was going.

The ship's quarters had been tight, but for the first time since delving below, Cynthia yearned for the cool air above.

Away from the magnetic heat of Liam Reynolds.

SIXTEEN

LIAM ROAMED AROUND *Harpeth Rose*. He acted like he was on a mission to the next area of the ship, but really he couldn't get his mind off Cynthia.

Ironically, bumping into her had been a complete accident. Standing face-to-face in the narrow corridor made his pulse thump. The cool belly of the ship had reached boiling level, the back of his neck and forehead sweating so near her body heat.

Damn Constance and her shampoo. What he would have given to run his hands over the blond strands falling out of her ponytail around her face and tuck them behind her ear. He didn't want to be caught staring at her lips, the plump pillows burning pink beside her fair cream skin.

Last night had been wonderful. He finally had a chance to listen to her story, hear her open up. And she was such a fun sport to attend a fancy dinner in her relaxed clothes. He had always been a sucker for a woman who chose practicality over vanity. She didn't need fancy clothes or makeup or dolled up hair. She was naturally stunning.

If any clarity came from last night, it was that Liam was falling for her. Possibly she felt the same, what with the chemistry he felt near her. But did he want her to? Because if she did, there was no winning on his end.

If he became greenhorn, he'd be back to doing what he loved and out of the plant, but Cynthia would have been denied her dream. If she became greenhorn, she'd be off on fishing trips with Nick and his crew throughout the year while Liam was stuck in Oakside, doing the same old routine. Even in the miracle scenario where they'd be dating, he'd have to cope with her being on the open sea at a dangerous job or constantly be thinking about her while he was away on fishing trips.

He couldn't wish for her dreams to be dashed all because his brain muddled and skin sizzled when she neared. All because he wanted her with him. And because he wanted the same job.

A commotion above drew him out of the hole he dug in his hypothetical future relationship with Cynthia. He climbed up on deck, the candidates and Nick and his temporary crew gathered round. Cynthia's grin ran ear to ear.

Liam nudged Miguel. "What's happening?"

"Cynthia won the scavenger hunt." He leaned away from Liam, arms crossed. "Surprise, surprise."

"What's that supposed to mean?"

"Huh? Oh, nothing. Better luck next time, man." He patted Liam on the back and retreated to the navigation bridge.

Shouldn't Liam have been the one saying that to Miguel? Was Miguel even trying? Now that he thought about the past three days of exercises, he hadn't seen Miguel complete any tasks.

Then again, he hadn't given this task his all. Hard to do, though, given the company.

The gang counted to three, and Cynthia swung the four-pronged metal grappling hook overboard.

The temperature rose, and Liam's ears rang. His breath quickened, and the world spun in a blur.

He closed his eyes only to vividly see what he wished he couldn't.

Flashing metal.

Sea spray.

Blood was the last thing he saw, on his shoulder, over his hands, before the world went black.

His body collapsed, knees buckling and hitting the floor hard.

He opened his eyes, blinking the blurriness away. The round bearded face of Ben Campbell above him stared back. "We lost you there for a second. You okay?"

Liam looked around, the sky coming into focus, his shirt sticking to his moist skin. "I think so." His eyes darted to his shoulder. No blood.

Ben held out a hand and helped Liam to his feet.

The crowd still gathered around Cynthia. She shot him a look, worry wiped over her face.

"I'm okay," Liam said. "I think I just need some water."

"No problem." Ben retrieved a bottle of water from the navigation bridge.

Nick continued on with the candidates, lecturing them about the importance of knowing the vessel and its contents, seemingly oblivious to what just happened. The less Nick had seen, the better. That went for the rest of the crew, too.

Liam had recurring nightmares of the injury a good year after it happened, but those went away with therapy and time. This whole week he worried whether he could physically manage the job and hadn't considered his psychological fitness.

Liam joined the group and sipped his water.

Cynthia locked eyes with him. "What happened?" she mouthed.

Liam shook his head, as if it was nothing. *It was nothing.* A fluke flashback he hadn't been ready for. Yep, next time he'll be better prepared. It almost sounded convincing. In any case, Cynthia need not be distracted by his personal issues.

"Pay attention," he mouthed back, then smiled.

Fortunately, the scavenger hunt was the only task for the day. By the time *Harpeth Rose* arrived back at the dock, Liam felt back to normal. Nick dismissed everyone for the afternoon. Cynthia headed out first, wanting to prepare for the interview. Liam wanted to follow, but she was too quick, disappearing around Campy's Bait and Bar before he even got off the ship. He really should consider adding running to his workouts.

"It's not what I signed up for." Greg stood in the doorway to the navigation bridge, Nick inside.

Liam stepped closer to hear.

"I can't do another day. I'm out." Greg turned away and marched toward Liam.

"Are you quitting?" Liam held up a hand to stop him. "If it's about the seasickness, you can work on that. I mean, I don't know if you saw what happened to me today. We all have our moments."

"When are you going to wake up?"

"Excuse me?"

Greg shook his head and walked away.

"Wait up!" Theo chased after him.

Nick stepped out of the bridge.

"What was that all about?" Liam strode over to Nick. "Wake up to what?"

Nick shook his head, swatting away the question. "Don't mind Greg. He wasn't cut out for this in any way."

"Then why did you invite him to compete?"

Nick scratched his head and returned the ball cap back to its place. "Sometimes there's a big difference between words on paper and reality."

Liam nodded. It was true. He'd seen it in applicants for the processing plant. Jobs in Oakside could be hard to come by, so when a spot opened, there was a pool of qualified applicants to choose from. Unfortunately not everyone advertised the truth. That, or they grossly overestimated their skills or level of commitment.

But something about Greg and Nick's encounter didn't fit the narrative, as if Greg had been referring to something else. What did Liam have to do with it? What was he not seeing that Greg had?

"You'd better get going if you want to make it to Josie's taping—which you promised to do," Nick said.

Liam checked his watch. After being out on the water—and out cold for a time—he didn't feel much like chatting about fishing. But a promise was a promise. "Right. I'm on my way." He moved to exit the boat, stopped, and turned back to Nick. "Where exactly am I going for it?"

Liam followed Nick's directions, which were simple enough.

KSMV Studios sat down the road from Bea's Bouquets at the southern edge of town. He crossed Pearl Avenue to Crescent Cafe and scarfed down a wrap, thankful they had returned early enough in the day for it to be open, before hitting the rest of the journey at a brisk pace.

The building at the corner of Hawkes Street and Pearl Avenue housed both the local news station and its affiliated radio station, 93.5 The Bay. The left side of the lobby had a chair underneath photos of news anchors from the past several decades. The right reminded him of the record stores he'd seen as a kid, with posters of musicians and framed vinyl albums plastering the walls. Back when buying music was an event, and record stores were hubs for people to gather over music.

"Can I help you?" A young man greeted him. His long dark hair reached between his shoulder blades in a low ponytail.

"I'm here for an interview. With Josie."

"I'm guessing you're Liam? Back here."

Behind the lobby sat two enclosed rooms. The room on the right had the door open, its desk stacked with CDs and records and rolled up posters. An On Air sign hung unlit, and two men chuckled over their take-out lunches.

Liam was led to the room on the left. Bright lights illuminated the right side of the room, three different sections of the wall dividing the station into weather, news desk, and interview area. Cynthia sat on a couch opposite of who could only be Josie in the latter section, the women exchanging light banter before noticing his entrance.

"Liam is here," Liam's guide said.

"Thanks, Josh," the seated woman said, her brunette head of curls somewhat tamed as if Medusa's snakes settled for a snooze. Freckles dotted across her pale cheeks and petite nose. She rose out of her seat and outstretched a hand.

"I'm Josie. So nice to finally meet you, Liam. Nick has told me so much about you."

"Really?" Cynthia sat opposite Josie.

Oh, no. He'd been trying hard all week not to reveal the full truth about him and Nick, keeping quiet around Nick when Cynthia was present. Now Nick's girlfriend was going to blow the whole thing.

Josie finished the handshake and turned to Cynthia. "In terms of the tryouts, of course."

Cynthia nodded, but her eyes read suspicion before meeting Liam's stare. "What are you doing here?"

Thank goodness she moved on from Josie's slip. "I was invited to do the show."

"Why didn't you say something?"

"I see you two know each other." Josie sat back down, smoothing her pencil skirt. "As I said, Cynthia, this month our special *Josie's Corner* segment has been about pursuing one's dreams. You know I've mentioned the tryouts here in Maiden's Bay several times."

Cynthia began to nod. Unconvincingly.

"I'm going to forgive you this time for not watching because you're my friend." Josie smiled, then winked at Liam. "She keeps pretending to watch, but…."

"I *did* watch at first," Cynthia pleaded. "Usually I'm working mid-morning, that's all."

"I'm just messing with you. Sort of. Anyway, I thought, what better than to interview some of the people trying out for the position? Especially you." She tapped Cynthia's knee. "I know you enough to know how big a deal this is. But I didn't want the whole segment to be filled up by your story."

"Nick asked me," Liam blurted. "Apparently the other guys weren't too thrilled to do this."

"And I'm so happy you agreed," Josie said. "Are you both ready to get started?"

"I guess so," Cynthia said.

"I'll have you both sit on the couch, and I'll sit across from you. Remember, this is a recording, and my editor will work her magic in post. But pretend it's live. The smoother the recording, the faster it can be processed for the morning airing. If you need to take a break, just let me know."

Josie referred to the seating as a couch, but it was more a two-cush-ioned loveseat. Liam stepped into the light, the sound woman micing him up and makeup team smattering him with some sort of powder, then squished down in the seat, brushing shoulders with Cynthia.

Cynthia leaned closer, the tropical scent of her hair touching his face. "It's like we're back on *Harpeth Rose.*"

"At least we're not rocking."

He shared a smile with her. Josie crossed her legs, elbows on her knees, smirk across her face. "Ready? Or would you two like some time to chat?"

"We're good." Liam leaned away from Cynthia. Hopefully, the microphone didn't pick up his drumming heartbeat, the pulse strong enough to feel in his pinky toe.

Josie sat up tall and gave a strong grin. "Welcome to another epi-sode of *Josie's Corner.*" She spoke flawlessly and effortlessly, never hes-itating on a word. "As you all know—" she gave big eyes to Cynthia, the non-watcher friend—"I've dedicated the month of February to the pursuit of dreams. Today I have two guests with me, Cynthia and Liam, both vying for a greenhorn position on a lucrative fishing vessel here in Maiden's Bay. Welcome, and thank you for coming on today." She tipped her head, cuing them.

"Thank you," Liam said.

"Yes, thank you Josie, for having us," Cynthia said.

"Let me start with you, Cynthia. I have known you for some time now, and locals probably know you best as one of our florists. How did this dream of being greenhorn come about?"

Cynthia cleared her throat gently. "I have always wanted to do something out on the water. My dad was a big influence in that. Be-cause of him, I learned to love boating and fishing, although I haven't done more than rod and reel up to this point."

"We won't tell Nick," Josie jibed.

"The good news is that I'm eager to learn, and in my head I've thrown out that hook so many times. I got to do it for the first time today, by the way. Most greenhorns never get the opportunity."

"How did that feel?"

"Honestly, I choked up a bit. I'm not ashamed to say it either because I knew as a teenager this is what I wanted."

She was so strong-willed and confident. Liam's cheeks hurt from smiling so much.

"What do you say to those who hear that and think, she's not cut out for that?"

"I refer them to the fisherwomen—East Coast, West Coast, and around the world—that are proving the naysayers wrong. I may not be as physically strong as some of the men on the crew, but as I'm learning this week through tryouts, strength isn't everything."

"I'd like to chime in, if I may," Liam said.

"Go for it."

"I didn't know Cynthia before tryouts. Over the course of the last two and a half days, I've seen in her someone determined, receptive to learning, and someone with great respect for the profession. And the next thing I'm going to say may not seem like it's a quality to have on a boat, but she's compassionate. She took care of a fellow competitor in a time of need, which is an invaluable asset when it comes to keeping a crew—a sort of hodgepodge of a family—together in trying times."

"It sounds like you're hurting your own chances there, Liam." Josie chuckled.

He looked at Cynthia. "It's only the truth." His chest warmed with the response of her smile.

"That's a lot to learn about someone in such a short amount of time. Did I hear you two are roommates for the week?"

Liam glanced at Cynthia, who eyed him quickly.

"Yes, that's right," Liam said.

"How has that been?"

Besides wanting to wake her in the middle of last night with kisses? Or restraining himself from snuggling in her bed, wrapping his arms around her? "Strictly professional," Liam said. It came out squeaky, and he cleared his throat.

"It has been interesting." Cynthia adjusted on the sofa, her body becoming more rigid the further Josie delved into the personal.

"Sounds like story time," Josie chimed in.

Cynthia bit her lip. "I'm just saying that I didn't expect to see him when my roommate came knocking on the door."

"Liam, didn't you say you didn't know each other before this week?" Josie asked.

"I did say that. It's not entirely true. I did meet Cynthia once in the flower shop two weeks ago. But it's true I didn't really *know* her."

"It's been great." Cynthia's words bordered on robotic. She was closing up by the second in front of the camera.

"You don't have to lie," Liam said. "I probably snore. I'm not sure I do, but I think I look like someone who snores."

Josie laughed, and Cynthia let out a chuckle, relaxing her rigid body. All he wanted to do was put her at ease.

"He's been very… accommodating."

Josie raised her eyebrows.

"We've taken turns getting each other coffee in the morning, and he walks with me to tryouts."

"Very gentlemanly of you, Liam," Josie said.

"I'm not so sure."

"Why's that?"

"I walk with her for my protection."

The two women laughed, Cynthia touching his arm. He knew it was her way of thanking him, for lightening Josie's inquiry. He wanted to freeze the moment, to savor it.

Because after this week, it would all be over.

SEVENTEEN

THE TEN-MINUTE interview flew by. Sweat moistened under her arms and around her neck, the room warm under the lights. It didn't help Liam sat next to her, her thigh or arm grazing his throughout the show.

Liam's words about her performance over the last two and a half days had taken her aback. She liked to believe all the things he said actually held true. She did take it seriously and respected the profession. If only her confidence matched everyone else's assessment of her. Did Nick agree with Liam's opinion? He was a man of few words—efficient, to the point. Even if his brother Ben teased him that he wasn't.

"That went really well." Josie typed on her laptop.

"I hope so. For your sake and your editor's."

"Thanks again for doing it."

"You know I'd do it ten times over if you asked." Maiden's Bay for sure was a small town, and Josie was one of Cynthia's closest friends. Cynthia had spent so much time helping Dad that she hadn't formed—or reinforced—many friendships locally post-college. It was Josie who stepped into her life and pressed her to join in on activities. Josie convinced her to attend a social one evening at the library, subsequently reconnecting Cynthia with her high school friend Elise. Cynthia would do it again despite the discomfort because their friendship meant more.

Liam stood in the darker half of the room. "Did you want to head back to the inn together?"

"Sure." *I'd like that. I'd like to take an afternoon nap in your arms.* It was what she felt. He sensed her unease in front of the camera, and he'd helped her relax. That was the connection they had. Why hide it? *Because it's wrong, Cynthia. Eyes on the job.* "Can you give me a few minutes?"

"I'll be out here." Liam left the studio for the lobby.

Josie approached one of the techs. "Are we all set for next week's segment?"

He gave her a thumbs up, and she swiveled around, facing Cynthia. "Now that Liam's not around." She checked the doorway to the lobby. "How's it going?"

"So far the tasks haven't been too bad—"

"That's not what I meant."

Cynthia shifted her weight to one foot. "There's nothing to tell we haven't already said."

"Oh, come on! He's *The Oakside Guy.* This is your chance. And you have to give me something to take back to Elise because she's driving me crazy. So... what do you think of him?"

"First off, I don't see this as 'my chance.' He's a fellow competitor up for the same position, and the last thing I need is a guy to distract me from achieving my dream." He had distracted her today on *Harpeth Rose.* That was certain.

"But...?"

Cynthia sighed, exhaling the strong façade, leaving behind the emptiness in her chest and ache in her bones. "I don't know. There's something there. There are times when he's next to me, or he says something to make me laugh, or...."

"Says beautiful, wonderful things about you on a local TV show?"

"Yeah."

"Cynthia, let me give you some advice."

"Here we go."

"Come on. You know my story. You know I wasn't looking for love, and Nick Campbell was the last person I thought I'd fall for. But when it's there, and you both feel it, you have to go for it."

"Even if it's logistically impossible?"

"It's not impossible. It might be difficult, but not impossible. We're talking Oakside here, not Antarctica. Look at me and Nick. I was back and forth East Coast-West Coast the first month or two."

"It's not just that. It's the fishing lifestyle, too. Whether it's me or him selected." Cynthia regretted saying the words. Josie lived it every day. She didn't need to be reminded of how unconventional and emotionally challenging it could be.

Josie cradled Cynthia's hands. "At least consider it."

"I have been. I feel like that's all I've been doing, figuring out how to be a part of the crew *and* give this a shot. What if he makes it instead of me? Will I resent him? It's so crazy. I don't even know if he feels anything for me. I mean, I have my suspicions, but I could be totally wrong. We barely know each other."

"You know how to change that."

"We'll see." Cynthia released herself from Josie's grasp and turned to the door.

"Oh! I almost forgot." Josie followed her. "I need one more favor, if you don't mind. You know about my Valentine's special on the show?"

"Oh. yeah, how's that going?"

"Seemingly well. Ask me again on Valentine's Day. We're doing a big event, and I think that's when we'll need to have the flower order ready."

"Did you get it in with Bea?"

"That's the favor."

"Josie. You know she's going to flip out giving her such short notice."

"Yes. I also know she'll provide the standard red roses or carnations at this point. I was wondering if you could have a visit this afternoon, maybe place the order for me? Pick out something a little more unique?"

"Not with the scraps left over."

"Exactly."

Cynthia looked at the ceiling, then closed her eyes. "Fine. I guess I can do it. I don't need to report to Nick until tomorrow morning. The last shipment in before Valentine's Day is tomorrow, so I'd better get the order in."

"Great. Thank you." Josie gave her a rough idea of the type of arrangements, amount, and her budget. Cynthia convinced her to up the latter by fifteen percent, since it was nearly last minute and the holiday tended to shoot up prices.

Cynthia left the television studio and walked to the lobby. "Ready?"

Liam examined a framed record on the wall, cream cover faded with a youthful Barbra Streisand sporting a bob. He hastily backed away. "One of my mom's faves."

"Uh-huh." Cynthia bit her lip, trying unsuccessfully to hold back her enjoyment.

"No, really. She and my sisters would listen to her when I was younger. Drove me nuts."

"One last thing!" Josie rushed over, dashing Cynthia's hopes of hearing more about Babs in the Reynolds family. "The Campbells throw a dinner on Thursday nights. I'll be going tomorrow night with Nick to Ben's house. Their mom is visiting, and I'm always a little nervous."

"So, where do I come in to play?"

"He's having the tryout crew over, which should make it easier on me. Especially if you joined."

"Both of us?" Liam pointed to his chest.

"Yes. I know Nick doesn't wear his heart on his sleeve, but he's all about family, and his crew is his second family. Although Ben is his actual family—I guess first family? Never mind. You get what I mean. Can you come?"

Cynthia couldn't believe it. The Thursday night dinner. Stories of their famous dinners spread throughout Maiden's Bay. A seat there was more coveted than one at Codfather's on Valentine's Day. It was an honor to be invited. Maybe she'd meet all of Nick's crew officially. If she won them over, it could help her chances.

"Are the other candidates going?" Cynthia asked. "I don't want any unfair advantage."

"Of course, they're all invited. Nick was supposed to mention it to them this afternoon. But he knew you two would be here, so he told me to tell you."

Cynthia looked at Liam, who shrugged. "Okay, sure."

"Great. I'll text you Ben's address, and I'll see the two of you there at six tomorrow evening." Josie clapped her hands together and ran back to the studio.

Liam tugged at her arm and guided her closer to the front exit. "Any idea what Nick is doing with the other four this afternoon?"

"No." To think they were getting another task without her, or special attention from Nick, was too much to process. But they, according to Liam, turned down the interview opportunity. Hard to believe they were doing extra anything right now.

They walked out onto Pearl Avenue. The quiet afternoon did nothing to block out the voice inside Cynthia's head. "I don't know if I should be saying this, but I've been getting a weird feeling about this whole thing."

Liam crossed then uncrossed his arms, finding a resting place in his pockets. "You mean with the other crew?"

"Yeah. Outside of you, and sometimes Greg, I haven't seen them doing much of anything. Even today on *Harpeth Rose,* I didn't really cross paths with them much. It's like they aren't taking it seriously."

"To be honest, I overheard Greg talking to Nick after today's exercise. He said something about this not being what he signed up for, and he quit. He left right then."

"Really? You're just now telling me this?"

"Was I supposed to tell you on *Josie's Corner?*"

Cynthia chuckled. "No, I guess not." She headed north, Liam at her side. "So I'm not the only one who's suspicious?"

"Not at all."

They walked along the shops, a few people walking the downtown streets on the rainless afternoon.

She recalled the day's task. She was so hyped up on adrenaline from being aboard *Harpeth Rose* she barely paid attention to anyone else. Had she passed the others looking for their next stations? Of course she had seen Liam. The memory made her smile, his body close to hers. She felt the tightness of his body, his arms, his chest.

But then she had thrown the hook overboard, and what had happened to Liam? She had been so worried about the interview she hadn't the time to ask. In fact, Liam's behavior added to the whole feeling of unease about the week.

"Friend?" Liam pointed to the waving old man across the street walking into the front door of an office. Cynthia waved back.

"That's Doc Bernie. He's been our family's primary care doctor since forever. He also takes care of most of the boating and fishing injuries around here. Knows more about everyone than the hospital up north, and charges a lot less. And, an interesting fact, his grandson Nathaniel is dating my niece Gwen."

"Geez. Do you know his favorite meal, too?"

"Definitely spaghetti and meatballs." She laughed. "I'm just kidding. I know what you're saying. Small town. Is Oakside not the same? Are you telling me you don't know the local family practitioner?"

"Which one? We have two."

"Oh! Mister Bigshot now. *Two* doctors' offices." She laughed, and he smiled.

"I couldn't tell you either one. Most of my adult experience has been with specialists and physical therapists. My mother probably could, though. She seems to know everyone."

"No, I get it. Most people go through life not knowing the everyday people around them. It's one of the reasons I stay here. I actually like to know who I'm dealing with and where things come from."

He slowed to a stop and turned to her. "You don't ever foresee living somewhere else?"

Oakside doesn't sound so bad. It was a millisecond of a thought. Not even a thought as much as a knee-jerk retort without serious thought. Still, it had popped in her head and freaked her out.

She stepped to the door of Bea's Bouquets. "I have to go in here. Josie asked another favor of me."

"Want some company?"

"That's okay. I'll be sifting through flowers and arrangements."

"I don't mind. Not like I have any other plans."

"You sure? You don't have another television appearance you're keeping a secret?"

"No, my visit on Jimmy isn't until next week."

"Okay, TV star. Come on in. Let me bore you to death."

She walked into Bea's. She had only been away from the store for three days, but it was the longest stretch away she'd had in who knew when. It felt like she was visiting her alma mater, the displays and aromatic sweet mix in the air both warm and unpleasant. She loved Bea, and for the most part enjoyed her time there, but she was beyond ready to move on with her life.

"Don't tell me you quit!" Bea yelled from somewhere in the store.

Cynthia stood on her toes, searching for Bea. "Where is she?"

Liam strained to see. "I don't know, but it's a little creepy she knows it was you entering."

Cynthia pointed to the upper corner of the façade. "Camera. Which means she's in the back."

Joanna, her replacement for today's shift, shuffled the display items at the register. She waved at them on their way toward the back.

Bea came out, apron on and shears in hand.

"I didn't quit," Cynthia said.

"Good. Because I didn't train you to be a quitter." She leaned in closer. "Between you and me, I thought you were a lot of work, but Joanna." She rolled her eyes. "What are you doing here?"

"Josie sent me."

"Oh, no. Uh-uh."

"Bea...."

"No, I know Josie too well. She expects too much for too little."

"You don't even have to be involved. I'll do everything. I just need to look at availability and put in the order. If I get it in now there's still a chance it'll all be on tomorrow's truck." She left out the part that Bea would have to take care of on-site delivery to wherever Josie needed the flowers on the weekend. One blow at a time.

"Who's this?" Bea pointed at Liam and gasped. Her lips curled up in a smile. A *wicked* smile. "It's that guy you like."

"Bea—"

"Oh, really?" Liam said.

"I remember you. Cynthia thought your face could use a little moisturizing."

"That's one way to put it."

"You two fit together. I can tell."

"How so?"

Cynthia pulled Liam's arm. "We're going now. We'll be out of your hair in a few minutes."

"Take your time." Bea chuckled. "You're good at that."

EIGHTEEN

IT WAS CUTE to see Cynthia flustered by Bea's remarks, just as she had been the first time Liam met her. So much had evolved since that day, and in such a short period of time.

The friend connection was certainly there. He hadn't been so comfortable around a woman in years. With Cynthia he could be himself, groggy and slow in the morning, quiet and focused during the tryouts. The best was joking with her. She got his humor—or at least acted like it.

No, Cynthia wouldn't pretend for anyone's sake. She was genuine, and it didn't take long to realize that.

They had spent twenty minutes in Bea's Bouquets, Cynthia thinking up flowers and checking on availability. Some of the names sounded like she made them up. His ex Sandra had been a standard red roses kind of gal, sometimes white or the occasional yellow. Cynthia said roses were a status symbol society had come up with, and there were plenty of flowers more beautiful and rare to leave an impression.

Flowers may not have ever been his thing, but he could've watched Cynthia all afternoon. She applied that same focus and drive he'd seen this week at tryouts, and had the breadth of knowledge as any expert florist—heck, botanist—would.

They had walked back to Constance's mid-afternoon. Cynthia opted for the shower while Liam relaxed in the breakfast room with coffee. The framed news clippings from *Bay Review* lining the first floor hallway occupied his time, recounting harrowing rescues and prize-winning catches. That want of excitement and rush of adrenaline got him on *Sea Prairie* in the first place. Then this week, another taste of it. But as he perused, his shoulder increasingly ached, as if taunting him and his ambition. Was he really up for that life again?

Liam retreated upstairs and showered for dinner, returning to the room with his worn clothes and belongings in hand.

"Are you sure you want to go to Campy's?" Cynthia held her jacket, wearing a scoop-necked red sweater and skinny jeans as alluring as any dress could be. "We could pick up something from the grocery store. The one up the street has a good selection of salads and to-go meals."

As much as he wanted a quiet dinner alone with her, they had a mission. "Did you not tell me you felt something was going on? Something Nick or the others weren't telling us? Someone, if not everyone, from tryouts will be at Campy's. Maybe we could get to the truth."

The irony was not lost on him. Guilt danced in his head like the little devil in movies that whispered in the protagonist's ear. He swatted it aside. Perhaps the suspected secret behind tryouts overshadowed the secret of why he came out to Maiden's Bay in the first place.

"So now we're sleuths being sneaky." She rubbed her hands together.

"I don't think you could sneak up on anyone."

Cynthia stepped back, a puzzled crinkle between her eyebrows. "What's that supposed to mean?"

"I'm saying that you'd be noticed."

"Why?" She pulled the hem of her sweater out, as if investigating a stain.

"I'm saying you look nice." *Nice.* Understatement of the century. "It's hard *not* to look at you." He was doing a fine job of not looking at her now, the words echoing louder and his face matching her sweater. *Is she going to say something?*

"Oh." She lowered her hands and bit her lip.

"I hope that didn't sound creepy or something. I meant it in a good way, like you draw the attention of the room." *You're making it worse.* He clapped his hands. "So what do you say?" His voice came out a little too loud and peppy. "Campy's?"

She inhaled deeply. "Yeah. Let's do it."

"Good." Good to the change of subject. Good to not completely ruining the evening before it started.

They walked out of Room 2 and headed downstairs. Constance greeted two arriving guests and waved to Liam and Cynthia before they slipped out onto Ocean Street.

Walking beside her, Liam resisted the urge to grab her hand. Instead he shoved both hands in his jacket pockets. The wind had picked up with the dimming of the sky, sending a chill along his neck. Yet his hands could've turned ice to steam.

Judging from the low bass thumping and the full tables by the second-story front windows, Campy's was busy. A chalkboard easel on the sidewalk indicated it was Work Week Wednesday, with all beer and appetizers half price.

They hiked the wooden stairs to the second story deck. Liam held the door for Cynthia, the music and chatter drifting across Pearl Avenue.

"What's the plan?" she shouted.

Finding a seat seemed unlikely. A handful of people formed a line near the door.

"Come on." He waved her on, scanning the occupied tables and booths as he moved toward the bar in the center. He stopped and leaned to her ear. "Just as I thought. Same place they were the other night." He pointed to the men at the booth, all four seated in the same configuration.

"You plan on just going up there and asking what's up?"

"Let's get a drink first."

They moved to the bar, only one stool empty in the middle.

A woman filled a frosted glass from the tap. Joel swiped a customer's card and punched buttons on the screen. Liam waved a hand for his attention.

"Ah, you again." Joel handed over a menu.

"Got two of those?" He pointed to Cynthia.

"Hey, Cynthia." Joel handed her a menu. "Want me to free up one of these stools for you? I'll Gus to get out of here so you both can sit."

"No, that's okay. Doesn't seem fair to kick him out when he's saved it all afternoon."

"Ah, don't be too kind to him. He's purchased one drink, and that was before I got back from our trip. Well over the allotted time for stool privileges."

Cynthia frowned. "Aww, give him a break. We're gonna join our friends in a second, anyway."

"Yeah, yeah," Joel said. "Good job today, by the way. *Harpeth Rose* isn't the easiest ship to get around."

"Thanks," Cynthia said. "I don't have much to compare it to, so it's fine by me."

Joel was right as far as fishing vessels went. *Harpeth Rose* was cut up, with no long straight companionways or perpendicular angles, as if spaces were sliced into the hull from every direction. It definitely wasn't the same as *Sea Prairie,* but no fishing vessel was, unless it, too, was refurbished from an old naval ship.

They ordered, and Joel fixed and delivered their drinks.

"Now what?" Cynthia said. "Are you going to stare the truth out of them?" She nudged Liam's arm.

"Let's have a chat. What do you think?"

She took a gulp of her drink. "You first."

They walked to the booth, and Liam's stomach churned. Why was he nervous? Was it because there was a chance they knew about him and would divulge that truth?

"Hey, there," Liam said. "Thought you'd all be here, so I figured we'd get the whole gang together."

Sean smiled briefly, and Miguel gave an unfriendly glare.

Liam and Cynthia remained standing, no available seats in sight. Best to have a quick getaway anyway, if the awkwardness worsened.

"Did I hear that you're no longer trying out?" Cynthia stared at Greg.

"Yeah. You heard right. I won't be there tomorrow. Or the rest of the week, I guess."

"Sorry to hear that."

She sounded genuine, though Liam couldn't for the life of him figure out why she was sorry about it. It was something nice people said, but Cynthia meant it.

"You did well." Sean wiped the sweat off his glass of beer.

"Thanks. I'm not sure if I could tell you where anything on *Harpeth Rose* is now, it was all a blur."

She most certainly could. Liam was sure of it.

"Hey." A heavy set man stood up out of the booth to the left. His face was young, like the four—now three—other men trying out. He wore a short-sleeved shirt under his vest, and sweat dampened his hairline. "Are you that girl?" He swayed and caught his hip on the edge of the booth, propping him up.

Liam opened his mouth, but Cynthia gently held his forearm. "Depends," she said. "Which one are you looking for?"

"The one that stole greenhorn from me on *Harpthhh—Har-peth Rose,"* he slurred.

"Excuse me? I didn't steal anything from—"

"You are, aren't you?" He stepped closer, finger pointing at Cynthia. "Hey, guys!" He swiveled to the booth behind him, and his words slurred together. "This girl thinks she can be a greenhorn. I'd like to"— he blinked hard—"see her hold a crab pot steady, dana-gul-ling from a crane. What a joke."

Liam stepped halfway in front of Cynthia, palm in the air, the other setting down his drink. "All right. That's enough. Why don't you go back to your group there?"

The man spit at Cynthia, more of an exaggerated noise of a spit than an actual one in his drunken stupor. Sean and Greg shot up out of the booth, Miguel and Theo rising in their seats, the men in the other booth shuffling to their feet.

Liam held a tight fist.

"Don't," Cynthia spoke in Liam's ear. Her hand held his arm back. "He's not worth it."

She was right. The last thing he wanted to do was fight, anyway. That wasn't him. He wasn't the angry boyfriend, fight-in-a-bar type.

He held both hands up at a truce. "We're leaving."

"That's right, you are."

Liam's shoulder exploded in pain before he had a chance to process what happened.

Sean and Greg formed a wall between Liam and the drunk guy. Cynthia helped keep Liam on his feet.

His eyes blurred with the pain, and a man approached, his arms spread out as he said something with enough authority in his voice to settle the rowdy bunch.

"Come on," Cynthia said. She clung to Liam's uninjured left arm and guided him through the bar, down the stairs to the street. His ears throbbed, even though the music faded and the street was light with traffic.

By the time they reached Room 2 at Constance's, his senses had returned. He replayed the scene, this time clear. The drunk man had swung at him, probably aiming for Liam's stomach or face, but missed either one. Liam's shoulder took the brunt of the force.

His bad shoulder.

It wasn't so much the injured shoulder that bothered him. It was the way the drunk man—no, *boy*—spoke to Cynthia.

And now Liam was alone with her, in Room 2 at the inn. It was how he truly wanted to spend the evening. The realization was the only thing keeping him still.

For all his fist itched to do was return to Campy's and let that drunk man know he couldn't be half the greenhorn Cynthia would be.

NINETEEN

CYNTHIA SWADDLED ICE from the kitchen into a towel, provided by Constance, and hurried back up the stairs.

The door to Room 2 swung open, Liam in a rush.

"What are you doing?" Cynthia pushed Liam's chest, guiding him back in the room and positioning herself in the doorway.

"I just have a few words to say to that un-gentleman."

"Oh, is that all?"

"It wasn't right." Fury overtook his pleasant eyes. It was charming and bullheaded at the same time. Cynthia appreciated chivalry, when applied appropriately. Physical retribution did not constitute chivalry in her eyes.

"That may be true." She shut the door. "But I was about to come up here and thank you for not beating him up."

"I wasn't exactly noble, was I? That man-boy deserves to be put in his place."

"On the contrary." She sat him down on the edge of his bed, the seashell duvet neatly arranged from Constance's housekeeping sometime during the day. "I find it incredibly noble to use one's brain over brawn. And don't worry. Joel cleared it up."

"Ah, *that's* who I heard."

"Yes. Fortunately, Joel doesn't have to resort to violence whenever a fight breaks out."

"What you may see as noble I see as common sense. Anyone who knows Joel is a Campbell would know better than to mess with him."

She smiled. "I'm sure your sisters would come to your rescue." She nudged him in the left shoulder.

"That doesn't make me feel better."

"It wasn't meant to." She laughed, and he broke a smile. "I'd bet you're stronger than Joel, from all that strength training of yours."

"Now you're just mocking me."

"I wouldn't want to fight you is what I'm saying."

"I'd hope not." He met her gaze.

It tingled just to be seen by him. She inhaled and composed herself. "Now let me see that shoulder."

"I'm fine."

"Stop it. What did I just say about brain?"

"Okay, okay." He unzipped his jacket and unbuttoned the flannel shirt. He winced, trying not to move his right shoulder as the sleeves slipped down his arm.

Those same carved muscles she had seen through the steam, the ones that came from doing and working, that had seemed so perfect, now showed his history. A thick rough scar arced across the front and down the side of his shoulder, the borders rigid and lighter than the skin around it. A branding from his past. In the middle, his flesh reddened in a swollen bump the diameter of a baseball. An awful, growing bruise she couldn't help but think was part of her doing.

"He got you pretty good." She sat next to him and placed the ice pack on his shoulder with one hand, the other holding his forearm. "Although, I think he meant to hit lower."

"That would've been better." He grit his teeth and sighed.

"What happened exactly? To your shoulder before? At sea."

He stared off into nowhere. His hand tensed into a fist.

"You don't have to talk about it if you don't want to." Although she really cared to hear.

"No, I—I guess there's no perfect time to talk about it. If there was one, this would be it."

She adjusted the ice on his shoulder and waited.

"I was on hook duty, retrieving the pots. I was good at it, too. Had the rhythm down. It was like my right arm could land the hook right where it needed to be to get that line. We'd been at it for several hours and were bringing in decent hauls.

"It became second nature. I started tuning other things out. During a throw, somehow the line caught on equipment. I can't even tell you much of what happened after. But if I think too hard about it, I can feel the hook digging through my skin, into my muscle, tearing me apart. I can feel it all over again."

It hurt to hear it. Cynthia couldn't imagine, not only the physical injury, but the realization his dream was injured, too. "Today," she said, "when I saw you on *Harpeth Rose,* just before I threw the hook. You looked like you had seen a ghost."

"Maybe I did." He raised and lowered his arm, readjusting the ice.

"Then after, you were flat on your back."

He sighed, eyes down. "I hadn't been on a fishing vessel since that day. It took a year for my arm to move in directions it should. Seeing you throw… my legs turned to jelly, I guess."

"It must've been hard." She shook her head. "Recovering for a year."

"Yeah, something like that," he joked. "You know my ex-girlfriend I told you about? Sandra? She couldn't handle the injury. Not the actual injury itself, although in the beginning it was bad enough to look at. But I couldn't sweep her off her feet anymore."

"She didn't help you with recovery?"

"At first I felt like she did. She visited the hospital. Even came to physical therapy with me during the beginning. But then, she just… wasn't having it."

"I'm so sorry. To have your dreams hindered like that, and then your girlfriend act… stupid. Sorry, I couldn't think of a better word."

"No, you're spot on. Stupid fits. I was injured, couldn't be there for my girlfriend. Fishing wasn't an option to pay the bills, plus medical expenses on top of everything. Thankfully, Nick stepped in. He found me a spot in the plant and vouched for me."

"Nick's a good guy."

"He is."

Which was all the more reason to work on his boat over anyone else's. "It really says something that you're putting yourself back out there. I thought I had a passion, but...."

"You *do* have a passion, believe me."

She shook her head. "I mean that it says a lot about your character."

He quieted, as if absorbing her words.

"Do you think you'll manage when we go out again?"

He grunted, shifting on the bed. "Hoping your competition is out of the picture?"

"That's not what I meant." The words were there, her mind fighting over whether or not to say them. "I'll worry about you."

Liam got up, his face turning pale, as if he was repeating the moment on *Harpeth Rose*. "Excuse me for a second." He walked out of the room, water dripping from the towel.

She considered following him in case he passed out again. *If talking about it puts him ill at ease, how was he going to make it through tryouts?* She pictured him on deck, hook slicing his shoulder. She closed her eyes, washing it away. Injury, even death, was a major risk of the profession. Throwing the hook was just one of a number of dangerous positions to be in.

But usually not for a greenhorn....

She sat up taller, stomach knotting.

Liam returned, towel wrung out and rolled up, color back in his face. "Didn't want to make a wet mess." He hung the towel over the desk chair and sat back down on the bed. "You okay?"

Obviously he caught her apprehension. His story didn't add up, but maybe not all captains ran their crew the same way.

"Yeah, it's just something you said." Her mouth felt dry. "I always thought greenhorns weren't trusted to throw the hook. Isn't that more of a deckhand's job?"

"Oh, well, that's... you know... sometimes—"

The ringing of the telephone interrupted.

"It's probably Constance." She walked to the desk and answered the phone.

"I wanted to see if everything was all right," Constance said. *"Do I need to call for help?"*

"No. As I said, it's minor. Nothing to be worried about. But thank you though."

"Are you sure? It doesn't hurt to have it looked at. I can get Doctor Jackson to come out."

"Really. He'll be swollen and sore, but nothing a few over-the-counter pain meds can't handle."

"Okay, you have a nice night, and let me know if anything arises, no matter the hour."

"Thank you. I will."

She hung up and placed her hands on her hips. "How many inn-keepers would personally check up on their guests?" Constance certainly lived up to her stellar reputation.

"Did you see her face when you brought me in?" Liam asked. "I don't even remember walking over here, but I don't think I'll forget that face."

Cynthia smirked. With Liam's moaning and wincing, Constance's face had gone from a warm smile to wide eyes and slack jaw. "I wonder what she thinks happened."

"We should've told her we tried to get in to The Codfather tonight without a ticket."

Cynthia laughed and sat back down next to him. "Payback for our poor wardrobe choices."

Liam let out a hearty chuckle. "With the violinist playing as they try to rip the shirt off my back."

They both laughed, Cynthia's cheeks hurting. She sighed, wiping the wetness from the corner of her eyes.

She didn't have to look at Liam, nor did she want to. She felt his stare as the air thickened and her lungs collapsed. *Don't look at him.* His hand on the bed between them crept closer to hers.

She had never connected with anyone like this in such a short period of time. There was a friendship there, a camaraderie. It wasn't two people thrown into a room, trying to get along on niceties. She had genuinely grown to like him and found herself wanting to be with him. All the time.

But as a greenhorn, she couldn't do that. Which was why she had to stop herself, and show him that they couldn't go there.

"You know, I think that guy wasn't all wrong," Cynthia said.

"What are you talking about?" Liam backed away, hints of anger returning, and her intentions received exactly as planned. Easier to push away than hurt in the end.

"I might not be able to steady an eight-hundred-pound crab pot dangling from a crane. I can only do what my body is capable of doing."

"Do you hear yourself right now?" He turned, facing her, and grabbed her hands in his. "Look at me."

I can't. If she did, she just might melt.

This man had taken a punch for her after she told him not to fight. The least she could do was look at him. She slowly gazed up, meeting his brown eyes.

"What did you tell me?" Liam said. "Brain over brawn? Survival out there is at least ninety percent brain. You have to have your wits about you. A smart, hardworking person—which you are—on a crew is better than pure muscle any day. It was my mistake, the accident. I let my guard down, not paying full attention to the task. And it ruined me."

She touched his aching shoulder, skin still cool from the ice pack, her pulse beating through her fingertips onto his flesh.

"You're not ruined."

His eyes met hers. He leaned forward, inch by inch. His fingers ran across her skin, up her wrist to her elbow. It was time to give in—to feel his neck, caress his face, run her fingers through his hair.

But this wasn't practical. It wasn't right to be so close, longing to be closer.

It would all be taken away if she got what she dreamt about. Or he got the position instead of her. She had never been so close to achieving her dream. It wasn't fair that in order to achieve it, she had to lose someone she had grown to care about. Someone who saw her for her, who stuck up for her no matter how fanciful her dream was. Even if he dreamt the same thing for himself.

"Cynthia."

"What?" It came out small and weak.

"There's something I have to tell you."

She drew her hand back, the pull of his skin tugging at her finger-tips to not let go, to not listen to her head.

He felt it, too. And he was going to say it. It was hard enough to back away, to put the distance between them and stop the roots of their relationship from growing. Hearing it out loud, from his mouth, would be too much.

"Don't say anything." She rushed to his lips, Liam's surprised soft-ness turning purposely powerful, returning the kiss. It was all she had ached for today, in the hull of *Harpeth Rose,* sitting next to him in the interview, catching his stares at her on their walk to Campy's.

His arms pulled her in. She touched his chest, his body flinching for a second, then relaxing as her hands crossed the scar and around his naked shoulders. One hand held her cheek, the other gliding down her neck. His lips followed, soft wet kisses past her cheek and cascading to the nape of her neck. Tension in her body dissolved with each lowered kiss, awakening her voice in a soft whimper.

He pulled away for a second, whether it was to catch his breath or stare into her eyes, Cynthia didn't care which. She wanted this mo-ment, wanted to be here with him. Close.

"I don't want to stop," he said.

She shook her head, loosening her grasp around his body for the briefest of moments. "Me, neither."

She pulled her sweater over her head and sat still in front of him, hair swinging down her back. His eyes washed over her, and it was almost too much to say nothing.

He reached out, two fingers slipping beneath her bra strap, curving down from her shoulder to the top of her breast. "You're beautiful." He let the words linger, sinking through her last bit of mental armor until she let it melt away.

She traced the scar on his shoulder, taking her time, her fingertips feeling the roughness of the ridge and the smooth skin beside it. "You're beautiful."

He smiled and kissed her again. She tasted his mouth, soft tongue licking her lips, then moving down her neck. His hand slid the bra strap off her shoulder, and he kissed her clavicle gently as if she'd break.

Her hands careened down his muscular back as she pulled him down on the bed over top her. He winced, shifting the weight of his upper body to his left side.

"Are you okay?"

"Yeah." He smiled, a devilish sneer. "I'll just have to reserve this arm for touching you."

She giggled, biting her lip to stop.

"What's so funny?"

"Nothing." She raised up enough to unsnap her bra behind her and dropped it on the floor. She touched his cheek, skin warm. "Thought I'd help you out."

This time his eyes tasted her skin, taking in every exposed inch.

She touched his chest, her full palm caressing his muscles down to his navel, fingertips grazing the waist of his pants. "I can help with that buckle, too."

He grinned. "Whatever the hell I did to deserve you, I'll be sure to keep doing."

For the first night at Maiden's Slumber Inn, Cynthia didn't have to bear the agony of Liam Reynolds sleeping across the room. She closed her eyes, absorbing every touch, every passionate kiss they shared, and let herself go.

TWENTY

Thursday, February 11

THE TRUTH HAD been there at the edge of his lips. He had been ready to tell her that yes, he was a deckhand. Probably would've been first mate in a year's time. And that trying out had been a ruse to assess her skills as future greenhorn.

That's all he had needed to say last night to start the discussion. To start laying out the truth and have their relationship lead on the right foot.

Then she kissed him. The virtuous voice in his head shut up, and emotions took over. It had been blinding pleasure.

Liam rose out of bed, his right shoulder stiff. He could still rotate it, which was a good sign. Physical therapy was not something he'd want to have to go through again. It wasn't something Nick could wait for in a new greenhorn, either. He'd just have to take it light, be extra careful during tryouts today. And try hard not to let the sight of the grappling hook cripple his ability to remain upright.

There were so many obstacles standing between him and the position, between him and his ticket out of managing the plant. Fortunately, being a deckhand had given him a valuable set of skills. Unfortunately, that skill set fit a limited number of occupations. Jobs in Oakside or Maiden's Bay, or most of western Washington for that matter, using those skills? Nearly extinct.

A slip of paper was neatly placed on the desk. It was from Cynthia. *Left early and didn't want to wake you. See you at the dock.*

Maybe she realized he hadn't fallen asleep right away afterward. He savored her warm breath on his skin and the floral coconut of her hair. While he loved lying next to her, it took willpower not to wake her to do it all over again, to feel their electric connection. Once sleep had taken over, he dreamed in broken nightmares. One he was in Oakside, and the plant couldn't keep up with the incoming catch, crabs stacking up on top each other. In another he fell off *Harpeth Rose,* his boots filling up with water, dragging him down. He yelled for Cynthia as the boat drifted away, yet his voice wouldn't sound.

It's the lying. It had to be. He had to tell her.

He checked the time. *6:52 AM.* That couldn't be right. He shuffled for a clean shirt out of his duffel bag and slipped on jeans and shoes. It hurt to pull the shirt up along his arm, but he muscled through it, grabbed the key, and left Room 2.

Constance waved him to stop. "Morning! How are you feeling?"

"I'm fine. Sorry, but I'm going to be late."

"Oh, okay. Would you like to bring something to go?"

He had already stepped through the front door by the time she said "go." The cool morning weather left him cursing himself for not grabbing his jacket, but there was no time for that. Hopefully, Nick could lend him something if they were going out on the water.

He flattened the longest bits of his hair, the crew cut starting to grow out, which meant strands branched out on their own in whatever direction they wished. It was why he could never manage to grow it out to one of the longer hairstyles younger men wore these days. He'd look nuts.

Everyone—minus Greg—already gathered around Nick and Ben by *Harpeth Rose,* Nick's hands on his hips. Out of the extra eyes from yesterday, only Joel rejoined Nick and Ben.

"Here he is." Nick motioned to Liam.

"Sorry," Liam said.

Cynthia glanced back at Nick as Liam caught her stare for an instant, long enough to quicken his pulse and forget the cold.

"I was just telling them that today we'll be on *Harpeth Rose,* but won't take her out. We're going to work on bait hooking."

Outside of throwing the grappling hook, Liam couldn't think of a worse exercise for his shoulder.

They boarded *Harpeth Rose,* Cynthia at the front of the pack, and Liam last. He positioned himself next to her as they gathered round for Nick's instructions.

"Early run this morning?"

"No. I just… was up early. Like I said in the note. Did you see the note?" She finally looked at him.

"Yes, thanks." Not sure what he was thanking her for really. "We need to talk."

The group waited as Nick and Ben discussed something—more like argued, based on the pointing and facial expressions. They weren't fighting loud enough though, the silence between Liam and Cynthia uncomfortable.

"Look, about last night." *It was amazing.* "I've been—"

"Can we focus on today?" Cynthia said. "There are only two more days left, and I really want to do my best."

"Yeah. Sure." How could he tell her the truth when she kept silencing him? Did she regret last night? She'd part ways in two days and forget any of this happened?

Nick and Ben finished their verbal brawl and approached the group.

"We'll break into teams again," Nick said. "Sean and Theo go with Ben. Cynthia and Liam with me. Miguel, you'll be with Joel. He's agreed to participate in the exercise with you."

"Sorry, Captain?" Cynthia raised her hand. "Can I talk to you for a second?"

Nick scratched his head up and down with his ball cap and stepped aside with Cynthia. Was she going to tell Nick about his shoulder? Did she worry she was going to have a weak partner?

"Okay, change of plans." Nick returned. "Theo with Cynthia, Liam with Sean."

Liam raised an eyebrow at Cynthia. She pursed her lips and turned off to her station. Nick stood amid the middle of the three stations. He gave Liam a quick shrug.

"You each are standing in front of one of our Dungeness crab pots. As a greenhorn, you'll be responsible for baiting the pots, which at times can be hectic, especially when we're pulling up pots and resetting them along the line. It takes practice to do it correctly and quickly. Like just about everything else on the boat, it also takes stamina."

And a functional shoulder. Liam grew nervous. He hadn't been separated from Cynthia yet this week. Being with Sean meant he couldn't show any signs his shoulder hurt. That's the way it'd have to be in reality if he was to work as a greenhorn. But why did that guy have to punch him there? Literally any other place would've been easier to cope with. Now eyes would be on him from everywhere. It was the first task they had in which all of the groups were in eyesight of each other.

"If you don't know already, I'll demonstrate." Nick picked up the bait sack, which from the smell of it probably held thrown out chicken from Mariner's Market last week. Or last month. He crawled inside the pot, snapped the clip on the bottom of the pot in the middle, scooted back out, and shut the trap door.

His movement was smooth and swift. Nick wasn't the most muscular man Liam had seen on a crew, but he certainly was familiar with the movements and kept himself that way.

"There you have it. Of course, in reality, there are more steps before and after, but you get the gist. Choose who will clip in. The other person will retrieve the bait. I'll signal when we're at an hour."

"Then what?" Sean shouted.

Nick smirked. "We'll see. Just do as many as you can, as quickly as you can. I want this movement to be second nature. Now go."

"How about it?" Liam nodded toward the pot. "You want to clip or unclip?"

"Neither."

Sean's response was shocking. What the heck was he doing on this ship? The only thing missing was a cell phone in hand, and Sean would've passed for a defiant teen.

"Do you or do you *not* want to be a greenhorn?"

Sean shook his head, eyeing Nick behind him. "I don't think you want to know the answer to that."

"What are you talking about?" The unease about the others trying out returned. He and Cynthia had planned to interrogate them yesterday evening at Joel's, but that didn't go as planned.

Liam looked around. Joel slipped into the pot, working diligently, his skinny frame an advantage to the task. Cynthia had opted to go first in her team, of course.

"Fine, I'll go first." Although he was curious as to why Sean even bothered showing up. "Just step aside, will you?"

"My pleasure." Sean took two steps back and folded his arms.

Liam grabbed the bait sack and got down on his knees. Man, it had been a long time. Luckily for him greenhorn lasted for six months before moving up. Maybe it wasn't lucky after all. Maybe more training and drills like this would've helped in preventing his accident.

He reached in the pot, pain thumping in his shoulder. He remained inside, looking back at Cynthia. Theo was already retrieving the bait bag. They both needed to pace themselves if they wanted to last the full hour, or possibly longer. But damn it if Cynthia didn't have fire in her eyes.

He clipped the sack in the pot and crept out, dropping the door. "That's one."

"You're getting beat by a girl," Sean scoffed.

"I don't mind actually."

Sean rushed to the ground and swooped in the pot, his long lanky body the perfect conduit for the job. He unclipped the bag, hopped to his feet, and handed it to Liam. "Here you go. Your turn again."

Liam had hoped for a longer rest than that, but he was going to have to push himself a little more if he was going to convince Nick he was truly capable for the spot. Not that Sean's attitude reflected the same.

Again he loaded the bait into the pot, this time not pausing, and breathed through the pain. If Sean wanted to make his rest short, then Liam could play that game, too.

He and Sean went back and forth. Somewhere around the thirty minute mark, the pain in his shoulder overpowered his will to stick it to Sean. He slowed down, huffing for air, and used his left arm for most of the action.

He came out of the pot, resting on his knees. A hand stretched in front of his face. Cynthia's. He grabbed it, and she helped him up.

"What's this about?" Liam asked.

Sean was over with Theo, and Joel and Miguel continued with the exercise.

"While I admire drive as much as anyone, you're torturing yourself. Let me take over."

"What, both parts?"

"Yeah. You can go every three or four turns. Nick isn't watching all the time."

"You don't have to do that."

"Yes, I do. It's what a good crewmate would do." She took the bait bag out of his hand. "It's what a good friend would do."

She worked diligently, in and out of the pot for what seemed like a hundred times. Whenever she'd catch Nick looking, she'd hurry and hand off the bait bag to Liam.

They approached mid-day when Nick stopped the drill for a lunch break. Liam's shoulder burned.

So much for an hour.

"I'm going to catch lunch with Theo and the guys." Cynthia squinted from the sun peeking through the clouds. "You coming?"

"I've gotta talk to Nick. You go ahead."

"Everything all right?" A sincere worry washed across her face.

"I'm fine." He took off his work gloves. "Hey, are we okay? Am I imagining things, or did you ask Nick to switch partners this morning?"

She sighed. "No, you're not imagining things. I *did* ask Nick to switch partners."

"Because you didn't want me."

"Not that. No." She put her hands on her hips. "I've learned a lot from you. But I want the chance to learn from the others, too. Get to know them. Who knows. Maybe one day more than one of us will be on the same crew."

He nodded. If it was an excuse to cover up any uncomfortableness with him, it was a darn good one.

She stepped closer and lowered her voice. "Plus, I didn't know if I could keep my focus working next to you. After last night…." She bit her lip. "It's not that I don't want to be around you. I don't want the others thinking—"

"I'll stop you right there," he said. "Although… you keep biting that lip, I may have to bite it myself."

Her jaw dropped, and she tapped his arm.

He chuckled. "You'd better go to lunch. It's always a good time to see people for who they really are, when they're hungry."

"You sure you don't want to come?"

"Nah, I'm good. We'll be dining tonight at Ben's, anyway."

"Okay. See you in a bit."

"Oh, and Cynthia?"

"Yeah?"

"Thanks. For coming to the rescue."

Cynthia nodded. "Of course."

She walked off, the three men waiting for her. Joel, Ben, and Nick gathered in the navigation bridge. Liam scanned the instrument panel, recognizing a GPS and fish finder, amongst other gadgetry and screens. The thick windows had seen some action, like a car windshield collecting bugs and chips on a long road trip.

"No, we're good," Nick said. "Thanks for your help today."

"You're welcome," Joel said. "Just keep working them to the bone so they come to the bar later." He slapped Nick's shoulder and headed out.

"Nick? A word?" Liam stepped back outside, and Nick followed.

"What is it?"

"I don't think I can go on like this." Liam couldn't meet Nick's eyes. Disappointing him hurt almost as bad as his shoulder.

"I caught you struggling with the drill," Nick said. "This afternoon will be less physical. Thought we'd go over charting and have a look at the engine room."

"That's admittedly a relief."

"Is your shoulder acting up again?"

"It's a bit sore at the moment. Nothing to worry about too much. But it's not just the physical part of it that's getting to me. I can't keep lying to Cynthia. We're around each other all the time, which at first was great to be honest."

"And now? Are you saying you don't get along?"

"No. We get along *too* well."

Nick lowered his eyebrows, puzzled.

"I care about her, Nick." He looked around. Heaven forbid someone like Sean would hear him. "We've, uh… gotten close."

"Jesus, Liam. Are you trying to say—?" Nick scanned the deck for listeners, then held up a hand. "I don't want to know."

"All you need to know is that I've fallen for her. I can't believe I let it get this far without telling her."

"It's only one more day, Liam."

"I don't see why I need to lie anymore, Nick. Cynthia has proven herself time and again. Did you see what she did this morning? She took up my slack, and did it well. I don't need to see any more. She'll do great as a greenhorn. As much as I want the opportunity for myself, I have to admit that. As for the others, I don't really know, because I haven't been around them much."

"But that's why you need to keep it a secret. One last day, to watch the others. Tomorrow will be the ultimate test that puts everything together."

"Don't you see?" Nick's nonchalance was aggravating. "How is it fair that I assess others while going for it myself?"

"How will Cynthia react when you tell her you were meant to evaluate her, and then decided to vie for the spot yourself?"

Liam knew the truth would be hurtful, but the way Nick laid it out—it sounded insurmountable. She'd never forgive him. What did he want more?

Nick threw his arm over Liam's good shoulder. "I can't make you decide what to do. Your desire to be greenhorn is fairly new to me, but so is your relationship with Cynthia. But before you make any decision, will you at least come to dinner tonight? Can you promise me that?"

Baited again. An evening spent with Cynthia. Another night of lying. It was hard to know which way the scale tipped with the weight of those two things changing by the minute.

Liam nodded. How was he to say no? Never pass up free food, as Constance said. Somehow those words were having a bigger effect on his life than he could have imagined.

"Fine. I'll be there."

"And no talking to Cynthia about all of this before."

He sighed and held up a hand. In a way, Nick's demand brought about a dose of relief from having to choose.

"Promise."

TWENTY-ONE

CYNTHIA'S MUSCLES ALREADY ached, and the heeled boots weren't helping.

The afternoon had been much easier than the morning drill. It wasn't so much as difficult to master as it was tiring. Yet in reality, out on the water with the boat swaying and the full crew out unloading and sorting the catch, she could imagine it requiring more skill. She wanted the chance to not imagine it, but experience it.

Seeing Liam suffering through the morning was almost as grueling as the task. She hadn't been completely honest with him when he asked about not wanting to be his partner. When she had awakened early in the morning, she thought it best to keep her distance. If she had stayed in bed, she'd give into her craving to touch him, hold him, kiss him. She'd want all of him again. Her pull toward him had the ability to mute the rational part of her that screamed it would never work out.

They had only two more days of tryouts, and if they gave each other space, they could get through it. Just two days. Then they could work out how they fit in each other's future. *If* they fit.

Then the baiting drills happened. All it took was one look at Liam wincing on *Harpeth Rose*'s deck, and her resolve crumbled.

As if it was impossible to be separated from him.

They had returned early afternoon and had a chance to get ready for dinner. Cynthia washed and straightened her hair, and applied makeup for the first time since arriving at the inn. While she occupied the bathroom, Liam took the opportunity to nap. Who could blame him? She herself had a tough time falling asleep last night. The option to snooze came in at a close second.

She buttoned her coat as Liam returned from his turn showering. Hopefully the black sweater dress and boots weren't too dressy for the occasion. Liam looked handsome in gray pants and a heather blue sweater, the crisp collar of the button-down white shirt peeking out the neck. It could have used some ironing, but the fact he packed them, in a duffel bag none the less, was part of his charm.

She grabbed her purse. "Ready?"

"Let me just grab my wallet here, make sure I have my key—" Liam froze.

"What is it?"

"You—you look—your eyes and—"

She touched her cheek. "Is it too much? I hardly ever wear mascara or lipstick."

"No, it's—you're beautiful." He stared with a grin on his face.

She remembered the first time he said those words, last night. And she said them back.

He stepped closer and gently touched her, lifting her chin and staring in her eyes. He leaned in and kissed her, a slow, soft, innocent kiss on the lips.

It's all it took to weaken her knees, like a marionette's strings losing tension. She stepped back against her body's wishes, foot as heavy as stone.

"I'm sorry," he said. "Did I overstep?"

"No." She shook her head and touched his chest. "I don't want you to think I didn't like what happened last night."

"But…."

She turned around, mulling over the right words, then sat down on her bed. "Could I ask a favor of you? Could we pause this, just until tryouts are over? I don't mean rewind or erase. Tomorrow is going to be the most important day of tryouts. It's the final day to show those guys what I can do." She stood up and reached out for him again, holding his hands in hers. "I want—I *need*—all of my focus on it. Please don't take that to mean I don't want this." She swallowed the last bit of hesitancy. "That I don't want you."

He turned aside, suddenly taking interest in the wallpaper.

Her words hurt him, no matter how thoughtfully constructed. "I'm sorry. It's not coming out right."

He turned back to her and cupped her face in his hands. "No, it came out perfectly. It's just when you say things like that, looking like you do, you make it damn near impossible not to touch you."

She leaned forward, and his forehead touched hers. They stood like that for seconds, minutes, before he moved. He kissed her forehead, the feel of his lips lingering on her skin. It was the last kiss he'd give her until the end of tryouts. She knew that with all her being, knew he cared for her enough to respect her wishes.

"Shall we go?" It was all too easy to get lost in his scent, his touch. He could've tempted her to skip dinner. Which was why they needed to cool off for twenty four hours at the very least.

"Yes." He snapped out of the trance. "We'd better."

They walked downstairs, out of Constance's, into the chilly evening. It felt good to be out of that room, out of each other's personal space, and into the open.

"Are you sure we need to bring something?" Liam asked.

"No offense, but I don't think you understand how big a deal this is." Thursday night dinners at the Campbell's were notorious in the fishing community of Maiden's Bay, oftentimes Ben and Angela hosting the entire crew of *Harpeth Rose*. Even the non-fishers of the community knew about the dinners and wanted in on the tradition. Cynthia had been friends with Josie for almost a year now, but never had been invited to the weekly event. It was like taboo or something to host someone outside of the vessel's crew and families.

"Oh, I believe you. Judging by those fancy shoes." He winked, and she shook her head, tightening up her coat collar in the breeze. With each step, they walked away from the seriousness of their talk, back to the night ahead.

"Right here." She opened the door for Liam, the bell jingling as they walked inside Mariner's Market. In a roundabout way, this place partly held responsibility for her pursuit of the greenhorn position. Since she was a little girl, she loved to walk in and get hit with the smell of fresh fish, most caught early in the morning by local fishermen.

It also smelled of sharp aged cheeses. However, that didn't motivate her to go into the dairy profession.

"You want to pick out some wine?" She pointed at an aisle to their left. "Down that way. I'll be in the back by the bakery section."

Liam wandered off as she clicked her way along the tile floor, forcing herself to ignore the seafood section and making a beeline for the bakery.

She settled on bringing a dessert. Everyone brought wine and bread, and she wanted to leave an impression on the host and hostess. And Nick, of course. Although if it took food choice to impress him at this point, she should probably back out of the tryouts.

"Can I help you?" the woman behind the counter asked.

"I wanted to see what sort of desserts you have."

"Will this do?" Liam held a bottle of red wine in one hand and white in the other.

"I think so. I don't know what they're serving, so that should cover it."

"Whatcha getting here? Ooh, look at those baguettes. Is that a Tuscan loaf?"

Cynthia looked at him, perplexed. "You can identify a Tuscan loaf, but you're clueless when it comes to carnations versus dandelions."

He shrugged. "What can I say? I like my carbs."

She sighed, undecided. "I guess we're doing bread." She pointed to the Tuscan loaf. "We'll take one of those."

"And a baguette," Liam chimed. "Please."

They checked out and carried their items out onto the sidewalk in front of the store. Cynthia checked about the car on her phone.

"You said you scheduled an Uber?"

"Yes, I promise," she said. "It'll be here on time."

"I'm fine with taking my car. Really. I'll keep it to one glass of wine, if that."

Alcohol was Cynthia's excuse for getting the rideshare, which may end up a good idea, depending on the amount she drank based on her level of awkwardness. Even more than that was the anxiety she would feel being alone with Liam. They were on the same page, keeping it cool for the next day. But being confined to a vehicle with no one other than Liam? She didn't trust herself.

The hired car—pickup truck, rather—pulled up. "Told you." Cynthia opened the back door, thankful the truck had a crew cab. It was awkward enough riding in a taxi or Uber in the front. Having to sit three across the front would've been agony.

"Hey there, Cynthia."

"Hi, Jerry."

Liam leaned in next to her. "You know the driver?"

Cynthia nodded. "I'll tell you later."

The car weaved up the mountainside north of town, leaving the rows of houses and entering the wooded hillside. Ben and Angela Campbell lived on the outskirts, just within range of the municipality. The view traveling up the mountainside, even through the firs and pines, was stunning. Maiden's Bay's beauty never ceased to impress her.

The car slowed, approaching a two-story house, the tires rumbling over the gravel driveway. "Here we are," Jerry said.

"Thanks, Jerry." Cynthia led Liam to the front door and rang the doorbell. She closed her eyes and took a deep breath. "I can't believe this is happening."

"If you're this excited about a dinner, what are you going to do on that first fishing trip?"

"Hi!" Josie greeted them at the door. "Come on in. Oh, hold on one second. Is that Jerry Bradley?" She waved to the truck driver. "Hi, Jerry!"

The driver gave a short honk of the horn before backing out of the driveway.

"You know our driver, too?" Liam asked.

"Josie knows *everyone*," Cynthia said.

"I don't know everyone. It's a funny story, actually." Josie urged them to come inside. She set the wine and bread down on the hallway table. The aroma wafting from the kitchen carried the buttery scent of biscuits along with the promise of seafood.

"My rental car broke down when I first arrived," Josie said. "At the crossroads to Jerry's street. He happened to be out mulching his garden, so he offered me a ride. Shortly after, he became an Uber driver part-time."

"That's not the funny part." Cynthia handed Josie her coat, who delightfully waited for it. "His ex-wife, Noreen, also decided to work part-time driving."

"They can't seem to stop arguing and competing," Josie said. "It used to be over who brought the best brownies to the bake sale. Now it's who can get the most five-star ratings."

"I purposely pick one or the other, depending on who is closest," Cynthia said. "Neither one would dare be late for fear of a bad rating."

"I guess the rivalry ends up being good for the customer," Liam said.

Josie walked them into the kitchen, white cabinets and appliances giving the space a cottage feel. Nick and Ben stood in the corner by the sink, sipping beers. An older woman and man were chatting in the adjoining dining room. She recognized the woman as Carol Campbell, former mayor of Maiden's Bay and mother to Nick, Ben, and Joel. She could only guess as to who the man was. Perhaps her boyfriend.

Cynthia and Liam placed their contributions to dinner on the counter beside the rest.

"I guess we're the first of the greenhorn crew," Cynthia whispered to Liam.

He leaned to look in the dining room. "Looks like it."

A woman entered the kitchen, holding a young child with hardly any hair. "I'm sorry I couldn't answer the door." Her hair pulled back loosely in a braid, and she wore a long floral yellow dress.

"Don't apologize for feeding your child. My goodness." Josie touched the woman's arm. "Angela, this is Cynthia and Liam."

"Nice to meet you," Angela said.

"So this is little Annabel?" Cynthia held out a finger, and Annabel clasped it, smiling a gummy smile. She knew not to bring up Annabel when lunching with Josie, else she'd have to hear the gushing until dinner time. "I've heard a lot about you. You do look like a little cherub, don't you?" Annabel wore a purple striped onesie with purple pants, but even with the pants Cynthia could make out the rolls of cute pudginess on her legs.

"Would you mind taking her, Josie? I need to wash my hands."

"Of course."

Angela handed Annabel off to Josie, who threw on a big smile and raised her voice two octaves chattering with her. "Let's go see your Uncle Nick." Josie walked to the corner of the kitchen, holding the infant on her hip as if she had done so a hundred times.

Ben joined his wife Angela by the stove, prepping dinner. The smell of the chowder overpowered whatever was cooking in the oven, in a good way. Cynthia raced through lunch and hadn't eaten since, her stomach empty.

"I'll take that off your hands." The older mystery man from the dining room stood next to Liam, taking the wine and bread.

"Thank you. I'm Liam."

"Robert." They shook hands, then Robert worked on uncorking the wine.

Liam pressed into Cynthia, the warmth of his breath tickling her neck. "Am I supposed to know who Robert is?"

"I really don't know what's going on. Where's Sean, or Miguel, or Theo?"

He shrugged, and they shared a quick smile. At least they were in it together.

"Josie, can I speak to you for a second?" asked Cynthia.

"Sure." Josie gave Annabel to Nick and crossed the kitchen.

"What's going on?" Cynthia kept her voice composed. "Who's Robert, and where are the others trying out?"

"Calm down," Josie said. "Robert is Carol's new husband."

"Who's Carol?" Liam asked.

"Carol is Nick and Ben's mom," Cynthia said.

"Oh. That's Missus Campbell? *The* Missus Campbell?"

Josie leaned closer. "Missus Clarendon now."

Robert Clarendon held two glasses of red wine, carefully making it to the table and handing Carol one. He was neatly dressed and handsome, with a strong jaw and lean physique. His salt and pepper hair was cut super short, in a way that signaled ex-military.

"What about the others?" Cynthia asked.

"Nick said they turned down the invitation."

Of course they did. No to the podcast. No to dinner. "And what about Joel?"

"He works the bar every other Thursday. This is his 'on' week."

"What about the rest of Nick's crew? Don't they usually come?"

Josie sighed. "So many questions." She shook her head. "They do, but since Carol is here, we wanted to keep it low-key."

"Low-key? So it's just us?" Cynthia felt her heart drop. They were crashing a family celebration. A family that wasn't hers. Then again, hers wouldn't get along so well.

"I'm sorry." Josie's face didn't look genuinely sorry. "Nick and I wanted you two to come, and Angela and Ben had all this food at the ready. Please stay. It would be wrong to leave now."

Nick tapped Josie on the shoulder, Annabel in his other arm. "She needs a diaper change."

"Okay." Josie stared at Nick, and he didn't move. Annabel gummed his shoulder, a circle of drool spreading through the fabric of his shirt.

Nick's shoulders slumped. "I didn't say it to imply you should do it. I just wanted to know where the wipes are."

Josie turned toward him and crossed her arms over her chest.

"I deal with fish guts for a living," Nick said. "Trust me, I can handle a dirty diaper."

"Totally not the same thing," Ben said. "You would think fish guts were the worst thing to handle, but you'd be wrong." He leaned closer and whispered, "That's the devil's work coming out of that one."

"Stop." Angela tapped Ben on the arm.

"You couldn't possibly have heard what I said."

"I didn't have to." She handed him a stack of bowls. "On the plates, please."

"My pleasure." Ben winked at them before moving off to the dining room.

"Looks like everything's ready," Angela said. "Go ahead and have a seat in there."

Cynthia was glad the awkwardness of standing around amidst the dinner-prep commotion was over, but didn't know if she was trading one uncomfortable scenario for another. She led Liam to the dining room. White plates dotted the red table cloth, and two tall pink candles stood in the center in glass holders. Cynthia veered to the left of the table, walking past Robert and Carol and sitting at the last chair on that side. Liam went around the other side next to Josie.

"Oh, you can sit on the end," Josie said. "Nick will sit here. And Angela and Ben like to be at the other end nearest the kitchen with the high chair."

"I'm not sure if the head of the table—" Liam flustered.

"Don't be silly. Please. That way you're next to Cynthia on the corner." Josie smiled. There was no arguing with Josie.

Which made Cynthia think. If Josie had asked the others, surely they wouldn't have been able to decline the dinner invitation. But she said Nick asked them, and he wouldn't have been as insistent. Or did he even ask?

Her suspicion must've been written on her face, because Liam got her attention. "Hey, you okay?"

"Yeah."

"You looked like you were going to be sick. You're not allergic to seafood, are you? If I remember, you had the freshwater option the other night at Codfather. That would be an ironic twist to your dream."

The tension eased a little. "No, I'm not allergic, and you're right, that would be tricky."

"Good, because from what I see, between the chowder and lobster bake, you'd be going hungry."

"Fortunately, no."

"What is it, then?"

She looked at the smile on Josie's face, and the pleasantries being passed among the family members. Nick, Josie, and Ben sat on one side, with Angela and Annabel at one end of the table, and Carol and Robert next to her. And of course Liam at her end of the table, right next to her. How had they planned to fit the other guys? Maybe she was being paranoid. Josie was a good friend. Why would she lie about dinner? Either way, they all seemed happy and welcoming and not to mind her presence at all.

"Nothing," she said. Voicing her suspicions might only make Liam feel worse for being there, and that wouldn't be fair. "Seeing their family like this makes me think of my own family." She placed the napkin on her lap. "And its shortcomings."

"Well, you have my attention now. Not that your dress doesn't demand it." His lips cornered in a smile. For a second, she was there with Liam. No one else. The chatter melted away.

"Are you saying there's more to it than your sister not talking to you? You don't have to tell me. If you don't want to."

"Oh, it's okay." The reversion back to her family was a welcome distraction from his flirting. The longer she waited to respond, the more she pictured him helping her take off the dress. "I'll tell you sometime."

Liam nodded and grabbed his wine glass. Ben stood up for a toast, and Cynthia grabbed her glass.

Liam leaned closer. "How about over lobster bake?"

TWENTY-TWO

THE WHOLE TIME Liam stood in the kitchen during introductions and pre-dinner chatting, he wondered what would be better. Sit directly next to Cynthia or across from her? Or should he sit on the complete opposite end of the table? Seeing her in that black dress hugging her silhouette knocked the wind out of him. She was beautiful in anything she'd worn this week, but it brought out her toned shoulders and the curvature of her clavicle underneath the fabric. The arc up her sleek neck to her gorgeous face had been the perfect spot to shower with kisses.

This dinner was going to last an eternity.

The decision had been made for him. He sat at the head of the table, she to his right, her left arm in agonizingly close reach. He wanted to hold her hand under the table. Connect with her without anyone else seeing. Instead he had to connect with words.

"It's so nice to finally meet everyone," Liam said. "I've heard so much about you, Josie. We didn't really get a chance to chat beyond the interview. And Ben never says a bad word about you, Angela. And Missus Campbell—I mean *Clarendon.*"

"Please, Carol."

"Well, Carol, you're notorious within the community, if I may say so."

"Notorious? I think that's a stretch." Her eyes wrinkled with fine lines, no doubt a testament to her life.

Liam knew little about Maiden's Bay, but most of what he *did* know tied to Carol Campbell. "You're Careful Campbell." At one point years ago, Maiden's Bay faced bankruptcy. The crabbing fishery, unregulated like today, was collapsing, forcing crews to sail further and longer. The fishing industry then suffered a major blow when two vessels collided competing over territory, urging a massive search and rescue. One crew member died while several others suffered from hypothermia and non-fatal injuries. It didn't rank as one of the deadliest, like The Armament or Bullion Run, accidents anyone with sea legs feared. But with Carol as mayor—and wife and mother to fishermen—she established a code of ethics adopted across the Crescent Coast and helped in drafting regulation guidelines, making those who made their living from the sea feel safer, hence keeping the economy alive.

"Enough, Liam." Nick sipped his drink. "Flattery doesn't look good on you."

"I don't mind taking some of it." Ben sat on the other end of Josie, dunking oyster crackers in his chowder. "If you feel the need to pass it around."

Nick rolled his eyes and shook his head.

"What about your family, Liam?" Josie asked. "Are they in the business, as well?"

"That's a tricky question."

Cynthia raised her eyebrows. In their private dinner the other night, she hadn't asked him, nor did he openly divulge that information.

"I have two younger sisters. Miriam is finishing up school to be a science teacher, and Chloe is in law school. She wants to specialize in maritime law, so that's probably the closest either one gets to fishing."

"And your parents?" Carol asked.

"My father worked on a fishing boat for ten years, then at Oakside's first local bank for twenty."

"So there's a bit of it in the genes then," said Carol.

"I'm actually adopted. Somehow, I still picked up the fishing bug, but not the banking one, which was okay by my dad. He passed away six years ago from a heart attack."

"So sorry," Angela said, and the other guests nodded in agreement.

"Thank you. My mom taught for years at the elementary school and now writes as a hobby. She's still in Oakside."

"I don't mean to pry, but do you know your biological parents?" Josie looked around at the company. "Is that too forward of me?"

"No, it's okay. I don't. I never really went searching for them, either. It was a closed adoption, and my mom and dad are my mom and dad. I was actually in the foster care system. The last family to take me in had to move suddenly, and they happened to live next to June and Barry Reynolds. The Reynolds offered to take me in, then fostering turned to adoption, and here I am. I couldn't imagine considering anyone other than June and Barry as my parents."

"Oh, wow." Angela clutched her chest. "It warms my heart to hear adoption success stories."

"I don't know if you can call me a success or not." He chuckled.

"I know we just met, but you seem like such a gentleman." Angela shoved a spoonful of applesauce into Annabel's mouth. "Ben and I were going through the adoption process. We tried getting pregnant for years, and it wasn't until we started the paperwork for adoption that the other way happened for us." She smiled at Ben, her eyes watering. Ben patted her hand.

"Do you think Annabel will want to follow in her father's footsteps?" Liam asked.

"Let's hope not." Ben wiped his brow. "My heart can't take it when she crawls across the room. And now she tries to stand! It's a nightmare."

"Now you know why I wanted you to check in every time you got back," Carol chimed, pointing to her boys. "I think by the time I hit sixty, my stomach was tightened into a permanent knot."

"What does your dad think about you being a greenhorn, Cynthia?" Ben asked.

It was an innocent enough question. At least Ben had meant well. Cynthia churned in her seat and feigned a polite smile. "My father passed away. It'll be two years this August."

"I'm sorry." Angela seemed to not wear her heart on her sleeve, but on her face. She had run the gamut of emotions in the last five minutes.

"It's okay. He knew about my dream and said that if he were captain of a ship, he would want there to be a full crew of Cynthia Pruitts on board."

The Campbell family chuckled.

"Of course, parents are biased when it comes to their children, but I at least got to know he supported my dream."

"Support means a lot in this business," Angela said. "Do you have other family around?"

"My mother lives in Spokane, and my sister Jackie lives here in Maiden's Bay. Jackie doesn't exactly have my father's take on the career choice."

"What is it about the job that she doesn't like? Is it because you're a woman when it's predominantly men?" Angela said.

"I don't think it's so much that. Although that would probably be an easier hang up to tackle."

"What is it, then?" Liam asked. Cynthia had closed herself off to discussing Jackie at The Codfather, and he never really had the chance to get back to the subject until now. Talking about Jackie changed Cynthia's whole demeanor. Her gaze turned downward, and her head hung low. Her body physically sheltered her heart.

"She thinks it's too dangerous. Not just for a woman. For anyone."

"It certainly is dangerous," Angela said.

"We know that all too well." Nick locked eyes with his mother.

"Again, why I hope for my sake Annabel takes after her mom and works at the school library." Ben rubbed Annabel's back. "Books are much safer. Aren't they, Little Bel? Yes, they are."

Annabel slapped her hand in a plastic baby bowl, the applesauce flinging onto Ben's face.

Ben wiped it off his eye. "This is what I mean." He excused himself from the table, Josie and Liam laughing.

"You can't let go of your dream because it's risky." Carol Campbell did not have the physical stature or heavy voice to command attention, yet she did all the same whenever she spoke. She had to, having been married to a fisherman, raising two others, and governing the town. "Yes, I was a nervous wreck whenever Thomas had gone out. I still am with my sons. But if I told their father he couldn't go…." She shook her head. "His spirit would've broken. And in the end? After all that time out fishing, he died in a car crash. You just never know."

"I had a brother." Cynthia blurted it out, and Liam could see her pulse racing in her neck. "I was one of those surprise babies my parents had later in life, so Jackie's twelve years older than me, and Owen was two years older than her. I didn't really know him that well because of the age difference. Or perhaps I did but I have forgotten, since I was so young when it happened."

The table was quiet, not a person moving outside of Annabel wiping her hand through applesauce on the highchair table.

"He had just turned eighteen, right before winter break his senior year of high school. His friend had been a greenhorn on a vessel all summer and was set to go out again before school started back up in January. By some stroke of luck—or misfortune—his friend caught the flu. However it worked out, Owen took his place. It was his first time on a fishing vessel. First time being a greenhorn. It was on *The Armament*."

Nick winced, and Angela covered her mouth after gasping. Even Liam had known about the tragedy. Word spread throughout the fishing towns from northern California to Canada.

Josie scanned around the room, out of the loop. "What happened?"

"Maybe we shouldn't talk about this over dinner." Nick grabbed Josie's hand, who swatted his away.

"I want to know." Josie looked at Cynthia. "Only if you're okay telling it."

"*The Armament* set out of Maiden's Bay on New Year's Eve. Three days later, an SOS was received, the captain stating engine trouble. By the time the Coast Guard arrived, there was nothing. It was as if the ship and its crew never existed."

Josie's mouth quivered. "My God. The entire crew?"

Ben leaned on the wall in the doorway as if he owed the history the common courtesy of standing. "To this day no one knows what really happened."

"I feel like I should feel more about it," Cynthia said. "Sad or angry. But I feel... disconnected. Like it's a matter of fact. I know the risk I'm taking going out there. It took my brother's life, and I know it can take mine or anyone else's."

"Excuse me." Josie placed her napkin beside her plate and left the table.

"Josie. Wait." Nick scooted his chair and followed Josie out of the dining room.

"I'm sorry," Cynthia said. "I didn't mean to offend anyone."

"It's okay." Angela released Annabel from the high chair and sat the pudgy baby on her lap. "Josie's been a little sensitive lately about Nick being in danger out there. Those of us who have lived it all of our lives know it and have had time to deal with it. For her, it's still fresh."

Cynthia scooted her chair away from the table. "Someone should tell her it was before the technology and regulations we have now."

Carol held up a hand, urging Cynthia to remain seated. "It's hard to want to be with someone for the rest of your forever when their forever could be cut short. Even with the advancements we've made." Carol's eyes held sorrow and strength. Robert held her hand on the table.

Liam longed to hold Cynthia's hand. She had some of that same strength Carol held, but that didn't mean she shouldn't or couldn't be held and consoled.

Her story reminded him that even with the best training and experience, a fisher's life could be taken away at any moment. This whole time he had been focused on whether or not she would be a good crew member, whether or not he could be with her beyond this one week, whether he could stand the time apart. He didn't stop to face the reality so many spouses and partners had to live with—the fact she could get hurt or die when she was out there.

And suddenly he didn't want her to go. He didn't want her to pursue such a dream. She was better than that world. She deserved better than what that pursuit could give in return.

Maybe he didn't want it for himself, either.

"How about we work on the dessert?" Angela stood, carrying Annabel.

"We'll help clear the table." Carol gathered her plate, and Robert followed, the two moving back and forth from table to kitchen, clearing the place settings and plating the leftovers. Ben grabbed dessert plates and passed them out, but only after Angela convinced him to do so.

"I didn't mean to scare everyone off." Cynthia's sad eyes met Liam's.

But she had scared him, and he couldn't bear to be near her at the moment while simultaneously wanting to hold her tight and never let go.

"I'm sorry about your brother," Liam said. "I didn't know."

"Most people don't. It was a long time ago, and the names of the crew are all but forgotten were it not for a plaque in the cemetery. I don't like to bring it up because…." She pointed out the empty table.

"It's amazing that you still want to do this, despite what happened to your brother."

"Trust me. I've received enough lectures from Jackie. It's the reason we don't talk anymore. Either I keep my sister and hate my life, or I pursue my dream and lose my sister."

"I don't want it to look like I'm taking sides, but—"

"Then don't." She took his right hand in her left, the warmth in her touch unbearable. "You've been so supportive of me this entire week. I haven't had anyone do that since my dad passed away. It's been me by myself."

"Cynthia—"

"I'm so glad you're here—at tryouts, at Constance's, at this dinner table. I didn't realize how much I needed a supportive friend. Someone who understands the call to be out there."

"About that." He pulled his hand out of her grasp, one of the hardest moves he'd had to make since physical therapy. He was her friend. But to hear her say that word to define them, as if she only saw him as that and nothing more, damaged his soul, despite her speech on pausing their relationship. "I don't think I'm going to make it through tryouts."

"What? What do you mean? Is it your shoulder?"

"That's a part of it. But—"

"You're sore and bruised now, but it'll heal. Think how far you've come since you first injured it. You didn't think you'd ever set foot on a boat again. You've done way more than that. Don't give up on it because of a stupid bar fight."

"I just—" *Want to be with you. Want to run out of here. Want to rewind to last week and never agree to this in the first place.*

"Please, Liam." She stared right into his eyes, and he wanted to cower, as if she could see him for who he really was, and he didn't like to be seen that way. "It's only one more day." She leaned away, sitting back deep in her chair. "I know you can do this."

"Hey, shouldn't you be discouraging me? One less person to compete against?"

"It's not about that."

"Then what's it about?" He nearly shouted the words. He paused, dampening his tone. "I've had my shot. Maybe I should step aside to let someone else have theirs."

She bit her lip, eyes watering up. "If it's truly not what you want, then fine. Quit. But don't say you're quitting in order to give me a chance. Because I can do it without you."

He caressed the back of her hand with his thumb. "I didn't mean it like that."

She took in a breath. "I don't want to do it without you." Her gaze landed on his.

She had struck his heart. He sat next to the woman who in a week's time had weaved a web of emotions for him to process. Liam was at a precipice in which any decision made would affect his future career, place of residence, relationship. Just about every facet of his life.

He sat, more torn than ever.

TWENTY-THREE

Friday, February 12

SWEAT BEADED ON Cynthia's forehead. The morning run started extra early, close to five AM. Who was she kidding, trying to sleep while Liam lay in the bed next to her? It was tough enough confessing she wanted him around for the final task in tryouts. That was on top of having already experienced the sensual pleasure of their bodies entangled, souls intertwined.

She had meant what she said last night. She didn't need him to help her, or teach her, or give her moral or emotional support. No, she could get through whatever task was thrown at her without that from him.

She *wanted* him.

Yet this felt like goodbye, like this was the last day she'd be near him. Who were they kidding? After today, he'd leave back to Oakside—or be out on *Harpeth Rose*—and maybe they'd start off promising to see each other. But time together would dwindle while resentment grew.

Why put themselves through it? Would it not be better to simply end it now?

She'd tossed and turned all night thinking about it. If it was truly an all or nothing deal with Liam, was she willing to go with nothing?

She ran past Jackie's house, eyes gazing up the driveway to the front door. No matter how much she tried not to be hurt by Jackie's actions—or inactions—the emotional strain was there. Had Jackie losing Owen felt worse than she felt now being shut out by Jackie? Wouldn't the loss of Owen, then Dad, bring Jackie closer to her?

Why were relationships with the ones she cared for always the most so difficult?

She turned off her sister's road and down to Pearl Avenue, beyond Campy's and the dock, the houseboats, and the strip of forested park by the beach. She stopped at the top of the outer steps at the base of the lighthouse and knocked, then tried the red door. It was open. She had never been out here so early, but suspected Mr. Ludlow would be up.

"Hello?" she shouted up the stairs. "It's Cynthia!"

She hit the stairs, pacing herself, but letting her calves burn by the twentieth step or so. It didn't matter how many times she had done these. There was no acclimating to the tightening spiral up to the top, and the hotter she became, the more likely she was to stop and freak out. The openness of the top motivated her not to stop.

She slowed, walking the last three steps to the top, panting and wiping her forehead with her sleeve. She stepped along the outer walkway, the wind steady at such a height, wiping away the heat she had built up in her body.

A noise came from inside, and she went back through the gallery door. "Mind your eyes coming up here."

She stepped up a set of six stairs, apprehensive, never having been near the lens before. The last three feet of wall height enclosed the lantern base, the actual light resting above surrounded by a glass lens, like a clear spiky Fabergé egg. The lens rotated, and she covered her eyes when its focused light swung around to her spot. It was so bright she could feel the light through her skin.

"You're up early." Mr. Ludlow sat on the floor, head below the light and feet up on the wall, as if the three feet of clearance was made for his exact positioning.

She crouched next to him, planting her feet along the wall and stretching her legs. "I wasn't sure if you'd be here yet."

"I usually am," he said. "You know, back when they used oil, I would've had to put out the light every morning and ignite it at dusk. Can you imagine that? The amount of oil, and the size of the wick."

"Sounds dangerous."

"Yeah. But exciting, too." He smiled, the wrinkles and sagginess along his weathered face smoothing out with the tight cheer. "Even though they've automated the whole thing, I like to be here when the sun comes up. Just in case one of these days it doesn't turn off."

She leaned her head back on the wall. The hard floor cooled her warm legs. "It's a little shocking when you think about it, with all the technology we have these days, that we still need lighthouses. You'd think all the gadgets would be better at guiding boats than a giant circling light."

"I'm sure the gadgets help, yes. But gadgets can fail. Information can be misread. The sea doesn't care about our tech and gizmos. The sea has proven time and again that she's unpredictable." He looked at her. "Your family knows that firsthand."

She nodded. Mr. Ludlow was one of the few people who knew about Owen without ever telling him. He'd had more than one friend on that ship. There was an unspoken connection between all of those families and friends that had to move on from the tragedy.

"Mister Ludlow, were you ever scared out on the water? Did you ever think you couldn't do it because it was too dangerous?"

"Was I scared? Yeah, sometimes. When you see a wall of black clouds in your path, and there's nowhere to go but through it, that's scary. But stay at home because I was scared? Never. Why? Are you reconsidering being a greenhorn because you're scared?"

"Honestly? Maybe. But it's not what you think."

"You're scared of something else."

She nodded.

"Hmm. The only thing scarier than being out on the water in a storm is not following your heart. If your dream is to be out there, do it. You won't be happy doing anything else."

"What if your heart is pulling you in two different directions?"

"Are you sure they're different?"

"What do you mean?"

"I'm gonna take a wild guess here and say that you care about someone."

"It's a good guess."

"Joel may have said something, if I'm being honest with you."

"That obvious to him, huh?" She sighed and rested her head on the wall. "I don't feel like I can have both. It's either pursue my dream, or pursue this relationship." She straightened up. "The funny thing is, we don't have a relationship, not technically. Yet I feel like all it would take is for one of us to say to the other how we feel. Almost like a game of chicken or something. But if we did, then I'd have to give up being a greenhorn, or he would, and be okay with that."

"You're looking at this all wrong." Mr. Ludlow swatted the air. "Your dream is your dream. That's that. But your heart also wants to be with this person. If I'm hearing you correctly. Has it occurred to you that if you can't pursue your dream because of who your heart loves, then that isn't the right person for you?"

"Are you saying he's not the right person for me? Or that I don't have to choose?"

"I'm saying the right person wouldn't ask you to choose."

It was a simple sentence. A simple concept. Yet it carried such a weight to it. And what about family? Did that mean her sister wasn't worth having in her life if she couldn't get past her job choice?

"Now help an old fellow up." He stretched out his arm, and Cynthia helped him to his feet. "She turned off. Sun's coming up."

Indeed the first glow of light crept over the hillside to the east.

"I'd better get going," she said.

"I'd better get cleaning. This glass doesn't clean itself."

She smiled. "Thanks for the talk."

"Any time."

She headed for the door.

"Oh, and Cynthia? Say something to the man, will you? You'll never know if he's the right person if you don't bother to ask, and believe me, not knowing is the worst."

"Sounds like you may have experience with that."

"Another time."

"For sure." She waved and took in the panoramic view for one more second before descending down the helix of steps. Sunrise meant it was at least six, which meant she had to hurry back to the inn, shower, grab a quick bite or drink, and run off to the dock.

The rest atop the lighthouse left her muscles stiff, but she quick-stepped it to the inn. The pep-talk from Mr. Ludlow was just what she needed. She had been torturing herself with what to do with her future when she wasn't even sure Liam felt the same. Mr. Ludlow was right. If Liam truly was the right person for her, she wouldn't have to lament over her career.

There wouldn't be time this morning. She'd tell him after today's tryouts. And Jackie? Well, one relationship at a time.

She hurried getting ready. Liam wasn't in the room or the bathroom down the hallway. For a second she worried he betrayed his word and left early, but his duffel bag remained in the room. She skipped grabbing coffee on the way out. The lack of sleep would eventually catch up with her, but for now her adrenaline more than sufficed to keep her going.

Unlike the early morning hours, graying clouds adorned the sky, with a stronger wind blowing than in the past few days. Not the best conditions for being on the water, but certainly not the worst. If they were going out on the water at all.

She arrived at the dock, trying not to fidget with her hands or tap her feet in anticipation waiting for the others to arrive. She turned with every new arrival, most lining up by the ticket booth for their early tour departures. No matter if fishing for Dungeness or awaiting the chance to photograph the slice of an orca fin through the water, it took time to hit the jackpot of wildlife frequenting the area. She'd been whale watching once, and it took more than two hours to locate the nearest pod. Finding crab took exponentially longer.

Liam strolled down the dock with Sean and Theo.

Nick strained around her to see who arrived. "What about Miguel?"

"He's out," Sean said.

"What do you mean he's out?"

Sean shrugged.

"Never mind. We have enough." Nick pointed to the deck of *Harpeth Rose*. "For our final day, I've invited half the crabbing crew to come out with us. I want them to have a say on all of you. They're my second family, and they'll be yours, too, if you make it on board. I value my crew and what they have to say. At the same time, we value the hierarchy. Experience and position are respected on my ship."

"We're going to run through setting and retrieving twelve pots just offshore past the bay." Ben pointed behind him. "This is not to be taken lightly. We had to get special permission from the Washington Department of Fish and Wildlife just to set since we're past season."

"Therefore, you won't be securing the doors on the cages," Nick said. "We don't actually want to catch crab during this exercise, not that we would here. What we do want to gauge is your ability to follow instructions, take what you learned all week, and make for a great greenhorn. Any questions?"

Surely there was something Cynthia needed elaborated, but this was it. This was the moment she had been waiting for, and she wasn't going to wait any longer.

"Everyone on board." Nick motioned them to move it.

She looked at the men, Sean and Theo quiet and expressionless, Liam apprehensive.

It was impossible to hide her relief that he showed up. "Thank you for coming."

"I told you I would."

"I'm glad you did." We need to talk, she wanted to blurt out. Now was not the time. "You look nervous."

"It's the first time I've truly been out at sea in two years."

"You can do it." She smiled, but deep down, his worried face choked her positivity.

Those trying out were assigned the navigation bridge while *Harpeth Rose* undocked. It gave them time to slip into their bibs and galoshes. Cynthia recognized some of Nick's crew as they worked. Familiar faces from around town and a few she knew names, although she didn't really know them. The closest she came to knowing anyone on the crew other than Nick and Ben was Ronald. He worked at Postal Port, next door to Bea's, and was Gwen's boss in the summer. Of course he was the ex-crew member not present today, whose retirement made this position possible.

Even with the heavier chop from the strong wind, Nick cleared the bay. To say with no issues would've been an understatement, for he sliced through so cleanly a surgeon couldn't have done better with a scalpel on a patient.

The waves of the open ocean weren't as white-crested as within the bay, but they rolled in bigger swells, rocking *Harpeth Rose* in a long, slow rhythm. The town sat to port, Cynthia's house up the hillside nowhere to be seen behind thickening clouds.

Cynthia longed for the day to be so far out she wouldn't see the town. She didn't want to see land at all. Only the endless horizon of water. But today the sights of downtown Maiden's Bay—the lackluster chipped white building of Campy's Bait and Bar looking as if it washed ashore, its back windows reflecting the clouded sky, the brick uniformity of the shops with Bea's tucked in the middle—were comforting. Like the town watched her, cheering her on.

"All right, listen up." Nick waved everyone to the crab pots on deck. "We're going to set three pots per person, in succession. We'll turn around and repeat the exercise bringing them up, so everyone will have the chance to show what they can do. Who's up first?"

No one raised a hand, or stepped forward, or made the slightest noise. Cowards. She could understand Liam's hesitation. The poor guy, with his injury, shouldn't have to go first. But Sean and Theo?

Cynthia raised her hand. "I'll go."

"Okay, let's do this. Everyone, this is Cynthia." Nick's regular crewmen nodded and waved. "She's greenhorn on bait. Let's move it like it's the real thing. Don't slack off on me today."

"Yes, Captain," they replied.

They shuffled to their respective positions and Nick returned to the wheelhouse. He kicked the boat forward and signaled for the first pot.

It was Cynthia's time to pass.
Or fail.

TWENTY-FOUR

WHEN LIAM HAD awakened, just after Cynthia left for a—ridiculously early—run, he had regretted his decision to stay one more day. Not only would he have to work through a still-achy shoulder, but he would be alongside the woman he was falling for. Having to lie, yet again, for one more day.

It had been a flight of fancy, a fool's wish, to pursue the greenhorn position. He had a taste of the water, the open air, and thought it meant he belonged back on a crew. But now he had a better picture of what he yearned for, and that was to get out of the processing plant and back to nature. He didn't know how he'd do that, or what job he'd have. He only knew he would put in his two weeks notice on Monday and pray something would open up anywhere in the surrounding one-hundred-mile radius. Ideally it'd be in Oakside, or Maiden's Bay, or any of the handful of towns dotting the Crescent Coast. Well, perhaps not Maiden's Bay. Nothing like starting a job near the woman who will soon hate him.

He wanted to tell her after dinner last night—about assessing her, foolheartedly going after the position, the growing depression of realizing he couldn't get back that life. Most of all, how he didn't want to say goodbye.

How could she possibly feel the same about him when she didn't know the real him? She knew a lie, and even if she fell for him through the lie, there was no way she would give him another chance. A do-over. They were simply out of time.

Now here he was, on the deck of *Harpeth Rose* as it rolled in the waves, watching Cynthia.

The woman who, in just a week's time, captured his heart.

Cynthia baited the pots smoothly, one after the other, as if she had been born to do it. She had a feel for the sway of the boat, the timing of the crew, everything. She was a marvel to watch, and he couldn't keep his eyes off her.

She was right. She didn't need him there. But he was glad to be able to see her in her glory.

Ben popped out of the bridge. "Next up? Move it."

Liam stepped up. Now that Cynthia had shone, he wanted to get his part out of the way. The darkening clouds and twinge in his shoulder signaled rain. The sooner they finished the better.

His nerves flared as he prepped the bait bag and set off into the first pot. *Only three pots, Liam.*

He secured the bait and slipped out. The hardest part was getting started, and he surpassed that hump. His nerves calmed as the routine kicked into gear and the second pot cleared off the boat.

Last one.

The crew held the third pot in place on the ramp, and Liam dove in. As he hooked the bag, his right foot wouldn't budge. He looked back, his boot stuck in the corner of the pot.

"Hurry it up, greenie!"

"Let's go!"

The crew waited for him to exit. The shouts and wind and waves lapping the hull brought him back to that day—the crew hustling, the sea foam spraying his face.

The glint of the hook before it struck.

He nearly panicked, but his boot came loose. He hurried out of the pot before they swung it overboard.

No, this was not the life he wanted.

He sipped water in the wheelhouse as Sean, then Theo, baited their three pots. Nick patted him on the shoulder with a nod of satisfaction. If only Nick knew how Liam's stomach churned and palms sweat.

Liam's chest felt heavy as *Harpeth Rose* came about. It was time to bring up the pots, and he wasn't ready. He'd never be ready.

Ben came out of the navigation bridge, Liam reluctantly following, and rounded up the competition. "Nick says we'll go in reverse order. Last person is first this time, and so on."

They nodded, and Ben returned to the bridge, the crew to their positions. Raindrops fell in a sprinkle, urging the contenders to hurry with their turns. Theo had been quick and agile with baiting on the way out and just as much on the way in. He unhooked the bait and backed out, giving the thumbs up. He'd be a perfectly capable greenhorn. His quietness could work for or against him depending on how the rest of the crew took it.

Sean was next, and although he had shown off to Liam during the exercise the other day, he slogged on—daresay irritated he had to do the task repeatedly. Was he in it just for the money? He wouldn't be the first. Many a crewperson joined just for the money, but usually quit after one season. It took more than greed to last out there.

Sooner than he wanted, it was Liam's turn. "Get this over with," he sighed. As if the sky heard his words, the sprinkle turned into a solid downpour, and the wind picked up, making it more difficult to land the swinging pot on the swaying deck. He retrieved the bait bag and gave the thumbs up, his boots squeaking on the wet deck. Another crewman dumped the contents and saved the bag.

By the third pot, his speed approached snail's pace. It might as well have been the thirtieth pot. Liam swore under his breath, locking his jaw shut at the arduous task done only as a favor at this point. The conditions moved into more dangerous territory, and he couldn't wait to finish. He got through the third pot, his shoulder not happy with him, but it was done.

Three more pots, and the trip was over, the last time he'd ever do work like this again. How easy it had been to reminisce in the positives of the job while on land. The brief foray at sea was a blunt smack of reality.

It was Cynthia's turn. The rocking of the ship had her stumbling at first, but she found her rhythm and worked with speed, the crew giving eyes to each other and nodding as she crawled out.

One pot down.

Two to go.

The wind slanted the heavy rain, water pelting their faces under the hoods. Liam repeatedly wiped his squinting eyes to catch the movement on deck, purposely avoiding seeing the hook thrown out. Now was not the time for weak knees. The second pot came up, and Cynthia and the crew cleared it to the thumbs up in no time.

Each movement stepped closer to Liam's freedom from the boat, and freedom from Cynthia. Only one of those he longed for.

The third pot rose out of the water, and two crewmen lowered it onto the ramp. They opened it up, going through the motions of the emptying process, and called in Cynthia. She slid in, unclipping the bag. The boat rocked, and Liam held onto the bridge's steel wall as his boots grasped for traction.

Cynthia lost her footing. The pot slipped along the ramp, Cynthia clutching inside. If the crew didn't gain control of it, the pot would skid across the deck.

Liam darted to Cynthia. He reached for the trap door but missed, grabbing the metal corner, as if his body weight could stop the movement of the pot.

Two crewmen pulled at him. "Get off the pot! Let go!"

Liam's world turned blurry, and his arms swung in the air. He fell down, wind whipping the shouts and water across the deck as the ringing started in his ears.

He wiped his eyes and shook his head, washing away the din and fuzziness into clarity.

Nick stood over him, the rainwater from his hood falling in large droplets on his face. "You okay?"

"I'm all right. I was—Cynthia was going to be—"

"I'm fine." She stood next to Nick, hands firmly on her hips. The crew crowded behind them.

"You were going to be hurt."

"No, I wasn't." She was practically shouting to be heard over the wind and rain. "I minded my hands and feet, the crew had my back with the pot, and I got out just fine. No thanks to your antics."

Nick helped Liam back to his feet. *Harpeth Rose* moved at a steady clip back east to the bay, the forward momentum reducing the lateral rocking.

"*My* antics?" Liam said. "You could've lost a foot if—"

"Well, I didn't."

"You're not invincible, Cynthia."

"I know that, Liam! But not everyone is going to get a hook in the arm, or will have their ship sink, for cryin' out loud. You've got to let me do what I do. Do you think you'll be there in the corner watching my every move so I don't get hurt? I have to trust the crew, and they put their trust in me. Do you think I'd put my life in the hands of someone who is hurt?"

Nick looked at him and back at Cynthia. "What's she talking about? Your shoulder was three years ago. You said you could do this."

"I know!" He huffed. He had thought he could do it. Maybe if he hadn't gotten in that fight, he would've been fine. But he wasn't fine, with his shoulder, with post-traumatic stress, even after three years. "I had a minor incident with it the other night."

"Are you kidding me right now?" Nick threw his hands in the air. "Liam, you shouldn't have been doing this with an injury. I thought it was harder for you, but I didn't know—that's a liability, for everyone!"

"I know!" He caught his breath amid his anger and frustration. "I'm out. I'm not cut out for this, and I don't even want it anymore. And I'm done playing your games. I'm sick of lying. To myself and everyone else."

Cynthia stepped in front of Nick. "What are you talking about?" She turned to Nick. "What games?"

"I wasn't up for greenhorn, Cynthia." He had struggled over saying the words all week. They poured out without effort.

"What do you mean?" Her eyebrows crinkled, face soaked. For a second the anger made room for confusion. "Are you trying for a higher position? You were greenhorn before. Nick, you know he had been greenhorn before."

"I wasn't trying out for anything at first. Nick asked me to come help him assess potential candidates for the position. It wasn't until we started that I thought I wanted it for myself."

"You what?" Cynthia grit her teeth, her nostrils flaring.

It was the moment Liam dreaded. All his worries culminated into the look she gave him right now.

"What's your assessment of me, huh? What grade do I get? Or how about Sean? And Theo? How'd we do, Liam, in your eyes?"

"Cynthia, please. I wanted to tell you that first night, when I found out I was rooming with you, but I had made a promise. I was ready to break it, though, the other night, when we were alone in the room."

"And actually…." Sean held up his hand in interruption.

"What could you possibly have to say to contribute to this conversation?" Liam asked.

"I'm not really trying out, either."

"Sean, come on." Nick gave him pleading eyes.

"Me, neither," Theo said.

"What?" Now Liam was confused. Were they extra pairs of eyes on judging Cynthia?

"We aren't really vying for the position," Sean said. "Nick asked us to help out. To put you, Cynthia, to the test, so to speak."

"I can't believe this," Cynthia said.

"I should've guessed it." Liam stared at Sean. "You're a terrible greenhorn. Along with Greg and Miguel. The only one with a fighting chance is Theo over here."

"Thanks," Theo said.

Sean chuckled, and Cynthia scoffed. "This isn't funny."

"Look, I did it to help Nick," Sean said.

"We all did," said Theo.

"I see." Cynthia backed away and addressed the crowd. "So you all put him above your own morals."

"Cynthia." Nick put his hand on her shoulder. "This is bigger than the tryouts—"

"No." She swung his hand off. "I'm done." She threw her gloves down on the deck.

"You can't quit now," Nick said.

"Yes, I can." She pointed her finger in his face, rain pelting her skin. "I didn't just want to be a greenhorn. I wanted to be a greenhorn on Nick Campbell's crew. But if lying like you did, and getting others to lie with you, is how you run a tight ship, I don't want any part of it." She stormed off to the bridge. Ben could barely be seen through the rain and glass, his arms up in confusion.

Nick sighed. "Secure the pots."

"What are we going to do?" Liam asked. He didn't care about the pots, or what needed to be done to dock, or even that the other men had been lying, too. He wanted to rush off to her, tell her everything he had been thinking all week.

"We're heading back." Nick scratched his short shadow of a beard, the rain slicker doing little to keep him dry. "It's over."

TWENTY-FIVE

"HEY THERE! I didn't expect to see you for another hour or two." Constance changed out the water in the vase on top of the anchor side table.

"I'll be checking out." Cynthia hadn't bothered to stop in the lobby, rushing up the stairs to Room 2. She stuffed the few clothes lying on the bed into her bag and swung her purse on her shoulder. If she had left anything on the desk or floor, so be it. As for her wet clothes she was wearing, she'd have to walk home anyway, and the rain didn't look as if it would give her mercy.

She hurried back to the lobby and placed the key on the front desk.

"Is everything all right?" Constance wrung her hands in her waist apron. "You still have one more night. It's all paid for—"

"I know." Cynthia took a breath. *Slow it down, woman. Don't take it out on Constance.* She slicked back the wet strands off her face. "I won't be needing tonight's stay. The tryouts are over."

"Oh, okay then. I do hope you liked your stay."

"It was fine." *Not her fault, Cynthia.* "It was good. You're nothing but wonderful to your guests."

"Thank you. I appreciate that." Constance looked up from the log book. "Now, will Mister Reynolds be checking out as well?"

"What?"

"Mister Reynolds. Liam?"

"Oh, I'm not sure." In fact, it was the reason she had been in a rush. Best to leave, out of sight, before Liam got there.

"I know it must've been a little odd staying here while your house is up the street."

"It was nice to have a mini getaway." *While it lasted.*

"If you don't mind, be sure to leave a review. That's all the people care about these days when they're shopping online."

"I will. Goodbye, Constance."

"Goodbye, dear. Have a lovely Valentine's weekend."

The word stopped her for a second, as if barbed wire caught hold of her clothing. Valentine's. She could take the rocking and rolling of *Harpeth Rose,* and the aroma of fish guts in her face. But that one word sent her stomach churning. It most certainly was not going to be a lovely weekend.

She exited the inn, looking left to her journey up the hill. It would be good to have a hot shower in her house, not that Constance's was deficient in any way. At least she wouldn't walk in on anyone else. She started the trek eastward for three blocks, then turned south.

The sight of home was supposed to be welcoming, but the two-story yellow house gave a sense of dread. She entered and placed her bag by the front door. The mid-day sun refused to show up for work today, leaving the house dark even with the lights on. The whole first floor was drab, the view outside nearly as depressing as the house.

She didn't want to be there. She didn't want to be in the house of her former family. The house of her dead dad, and divorced then widowed mom. She wasn't supposed to be here today, and the house told her as much. She was supposed to be pursuing her dream.

She walked upstairs and opted for a soak in the bath. She put on an oversized navy sweater and reshaped her ponytail. Even though she didn't want to be around Liam or Nick or the boat, she didn't want to be alone, either.

Cynthia grabbed a rain jacket and umbrella and slipped into rubber rain boots. Locking the front door behind her, she walked south, appreciating the shelter of the umbrella. She had no destination in particular. Just walking, the slower version of her run that gave her more time to think and more time to actually see the world around her.

Spring felt far off, but the trees hinted their readiness with the tiniest of buds jutting out of their branches. No matter how brutal the winter was or could be, nature pushed through and flowers would appear come April. They didn't care about past drama or future perils. They merely did what they were meant to do.

She thought fishing was what she was meant to do. If it wasn't....

She stopped in the middle of a puddle on the street, her boots doing a better job than the hidden sun at keeping her feet dry. She looked out from under the umbrella.

She stood in front of Jackie's house. She hadn't consciously aimed for it. But there she was, in front of the two-story white house with black shutters. She knew the driveway as well as she knew her nautical knots, the crack that shimmied from the right side up to the left corner. Light shone in the window above the front door.

She made her way up the driveway to the front porch stairs. "What am I doing?" She closed her eyes. If Jackie turned her away, then that was it, wasn't it? If she still couldn't accept Cynthia after failing to be a greenhorn, when could she?

Cynthia pushed the doorbell and heard the faint ring coming from inside the house. A dog rushed the door in a thunder of barks. The front door opened, and a woman stood behind the screen door.

"Shush, Snickers. Sit." She pointed her finger until the dog sat at her feet. "Good boy." She finally looked up at the guest. Her brunette hair was cut short in a bob, but her green eyes still burned as emerald as they had in her youth.

"Hi, Jackie."

Jackie stood at the door, breathing.

That was a good sign. At least she hadn't slammed the door closed.

"What are you doing here?" She still held the knob of the screen door, apparently undecided.

"I, uh...." Cynthia hadn't thought this through. She was surprised thirty seconds ago that she walked here. "I think I'm done with my dream." She bit her lip, holding back the wash of emotion flooding to her eyes.

Jackie opened the screen door. "Come on inside."

"Really?"

Jackie huffed. "Yeah, really."

Cynthia folded the wet umbrella and took off her boots inside. She followed Jackie down the corridor, past an office and into the kitchen. The dark cabinetry and countertops dated the house, but gave it a homely lived-in feel. It was the exact opposite feeling Cynthia got from Mom and Dad's house.

"Some coffee?"

"Sure." Cynthia took a seat at the kitchen table. The chocolate and mahogany pointer sat at her feet. "A dog owner now?"

"Yeah." Jackie filled two mugs with coffee and grabbed the sugar cup. "That's Snickers. We fostered him for a few weeks, and then we couldn't end up not keeping him."

"I get it." Owen and Jackie had a dog during their childhood, but Cynthia missed out. She had wanted a dog when she was younger, and most of her adulthood life involved college or taking care of Dad. Perhaps it was something to look into, being in the house all alone.

Jackie handed her a mug and sat down at the table. She sipped her coffee and stared at Cynthia. "So what brings you here?"

The coffee did anything but roll down Cynthia's throat. She gulped hard. "I know you were probably aware that I tried out for greenhorn this week. For Nick's crew."

Jackie stayed quiet but nodded in affirmation.

"I thought it was what I wanted. I'm not so sure I don't want it."

Jackie cleared her throat and waited for further explanation.

"I was invited to dinner last night at Ben Campbell's house. Somehow they got the story of Owen out of me. It's not one I tell very often."

"Nor do I." Jackie leaned down and stroked Snickers on the back.

"I know you've always thought my dream was crazy. Telling Owen's story reminded me just how crazy it is. Anyway, today was the final day of tryouts. We went out on *Harpeth Rose* and went through the motions of setting out the pots." Cynthia knew Jackie couldn't care less about the details. In fact, the more she heard about the process, the more uncomfortable Jackie would get. Judging by her adjustment in the seat, not much had changed.

"Anyway, I was good at it. I was really good at it. I don't know if there had ever been a time I felt so confident and comfortable doing something. But then there was an accident."

"What?" Jackie sat up taller.

"It was a minor one. I had control of my actions, the rest of the crew were spot on with their duties. We worked together, and it worked out fine."

"Why are you here, then? Are you here to tell me you can survive anything on a boat? That you can make it through no matter what?"

"No. I'm here to tell you that even though it went smoothly, I got the first glimpse of it not going smoothly. I have always put off hearing about the dangers of the job. Even if I heard about them, I brushed them aside." She leaned her elbows on the table. "I always knew why you didn't want me out there. But today I finally understood why."

"Oh, Cynthia." Jackie inhaled deeply, then let it go, shoulders lowering with the exhale.

"I guess I'm here because I wanted you to know I quit."

"You *quit?* Cynthia—"

"You can spare me the 'I told you so,' please. It's extremely fresh, and I'm still processing it."

"One accident shouldn't shatter your dreams—"

"It wasn't just the accident. There was this guy, and for the short story, he ended up lying to me. The whole thing was a lie." Cynthia stared down into her coffee, then looked at Jackie. "Wait. Are you telling me I shouldn't have quit? Am I hearing you correctly?"

Jackie stood up and brought her mug to the sink. She set it down and turned around, leaning on the counter. "I did know you were trying out this week. In fact, I saw you the other day on *Harpeth Rose.*"

"But how—"

"It was docked. I had heard about tryouts and wanted to see for myself. I don't know why. I was curious, I guess. Perhaps I wanted to see if you would be rotten at the whole thing. I think I've given you a hard time because I worried you did it all for Dad. That you followed this dream because Dad wanted you to."

"Jackie—"

She put her hand up. "Please let me finish."

Cynthia hushed and nodded.

"I couldn't see everything that was going on up on that deck. The dock didn't afford me a great view. But I heard enough. I heard you having your turn. I heard the praise and the speed compared to the other groups. And Joel told me about throwing the hook. He said he'd never seen such a big smile on your face."

Cynthia couldn't stand hearing it. Jackie had captured her pouring her heart out on the boat. It had been a dream so close to attaining, but now was only a memory. One week of happiness, tainted by falsehood.

Jackie sat back down at the table. "I didn't know you, Cynthia. I didn't know what part was you and what was Dad. But now I do. I know you really did want this. And you're brilliant at it."

The tears fell onto Cynthia's cheeks. It was useless trying to stop them. "I didn't want to have to choose. Nick and Liam made it easier to choose."

"Choose what, honey?" Jackie took Cynthia's hands in hers.

"Between my dream and having people like you in my life."

Jackie shook her head, tears rolling from her eyes as if they were contagious. "I'm so sorry. I never wanted you to give up on your dream because of me. Okay, maybe I did there for a while. But I was wrong."

Cynthia hugged her sister for the first time in years. She felt solid yet feeble, shaking from emotion.

Jackie wiped her eyes. "Now we've settled that."

Cynthia chuckled her tears away.

"You didn't quit just because of me." Jackie raised her eyebrows. "You said a man had something to do with this? And lies?"

"Yeah. It's complicated."

"Hm. I guess you're staying for dinner, then."

"You don't have to—"

Jackie waved at her. "I know I don't have to. I want to. You're going to stay for dinner. Jonathan is out of town until tomorrow, so you're going to keep me company."

"Okay." Cynthia smiled.

"And you're going to tell me all about this man and the number he's done on you."

TWENTY-SIX

HARPETH ROSE COULDN'T reach the dock fast enough. Liam had stayed outside while Cynthia occupied the navigation bridge with Ben. Not even Nick wanted to be in her vicinity. With the vessel moving at a clip, the afternoon breeze and rain frigid, Liam sought a bright orange jacket from the gear room. It smelled of fish and felt damp, but the heaviness added insulation and blocked the wind.

The crew secured the vessel at the dock. Nick had a list of tasks to perform and divvied them between the crew. Sean and Theo stayed to help, so Liam bid Nick the same respect, despite the mountain of lies they all told over the week. Cynthia stuck to her guns and left as soon as she could, adamant to stay away from any and all men on the ship.

"I really should go after her," Liam said.

"She doesn't want to talk to you right now," Nick said. "Or any of us, for that matter."

She was mad at everyone, but Liam had to have been the worst in her eyes. They had spent most of each day—and technically night—together, only for him to betray her. It didn't seem like any amount of explaining would wash away the hurt she felt.

"Give her some space. In time you'll be able to talk it out. Trust me, Josie and I have our moments at this."

"Oh, so you two lie and keep secrets from one another?"

"Heavens, no. That would be awful." Nick chuckled, and then wiped his amusement away after looking at Liam.

The problem was Cynthia would take infinite time and space if he didn't go after her. He wallowed in his guilt for the next hour, checking off the task list Nick had given him. By the time he finished and Nick pardoned the crew, there was no telling how far Cynthia could've gone.

Even so, Liam rushed to the inn. The couple of blocks seemed like miles, as if every second apart from her was a year of time missed out. He aimed to go straight to Room 2, but Constance stopped him in his tracks.

"She already checked out." Constance gave Liam the sad eyes. He didn't need sad eyes. Pity wasn't something he deserved from anyone. He had lied, and the truth set him free. Free of any possibility of a future with Cynthia.

"Any idea where she went?"

"Probably back to her house, I'd assume."

He pictured the roof of her house from the window of The Codfather. Based on his memory, he'd have to walk a few blocks up the hill, but probably guess the road and the house. Knocking door to door didn't seem like a good option, but it was the only one he could think of at the moment.

"I know I don't know you very well," Constance said. "But if I were you, I'd let her cool off first."

It wasn't Constance's business, but then again, they had stayed there and gotten to know her. She most likely saw how upset Cynthia had been. "It was that obvious, huh?"

"Darling, if I had a dollar for every time I witnessed a lover's quarrel."

"Oh, we're not lovers."

"And a dollar for every time two people were in denial of their true feelings." She gave a look of a schoolmarm scolding a student for not doing his homework.

"She doesn't want anything to do with me."

"Maybe not right this second."

"Even if she did, I don't think I could stand her being out there on the water, anyway." He sighed and turned away from the desk. Why was he telling her all of this? It didn't matter. Some wounds just couldn't be mended.

"Let me show you something." Constance came out around the desk and pointed to the hallway. "Come on. Over here."

Liam followed her.

"You see all these clippings?" She pointed to the framed *Bay Review* stories.

"Yeah. I read some of these the other day."

"Then you're familiar with them."

"Yes." He placed his hands on his hips, wondering what she was getting at.

"Just about every one of these accomplishments could have ended in tragedy. Look at this one." She pointed to the story of the 1997 US second place marlin catch. "David Laramy reeled that sucker in for three hours. Three hours in six-foot waves. His radio went out, and no one had heard from him. He showed up at the dock with that winner."

The article failed to mention some of those details from what Liam could remember.

"Or this one. Abigail Chaucer, the first woman—or *human* for that matter—to kayak from Maiden's Bay to Lookout Station and back. Had one of the worst rain storms that spring."

He appreciated her knowledge but didn't get the point. Constance must have registered the confusion on his face.

"These people all experienced a high moment in their lives. A joyful, happy triumph that they wouldn't trade for the world. They couldn't imagine getting that feeling doing anything else. Yet at any moment during their journeys, they could have experienced tragedy. Some did." She pointed to another article about a rescue in a winter storm that resulted in losing expensive equipment and injuring two people.

She turned from the framed articles and faced him. "You experienced tragedy, didn't you?"

The ache in his shoulder awakened.

"You were injured."

"How did you know?"

"Honey, haven't you learned a thing about Maiden's Bay?"

"Everyone knows everything."

She nodded. "Except for what's right in front of them. You followed a path you thought you'd take for years. I'm willing to bet you weren't going to listen to anyone who told you not to follow that path, am I right?"

He sighed. "Probably not."

"You were injured, and then suddenly it wasn't your path to follow."

"Why show me these stories?"

"Because your path isn't everyone's path. You had your chance to figure it out. Don't cut someone else off before having a chance to figure it out. The results may be similar to yours. Or who knows?" She pointed back to the fishing hall of fame in her hallway. "Imagine if these people weren't encouraged at any point in their lives to follow their dreams."

Liam had been encouraged. By Dad. If he didn't get that, would he have been strong enough to go through with it on his own? Cynthia certainly was.

"Wait a second." Liam straightened up and folded his arms across his chest. "Are you trying to give me relationship advice?"

"I'm not saying what you should do." She held her arms up in surrender. "I'm just trying to open your eyes."

He smirked. "This is coming from someone who—from what I hear, because you know, Maiden's Bay there are no secrets—you let go of the man you possibly loved, who now sits at Campy's on a barstool, alone and forlorn."

"I don't know what you're talking about." She scuttled away, rushing to the safety of her desk.

"Uh-uh, you can't give me a lecture on relationships and then dodge your own problems."

"It's not a problem," she said sharply. "It's a non-issue at this point."

"If it's not an issue and you're done with him, why is it making you so uncomfortable to talk about him?"

"Because that man—" She pointed at him, wrinkled hand quivering. "That man—much like yourself—didn't know how to handle a successful independent woman."

"Ah, is that what this is all about? It didn't work out because you are a successful owner of a business, and he...?"

"He manages the dock. Wouldn't quite call it that nowadays. But that's beside the point."

"He loves you, you know."

Constance hung her head low. "If that were true he wouldn't have gone back to drinking. He would've fought for us."

"Drinking? Constance, I know as well as you he's at Campy's most of his waking hours. But I assure you, it's not to drink and forget his problems. He's as sober as you are. He's there to be around people. He's lonely. Very lonely without you. He tried to join our tryouts."

Constance chuckled.

"No kidding. I swear."

"He would've hurt himself for sure."

"I don't doubt it. What is he, a hundred and twenty?"

Constance broke into a full hearty laugh. "He's my age, so you be careful."

"You get what I'm saying, though? He hasn't changed from the person you knew. The person that, I'm guessing from your face, you love. He's heartbroken."

Constance straightened her apron and touched her cheeks as if the action would wipe away her feelings. "Well, that's some story you tell."

Liam couldn't blame her. He didn't want to listen to what she had to say about him and Cynthia. It was easier to judge others and tell them what needed to be done than to face one's own troubles.

"I guess I'm going to pack my things."

"Are you checking out a night early, too?"

He nodded. "I don't suppose I have a reason to stay anymore."

"No." She looked somberly at him. "I suppose you don't."

TWENTY-SEVEN

Saturday, February 13

"WE'LL BE OUT by this afternoon, so if you want more you'd best get them now. You can combine them for a larger impact." Cynthia stared down the customer. The middle-aged man scratched his chin and surveyed the store.

The pre-arranged bouquets would go fast. Even though Valentine's Day was officially tomorrow, most couples were celebrating today. Easier to stay out on a Saturday evening than Sunday.

"You know what, I'd better take two more." He pulled out his wallet, and Cynthia rang him up.

"Here's your receipt. Happy Valentine's Day." She forced a smile, barely lifting the corners of her mouth. He walked out of the store, and Bea walked over to the register.

"You're not very good at pretending to be happy." Bea shook her head. "I do like that you upsold him though."

"Don't you think being a bad liar is a good quality to have?" Unlike Liam and Nick and literally every other guy involved in the fake tryouts all week.

Throwing off the gloves, standing on the deck of *Harpeth Rose*, was like throwing her dreams in the trash. But she had no choice. It was all a sham. She had meant every word spoken. She couldn't work for a group of liars. Even if her sister now supported it, trying to talk her back into it.

The store bustled with customers since it opened this morning, the last-minute shoppers scrambling to have something for their significant others. She was surprised to see Greg five minutes after opening, opting for a bouquet to accompany the watch he bought for Theo. She was not in the mood to talk to anyone from tryouts, but Greg was different. He had quit early, and admittedly she still felt a little sorry for him that he had gotten sick on the boat. Seasickness really was the worst feeling in the world.

Well, maybe second worst. This—the way she felt now—was the worst. Having her dreams dashed was rough. Realizing someone she cared about and fallen for was actually an imposter on top of it? Devastating. If she thought too long about it, the tears would well up in her eyes again.

Still, her heart had a mind of its own, jumping at each sound of someone walking into the store. Maybe it was Nick, coming to apologize. Or maybe….

No. Liam surely had moseyed back to Oakside, where he ought to be. She didn't have anything to say to him anyway. He had tried to explain himself on the boat, but there was no justification, friend of Nick's or not.

"I know things didn't turn out like you wanted them to," Bea said. "Life usually doesn't."

"That's reassuring."

"But if you depress my customers on Valentine's Day, you'll have to find another backup job."

"Bea, it's not my backup job."

"Now who's the one lying?" She walked off to help a customer reach a higher wall display.

Bea had a point. In fact, Cynthia had rushed to the store and asked if she could work today because she didn't know what else to do. Part of her held out hope it would be a distraction to get her through the day. The first full day of her dream being dashed. But all it did was drag it out, seeing the happy customers buying gifts for their loved ones. Only because someone decided to make one day of the year a day to do just that.

The front door opened, the crisp breeze a welcome reprieve from the stagnant floral air reminding her of her failures in life and love.

"Cynthia, can we talk?" Josie stood in front of her, chestnut hair streaming out of the knit purple hat on her head.

"Your order will be delivered this evening." She thought Bea would have her do it, but astonishingly Bea agreed to take care of it. "That's one thing I *did* get right this week. Those buds will open up fully overnight, just in time for whatever you have planned for tomorrow. They'll be beautiful."

"That's what I need to talk to you about." Josie wasn't a television host and social media director for nothing. She genuinely looked at the bright side and carried a smile through awkward situations. It was a gift.

Which was why it was surprising to see her face so concerned, her eyebrows scrunched in worry and mouth curved downward.

Cynthia sighed. "All right." She stepped away from the counter. "Bea? I'll be in the office for a minute."

She walked Josie toward the back of the store, stopping to ask Darrell to man the register for the time being.

"Okay. I can try to guess why you're here, but just tell me."

"Nick told me what happened yesterday."

"It was bound to get out. That Cynthia Pruitt was made the fool."

"That's not true at all."

"You're actually going to *defend* Nick?"

"I sure am. Not because he's my boyfriend, and not because I love him. Because what he did wasn't all his fault."

"No, you're right. It was also Liam's, and Sean's, and—"

"I get it. You're upset they were all in on it. But again, that's not entirely true."

"What are you saying?" Cynthia sat down behind the desk. "Are you telling me you had something to do with this?"

Josie slipped her hat off and unbuckled her coat. She sat down in front of the desk. "You know the Valentine's special I'm doing?"

Cynthia racked her brain.

Josie's shoulders slumped in disappointment. "Remember, the vacation for two lucky people?"

"Oh, yeah. The one Elise jokingly volunteered for. What about it?" *Get on with it. I have a miserable job to get back to.*

"I decided to go with two locals to match up this year." She paused, staring at Cynthia. Her focus turned to her hands, and she bit her lip.

"I'm not good at guessing here. Just tell me."

"You and Liam." Josie shook her head. "Geez. I was so worried you'd catch on, but obviously that wasn't an issue."

Cynthia stood up and walked to the office window, staring out at the store, yet looking at nothing. "How could—how did you even—"

"I thought it would be a good surprise, but I can see now that it was all too much. What with Nick's fake tryouts and—"

"Stop. Just stop!" Cynthia rubbed her forehead. She sat back in the chair. "Tell me everything. Tell me what you did, in the order you did it."

"Right. You deserve to know."

"I sure do."

"Okay." She paced the room. "You told me about Liam over lunch that day. And I was looking for an interesting twist in this year's Valentine's contest. I figured, why not utilize the contest as a way to give you two a shot at love?"

"Because you found Nick, and everything is happily ever after." It sounded overboard snarky once it came out.

"But it's not, is it? Yes, I *do* love Nick. But it's not always easy for us. I don't even think it's on his radar to do anything for Valentine's Day."

"He was too busy conning me."

"Cynthia, please. Can I explain?"

"Go ahead."

"In order to have you as one of the couples in the running, I spoke with Nick on one of our phone calls while he was out for the last trip of crab season. I told him about my idea, and I didn't know how to get a hold of this Liam person. I told Nick his name and that he worked at the plant in Oakside. Nick gave me his last name, I found a picture of him on a conference website, confirmed his photo with a source, and it was a match. And that was when I really got Nick involved with incorporating

the tryouts with the contest. By then everyone knew about Ronny's retirement, and knew that Nick would shift his crew up a position, leaving
a greenhorn slot to fill. You have to trust me when I say Nick intended
to speak with you about the position before I got involved with my she-
nanigans. Everyone who knows you knew you wanted it for years. So we
used it as an opportunity to get you and Liam together."

This wasn't happening. Josie was one of her best friends. The ma-
nipulation and lies…. "The tryouts." That was why they were staged.

"Exactly. They'd not only give you and Liam time to know each
other, but it would give Nick confirmation that you'd be a good choice
for the spot."

"Josie, what were you thinking? You know I'm not into the
whole Valentine's Day hype, or forcing people together like a crazy
reality show."

"That's exactly what I was thinking. You would never have given it
a go if I had asked you. I knew the only way it would work was if you
were oblivious to it."

"Was it just the two of us on your show this entire time?"

"No. We had the stories of three other couples. We featured their
stories, as we did yours, and viewers voted online for the winner. You
were our clear winners. After that, we went to work putting everything
in place. I promise we only revealed your names when you came to be
on the show."

"I can't say that makes me feel any better."

"I'm sorry you're hurt by it. And I'm sorry it required being sneaky."

"That's a more fun way to say *lying.*"

"Call it what you want. But I'm not completely sorry for doing it."

"Some apology there, Josie."

"Because it *did* work, didn't it?"

"You don't know what you're talking about."

"Yes, I do. I saw the way Liam looked at you when we did the
interview together. I saw the way you opened up over dinner at Ben's.
It wasn't because of me or the Campbells. It was because Liam was at
your side. You wanted to let him in."

"It was all a lie."

"You can't fake that, Cynthia." Josie got up and stood in the door-way. "Nick wanting you as greenhorn wasn't a lie, either. He still would love to have you on the boat. *If* you'll forgive him. And me, for that matter. I was the one who pressured him to go along with it."

Cynthia sighed. It was a lot to process. If anything, she felt fool-ish. How could everyone be in on it but her, and she didn't realize it? Something felt off all week, but she never would have guessed the real reason. "You're supposed to be my friend. It feels like you want-ed a great show and didn't care at what cost. As if my feelings—my *life*—didn't matter."

"That's the opposite of the truth. I did it because I care about you. I want to see you live your dream. I want to see you happy, Cynthia."

"It's going to take time, Josie."

"I understand. Please know that Nick and I are around if you want to talk about it anymore. We really didn't mean to hurt you or Liam. Honest."

She nodded. Josie did have a good heart, even if it made her do crazy things. "Thank you for eventually telling me the truth. Even if it was hard to hear."

"You're welcome." She put her hat back on and stepped back into the store.

The lengths she had to go through to pull the whole thing off.... It was mind boggling. "Hey, Josie."

Josie turned around in the middle of the store.

"Who was your source... about Liam?"

"What do you mean?"

"You said you confirmed his photo online with a source. Who con-firmed it?"

She stared at the black-haired stubborn owner of the shop. "Some-one close to you."

"Bea?"

"Yes?" Bea placed a potted plant on the ground.

"You talked to Josie about Liam?"

"All I did was confirm whether I had seen a particular customer in the store or not."

Cynthia's shock left her with her mouth agape. "You were in on it the whole time? Even when you made me feel awful for leaving you for the week to pursue my dream?"

"I had to keep up the ruse." She smirked. "Besides. I was mad you left me. Even if it was my own doing."

Cynthia searched for words, but there was nothing to say. What do you say to Bea, the world's most unsatisfied, demanding boss who happened to have a soft spot for love stories? And conniving apparently.

"One more thing," Josie said. "Please remember that, although Liam lied about why he was at tryouts in the first place, he was innocent in the whole match up."

"He didn't know, either?"

"No." She put her hat back on. "What you felt between the two of you was the most authentic thing of the whole week."

TWENTY-EIGHT

LIAM SCANNED THE logbook of the past week's productivity. The computer held the same information, but he was a stickler for keeping information in two formats. Who knew he had so much in common with Constance?

He hadn't planned on being around Oakside Processing today. In fact, his "vacation" was through the weekend, with only half a day scheduled on Monday. But he had no need to stay in Maiden's Bay.

Nor did anyone care for him to stay.

It didn't matter what he said or could say to Cynthia. She couldn't get past the fact he lied about who he was. In his mind, it was more a lie about what he was doing—why he was there. Otherwise, he had been nothing but genuine with her. At Constance's, Joel's, dinner at The Codfather, that night in Room 2.

Those were all real moments, not faked. The fact she saw it otherwise hurt.

He had known better, though. His gut had told him every day, every *hour*—the longer he kept his secret to himself, the worse things would be. Here he was on a Saturday morning, double-checking last week's shipments.

It was better than being at home. Mom would've come over and been in his business about Cynthia. She had probably spread the word to Chloe and Miriam by now. All he needed to do was tell her he planned to put his two weeks notice in first thing Monday and full-blown Reynolds interrogation Armageddon would ensue.

The phone on his desk rang. *"Mister Reynolds, there's a Nick Campbell here to see you."*

His chest collapsed. He half expected Nick to visit, coming through the back way via the dock, like every other time he'd arrived.

The fact he went through the front door to the lobby meant he wasn't here for business. It was personal.

Liam couldn't send him away. He had driven over an hour to come down. "Send him up."

He opened the office door and heard the clang of the metal steps as he seated himself in his chair.

"Liam." Nick held his UW hat in one hand, the other holding a brown paper grocery bag.

"Nick. Come on in."

Nick set the bag on the floor and took a seat.

"I'm not sure what you could possibly tell me that we haven't already hashed out." Liam tied the loose ends by phone on the drive back to Oakside. He had confessed about the barroom brawl—one-sided, really—that agitated his shoulder, how he came to realize he didn't want the position, and how Cynthia urged him to continue on, not knowing the full truth. Perhaps harder still, he delved deeper into his feelings about Cynthia.

Nick in turn discussed how, despite Liam having put forth a good effort, he had chosen Cynthia at the start. It pained Nick to see Liam try his hardest for something that really wasn't up for grabs.

None of it mattered, though. Cynthia was right. They were all a bunch of liars, and she was better off away from them.

"I wanted to say I'm sorry again," Nick said.

"I said yesterday we were straight. No sense in dragging it out."

"I know, but you don't know the full story. I wasn't sure if I should tell you since it probably doesn't make a difference at this point."

"What more is there to know? You asked me to help you scout greenhorns, everyone else except Cynthia was in on the fake tryouts, and that's that. I don't really get why you had fake tryouts. Seems like an odd form of hazing in a way. You could've at least told me not to bother."

"That's the part you don't know. I thought if you never heard why, things would move on as if the plan never existed. You'd be none the wiser kind of thing."

"But you're here, so tell me."

Nick rubbed his hands on the arm rests. "It wasn't my idea to have tryouts. It was Josie's."

"Josie's?" No, he wouldn't have suspected such a thing. "What did she have to do with it?"

"She's been running a Valentine's segment on her morning show where she tries to bring two people together, send them on romantic dates and activities."

"And?"

Nick blinked and wiped his shaven jaw. "I should've said no."

"What are you saying, Nick?" The realization washed over his body. It couldn't be true. "You mean—me and Cynthia?"

Nick raised his eyebrows and shrugged.

Something hadn't felt right all week, but that was because of the fake tryouts, right? Thinking back, it wasn't just the other contenders who had made him feel uneasy. "The whole thing was a ploy to get me and Cynthia together?"

"Now hold up. Josie did put on the pressure to find a way to get you guys together. I came up with the idea though. Not to torture Cynthia or make you two feel uncomfortable. But it was for Josie's sake. She's been on me lately about the safety of the job."

"It's a little too late in your relationship for that talk, isn't it?"

"I know, I know. I just—we're in deep, and I think it's hitting her now that Ron won't be with us. She trusted him, as did I. We all did. So I thought, if I not only had these tryouts to get you two together, but to actually see what Cynthia was capable of, it may alleviate some of Josie's worry."

"Knowing the new person is someone you trust."

"Exactly."

Liam's head hurt, rushing through the events of last week. "What about the interview? Was that all fake?"

"No, that was for the segment. It was all a part of her audience getting to know this year's couple."

Liam snapped his fingers. "The room at Constance's. That was on purpose."

"Actually, Constance did have separate rooms for you two. Apparently, Cynthia suggested rooming together. Did you two ever notice the other guys weren't around at the inn?"

Liam thought it over. Laughter crept out. "I can't believe we didn't notice that. We both sensed something was up with the other guys. We even went to Campy's to talk to them. I can't believe we didn't consider whether they were really staying at the inn."

"That's because you were so smitten with each other."

"I don't know about that." Liam leaned back. "On my side of things, maybe. Cynthia was focused on the tryouts."

"Or someone else participating in them." Nick smiled.

"The dinner! The dinner at the restaurant, that was all a part of it, too, right?"

"Yes. Josie's idea. Constance's execution."

"So Constance was in on it? Who else?"

"Oh, the wait staff at the restaurant. Joel. The hired competition of course."

"Apparently the pay wasn't enough for Greg or Miguel to stick through it."

Nick chuckled. "I guess not. I tried to give them as little work as possible. That's partly why I kept pairing you with Cynthia. The others would come back at the end of the day."

"I knew they weren't doing it!"

"They felt bad about the whole thing. Poor Greg got the worst of it. I think that was the first time he'd been on a boat."

Liam laughed.

"They're not as bad as you think," Nick said. "Let's see, who else? My entire crew, even if you didn't see them all. And everyone at dinner Thursday night. Which, by the way, I thought we were going to lose you because of the downed generator. That was a close call."

"We both got lucky on that. I didn't really want to have to drive back to look at that thing. I think part of me really wanted to go to dinner. We were the only ones invited to dinner, weren't we?"

"Yep."

"I feel like such an idiot for not seeing it."

"Well, sometimes it's hard to see reality. We all feel the fool sometime or another."

Liam stood and walked to the window overlooking the workers below. The plant hours aligned with fishing seasons more so than regular nine-to-five hours. Today the floor operated at half capacity, the employees cleaning machinery and taking inventory.

"Does Cynthia know?"

"She does now." Nick checked his watch. "Josie planned on telling her this morning while I drove here."

"I think you got the better part of the bargain."

"Well, that leads me to the second reason I came here." He opened the brown paper bag and revealed what was waiting inside. A vase of red and white peonies, nearly in full bloom, a small sample of what Cynthia had ordered at the flower shop on Josie's behalf.

"Is that—are those the flowers for Josie's event?"

"Yes. One of the arrangements."

"What are you going to do with those?"

"The question is, what are *you* going to do with them?"

Liam's head hurt enough from retracing his steps this week. "I'm not following."

"Josie had a main event, a big reveal at the end planned. These flowers were a part of it. Now that things have disintegrated as they have, we're stuck with a lot of flowers and no event."

"I'm still not seeing where I come in with all of this."

"Let me ask you something. And be honest with me."

"Why? You think I'm a good liar or something?" He smiled and sat back in the chair behind the desk. "Shoot."

"Do you have feelings for Cynthia… beyond friendship?"

"Of course I do. I told you that yesterday, but I don't see—"

Nick held up a hand. "You think she feels the same way about you?"

"I thought for a time there that she did. I mean, we…." It had been so electric, emotional, sensual. How could one person feel all that without the other feeling the same? "I'm not so sure now with everything that has gone down. It has only been a week, Nick. And in that time I managed to build up trust and throw it all away."

"Stop with the excuses. Throw out the lying. You were being lied to, too. You didn't know about the Valentine's scheming just like she didn't. That may make things a little more forgivable."

"I don't know." Liam shrugged. "I don't know if she'd even talk to me."

"Do you want to find out?"

"Sure, but—"

Nick stood, waving his hand once again to shut him up. He slid the bouquet across the desk, the red and pink flowers swaying in the vase.

"Then I have a plan."

TWENTY-NINE

Sunday, February 14

TO RUN OR not to run?

Cynthia hadn't set the alarm last night because she planned to spend her Sunday morning in a coma, sleeping off her feelings so she wouldn't have to deal with them. Her body and mind had other plans apparently, considering it was six AM and she was wide awake.

There was no stopping the motion of thoughts now. Running would expend energy, yes, but it wouldn't stop the thoughts. If anything, she'd lament over them too much and not pay attention to where she was running.

Instead, she showered and took her time getting ready. She listened to internet radio on her phone, the closest thing she could come to a house full of life. Otherwise the only noises ringing through the two stories were those of creaks and crackles when the heat kicked on and off, expanding and retracting the floorboards. After dinner with Jackie on Friday, the house never felt more desolate.

She sipped her coffee, reading the news on her tablet. A bird flew to the window, swooping away in time to avoid a collision and catch up with its friend.

She set the coffee mug on the table. Something wasn't right out there.

The town appeared normal for a Sunday—few cars on the road, a trawler bobbing in the cape, the lighthouse—

Cynthia gasped. Even though the sun lit the sky bright enough to drown out the stretch of light, the lighthouse was operating.

She checked the clock. 7:25 AM.

If something happened with the automatic settings, then Mr. Ludlow should've been there to manually stop the light. It wasn't like him to not be there. In the months she'd been running the stairs, the only time he missed his volunteer shift was the week he was ill.

She dialed Campy's on her cell phone. It rang until a recording played, reviewing the pub hours and weekday drink specials. Of course Joel wouldn't be there so early. Who else should she call?

There may not be a problem at all. But wouldn't others notice the lighthouse running? *Sunday in Maiden's Bay, Cynthia.* She was probably one of the few people up so early, other than Mr. Ludlow. Which was more reason to suspect the worst.

She flung out of her seat and grabbed the cream cableknit sweater hanging on the door hook. She didn't even bother to lock the front door. Her heart raced, and she took to the street, feet hitting the pavement in a run. She had run the route to the lighthouse countless times. So why did it feel lightyears away?

If something happened to him and no one else noticed the lighthouse, then he would've been suffering or passed out or who knows what for at least an hour. She crossed Pearl and ran past the dock.

She sped through the empty park, sprinted up the handful of steps to the red door, and pushed it open. She stared upward, catching her breath. "Hello? Mr. Ludlow? Wyatt?"

She ran up the stairs. Three-quarters of the way up, she slowed, her chest heaving and brow sweating. She cooled off, fanning the sweater. Cooler air hit her as she approached the gallery doorway.

Although the sun shone, the steady wind negated its warmth, and she closed the sweater beneath her crossed arms.

"Mister Ludlow?"

She didn't walk the entire circle, but sensed he wasn't outside. She hadn't even glanced inside. Hopefully he didn't get hurt trying to turn off the light or clean it. It would be hard to carry him down. She'd have to call for help, and she didn't have her cell. Just wasn't thinking straight.

She climbed the smaller set of stairs onto the landing, half-expecting to see Mr. Ludlow seated with his feet up against the wall. She shielded her eyes from the rotating light, waiting for it to pass to search for him.

The light was off. Rotation had ceased.

"What—what is this?" Thick bouquets of red and white peonies in glass vases sat on tall black plant stands, one in the middle of each facet of windows. The morning light danced off the glass prisms of the vases, speckling the glass room.

She touched a crimson petal, the aroma sweet and fresh. These were her arrangements. The ones she ordered for Josie.

She turned to the entranceway at the sound of feet up the stairs.

Through the brightness of light mixed with red and pink, she made out short hair and broad shoulders. Her eyes focused as he neared, catching his deep brown eyes.

Liam.

It all felt like a dream. "What are you doing here?"

"I knew you probably wouldn't talk to me on the phone. I thought maybe the tallest, brightest structure in Maiden's Bay might get your attention."

"You kept it running? What about Mister Ludlow?" She wrapped her sweater tighter. "Is he okay?"

"He's fine. He's the one who let me in. I couldn't have done it without his help."

First the lies, and now a ploy to get her to talk? For what? "What exactly is 'it'?"

"I wanted to apologize. Again. But with no excuses. I shouldn't have let the week go on the way it did. I should've been up front with you, and I'm sorry."

She put her hands on her hips. "I'm tired of lies and deceit."

"I know. I'm so very sorry. I shouldn't have agreed to any of it." His hands shook and eyes turned moist. He looked pitiful and remorseful and gorgeous all at once.

Cynthia closed her eyes and sighed. "Look, there was a lot going on behind both our backs that I've found out since then. Josie told me everything."

He nodded. "Nick told me."

"You know then, how we were pawns in a game."

"I wouldn't quite call it a game, but that doesn't change how it made me feel. I guess it's comforting our instincts were right."

"What do you mean?"

"That something was off. With everyone around us. And I do mean everyone. Can you believe Constance was in on it?"

Cynthia shook her head. That strong-headed elderly woman who looked so innocent at first glance. "I know. And everyone working that night at the restaurant. Did he tell you about the interview?"

"It was actually real, just not for the reasons we thought."

"They're terrible."

"The whole lot." He smirked. "But, when you look at it, was it really that bad?"

"That practically the whole town around us was lying to us? It's pretty bad. At first it was hard for me to believe Josie could have such influence on people. That woman gets an idea, and look out."

"She's formidable." He stuffed his hands in his pockets. "I meant more you and me. Was that so bad?"

Cynthia looked at the peonies, then down at her feet. "No." She looked at his face, but couldn't bear to look in those eyes. "That wasn't so bad."

He stepped closer. "Dare I say nice?"

She stepped back between two of the flower displays. "It was nice."

He took another step. "Do you think maybe it could be great even, if we let it?"

"Liam—"

"Just let yourself feel, Cynthia. I'm here, right in front of you. I've come all this way this morning. I'm putting myself out there because I think it's worth giving us a shot."

"Nick actually does want me to be greenhorn."

"I heard."

"Will you be okay with that?" She stood straighter and stepped closer to him, Liam pulling back. "Will you be okay in Oakside, or wherever you'd be on land, waiting for days—sometimes weeks—at a time for me? Knowing I'm out there in dangerous conditions, and you couldn't do anything to help me?"

"I could do something to help you." He grabbed her hands in his and stared at her straight on. "I'd support you. One hundred percent. I'd send you off with care packages of snacks and extra hats and gloves, and of course pictures of me." He smiled. "And I'd shower you with kisses when you'd return. I'd hold you as if I hadn't held you in years. Because I know what it's like not to have you in my life at all." He placed his hand on her cheek. "If you didn't go out there, you wouldn't be you. You wouldn't be the woman I've fallen for."

It was what she needed from him. Not the apology, not excuses. She needed to know he wasn't making her choose.

"If you tell me you felt nothing this week—if this has all been in my head and not real to you, then I'll go."

I did feel it. It's not all in your head. It's real. Her pulse pounded and heart throbbed.

"Cynthia?"

She grabbed his shirt, pulling him closer until her lips met his. He kissed back, hands holding her face. She breathed him in, tasting his lips, wrapping her hands around his solid shoulders to his back. He tugged lightly at her hair, exposing her neck, which he grazed with gentle wet kisses. The thrill sent goosebumps down her back.

Her knees buckled, and she stumbled back on the window.

Liam gently pulled away. "You okay?"

Don't stop. "Perfect," she said.

The passion in his eyes melted her like sand into glass. She yearned to taste his lips again. Was this it? Time enough to rethink what they were doing?

He leaned in and softly touched his mouth to hers, defying her insecurities. Even his simple kisses were heaven.

He stepped back, holding her hand and pulling her away from the window. "So, does that mean we can put the lies of the past week behind us? I promise. No more lies."

She swayed her head as if staring at a pendulum, weighing her feelings. "Maybe."

"Oh, come on." He stretched out his arms. "If these arrangements don't win you over, then I'm at a loss."

She smiled. "It helps when the lady picks them out, huh?"

"They're nice. I'll give you that." He leaned his forehead on hers. "But I'd rather look at you."

"Keep saying things like that, and I'll soon forget what lies you're talking about."

He chuckled. "Keep kissing me like that, and we won't be talking about anything."

Cynthia turned around and pulled his arms around her waist. He rested his chin on her shoulder.

She took a deep breath and closed her eyes. "If we're being completely open and honest, then I have a confession to make." She opened her eyes as the weight of Liam lightened on her shoulder.

"I'm listening."

"You said you received a call from a Maiden's Bay area code before the tryouts. That was me."

His arms loosened from her waist.

She turned around, and he stood, jaw agape. "I knew it!"

"I chickened out at the last second."

"Why didn't you tell me? On that first day at the inn?"

"You're kidding, right? Tell my fake-competitor-judge-turned-real-competitor roommate I almost asked him out?"

He nodded, grinning. "Fair enough. Come here." He held her, and she buried her face in his chest.

"There *is* one thing that bothers me," Cynthia said. She could feel his heart beneath his shirt, pounding in his chest.

"What's that?"

"That Josie was right in the end." Cynthia glanced up at him. "She's my friend and all, but it's so irritating when she gets her way all the time."

"I think I have something that may help with that, actually."

"Oh, really?"

"There's still one recording left for Josie's Valentine's special. It was supposed to be a live reveal of the truth about this week."

"Oh, no. I don't think I want to do another interview, especially if it means talking about us and admitting her ruse worked."

"I think you'll change your mind when you hear the plan."

He did have success with plans so far today. Plus would it be so bad to give Josie a taste of her own medicine?

Cynthia raised an eyebrow. "Go on."

THIRTY

"THANKS AGAIN TO both of you." Cynthia had Josie on speaker-phone, and Liam leaned in to hear. *"I wasn't sure after the way events unfolded if you'd participate in another segment, let alone a live one."*

"No problem." Liam's hand grazed Cynthia's as she fought to keep composure. She had seemed ecstatic when he told her the plan. Nick had it in the works for weeks, flying out Josie's mother and old college friends. It just so happened to fall in place with Liam and Cynthia's story not working out as planned.

They stood in Campy's Bar, the crowd of townsfolk gathered around but trying to stay quiet. "You know, I thought you'd have it at the television studio like before," he said.

"I was going to, but then we decided to include everyone—get the perspectives of Greg and Sean and the gang, Constance. There really were a lot of people in on it that helped."

"Well, we're here ready to go." Cynthia's grin grew.

"I'm almost there. Crossing Pearl as we speak."

"Okay, see you in a few." Cynthia quickly ended the call. "She's almost here!"

The attendees gasped and found their places. Carol and Robert leaned outside the door while Ben and Angela surveyed through the front windows. Angela held the pacifier in Annabel's mouth, keeping her complacent.

"Here we go, everyone quiet!" Nick's voice quivered.

The sound guy held out a boom microphone toward the door and gave a thumbs up to Nick. The room's silence held enough to hear Josie's footsteps up the outer deck stairs.

Josie opened the door. She let the door softly close behind her, confusion written on her face. "What's going on? Mom? Oh, my goodness! What are you doing here?"

She froze, as if her brain had to stop her body in order to process what was happening. "Why are you filming me right now?"

Nick stepped right in front of her, the boom guy adjusting the microphone to give him room. He took off his cap and straightened his hair with his hand.

"A man has to look presentable, after all," Ben said. Angela elbowed him, even while holding Annabel.

"Josie Morrison—"

"Nick, what's going—"

"Fourteen months ago you walked—crashed, really—into my life. It hasn't been the same since. And I never want it to go back." He lowered to one knee. "I know the past year has been crazy. I wouldn't want to go through life without all of it if it meant not being with you. Josie, will you marry me?"

He had no box to open. Instead he nodded to Ben, who held out the fishing rod so that the hook swayed in front of Josie.

She focused on the hook, hands over her mouth, the diamond ring spinning on the line.

"That was my idea," Carol whispered to Robert, loud enough for everyone to hear.

Josie carefully stopped the ring and cried. *"Yes.* Yes, I'll marry you!"

The store erupted in applause and cheers. Nick took the ring off the hook and slipped it on Josie's finger.

The group broke into chatter as the newly engaged made the rounds greeting the proposal guests.

The KSMV team wrapped up the live broadcast with a promise to post more on the event later. "This definitely will make for quite the show," one of the crew said. "Not to say you two wouldn't have been exciting."

"I think we've had enough excitement for one week." Liam caught Cynthia's glance and winked at her. The drama and excitement was worth it if it meant he could be with Cynthia.

Greg and Theo inched closer.

"Well, well, if it isn't the crew of liars." Liam smirked.

"Come on," Greg said. "It was for Nick and Josie. I don't just mean right now, either."

"We know," Cynthia said.

"Sean and Miguel couldn't be here, but they wanted you to know they're sorry," Theo said.

Liam wrapped his arm over Cynthia's shoulder. "Maybe we can go for a drink for real sometime."

"On your tab." Cynthia's eyes widened as she pointed.

"Fair enough." Greg and Theo shook their hands.

"Did I hear someone say tab?" Bartender Joel shuffled over to them. Mr. Ludlow joined him by his side.

"I see everything worked out," Mr. Ludlow said.

"With some luck, it did," said Liam. "Thank you."

"I was talking to her." He pointed to Cynthia, and she nudged Liam.

"I may have told him about you before you concocted your light-house scheme," she said.

Liam eyed Wyatt Ludlow. "You know, I thought it was a little too easy to convince you to let me up there and keep the light running." Something about the older generation in this town. They certainly had the smarts and youthful sly streak about them.

"That wasn't funny, by the way." Cynthia tapped Mr. Ludlow on the shoulder. "I thought you were injured, or even dead."

"Who me? No, my candle hasn't burned out yet." He winked, and Joel pulled at his arm. "Come on, let's leave the other lovebirds here be."

"Cynthia! Can you believe it?" Josie broke up the conversation and hugged Cynthia. Her ring dazzled in Cynthia's face, and Liam shook hands with Nick. "You were in on this, weren't you?"

"I sure was. Serves you right tricking us."

"Don't get used to it. It's addictive. And don't you think this means I'm not getting a closing piece on your Valentine's romance."

"Yeah, yeah," Cynthia said. "This is your day, though, so go enjoy it."

Josie hugged her briefly, then scanned the room. "I'd better go talk to my future mother-in-law!"

"Congratulations again," Liam said.

They were amongst a sea of celebration, but as Josie and Nick left, Liam was finally alone with Cynthia. She turned to him, and he hugged her.

"So, what now?"

"Oh, there's Constance." Cynthia pulled away from him to look. "Care to give her some heat about her trickery?"

Liam chuckled and looked behind him. Constance chatted with someone. The person turned, and Liam recognized the emotionally beaten man.

"She's talking with Gus. I don't believe it."

"I'm shocked," Cynthia said.

Liam's heart warmed watching the two talk. No hands were flailing or voices raised. He'd like to think he had something to do with her openness to it, but who knew with Constance? She was a strong and intelligent woman. She sure saw through Liam and Cynthia.

Gus caught his stare and came over. "There's something I wanted to talk to you about."

Liam touched his chest. "Me?"

"Yep. The whole week I'd been seeing how hard you worked out there for the tryouts."

"The whole tryout thing is a little complicated," Liam said. "Are you saying you were spying on me?"

He gave a hearty laugh. "Why do you think I sat at the bar all day? It's a good vantage point."

Liam opened his mouth but didn't know what to say.

Gus held up a hand. "Constance filled me in about your injury and what happened. Now, I know you're a manager over at the plant south of here, but I wondered if you'd ever fancy the idea of managing the dock."

"You mean here in Maiden's Bay?"

"I think it's about time I retire. I'd help train you, of course, but I'm sure you'd pick it up just fine. I know the Campbell boys would feel better knowing someone they trust is taking over."

"I'm—" *Speechless. Shocked.* He looked at Cynthia, who squeezed his hand tighter. It was the perfect opportunity. Outdoors on the water, but not on the water, and right here in Maiden's Bay. "I think I'm inclined to say yes."

Gus tapped his shoulder. "How about you come around later this week, and we'll talk logistics."

"Sounds great."

Gus headed back to Constance, who nodded to Liam with a smile.

"Liam, that's amazing!" Cynthia hugged him.

"I was itching to put my two weeks notice in tomorrow." He touched her arm, speaking directly. "I want you to know I'd meant to leave the plant for something better. I don't want me moving here to scare you. I know it's soon—"

She kissed his cheek. "I think it's wonderful."

God, he loved this woman. *Truly* loved her, with all her quirks, her drive, her heart. Her acceptance.

"Okay, you have a lot of explaining to do." A raven-haired woman scolded Cynthia. "We go a few days without communication, and now you have a boyfriend?"

"Putting it that way sounds like I should not talk to you more often." Cynthia laughed.

"That's not funny!"

"Elise, this is Liam. Liam, Elise."

"Nice to meet you." Liam had a lot to learn about Cynthia—friends, extended family, hobbies. It was exciting to know there were layers left to peel.

"How about lunch tomorrow?" Cynthia asked. "I'll gather up Josie if she can get away from Nick after all this, and we'll catch up."

"Perfect."

"Now, if you don't mind," Liam said, "I think it's time we spend some of Valentine's Day to ourselves." He'd wanted time with her since seeing her in the lighthouse. Heck, since seeing her in Bea's Bouquets.

Cynthia nodded. "What do you suggest?"

He led her out of Campy's Bait and Bar, out of the crowd's laughter and chit chat and into the quiet Sunday streets of Maiden's Bay.

He stopped her on the sidewalk and looked into her dazzling gray eyes. With as much seriousness as he could muster, he popped the question. "The Codfather?"

Cynthia rolled her eyes. He pulled her in and met her lips. Their laughter broke the kiss. "Maybe we can hire that violinist to play at our table for the whole dinner," he said.

Cynthia held his hand tight in hers. "And I'll be sure to wear my best hoodie."

"Should I even bother wearing a shirt?"

The sound of her laughter made for the best Valentine's Day ever.

EPILOGUE

NOTHING FELT BETTER than the warmth of the sun and salt of the air as Cynthia stood on the deck of *Harpeth Rose*. The summer salmon fishing was on the steady decline, but Nick said it'd be a good way to see how the crew functioned with their new greenhorn. Cynthia had never pushed herself harder, the physical labor intense. They had only been out for a week, but long enough to better understand the mental toll the lifestyle could take on people.

It wasn't enough to deter Cynthia. In fact, she knew as *Harpeth Rose* pulled up to the dock in Maiden's Bay that she had chosen the right career path.

Every crew member had a list of to-dos to complete before disembarking. The tasks were easy enough, but torturous knowing that Liam was near. She could almost feel his arms around her as she checked off her list. It would've been longer if they hadn't stopped at Oakside first to unload the catch. For a second she had wished Liam worked back at the plant, just to see him sooner.

She reported back to Ben upon completing her jobs, and he gave the go ahead to leave. Her feet hit the planks of the dock, and she ran past the other crew finishing up. She rushed headling into Campy's, shuffling through the racks to the back office. Nick was discussing something with Liam, but she didn't care. She burst in and attacked Liam with a hug, legs wrapped around his hips, and Liam exhaling with an *oomph*.

"Were you dismissed?" Nick asked.

"Yes, Captain." Cynthia goofily grinned, planting her feet back on the ground.

"I'll come back in a few." Nick tipped the brim of his ball cap and exited the office.

Cynthia kissed Liam over his cheeks, with a last one on his lips before lowering to stand.

"You know, not many men would find the smell of fish guts and all that a week on a boat encompasses very flattering."

She pulled away, smirking.

"I didn't say I was one of them. Come here."

He pulled her close, his broad chest pressed against hers. "I have to get out there you know, and finish paperwork with Nick."

"I know," she said. "Just one more minute alone." She sat in the chair, and Liam leaned on his desk. "Anything new I should know about?"

"Oh, you know, the usual. You officially have a new roommate. *Housemate* I guess is more the appropriate term."

"Hmm. Do I know this person?"

He walked behind the desk, leaning over her on the chair. "I believe you and your friends called him The Oakside Guy?"

"I heard he's handsome."

He kissed her on the lips, stopping the growing smile. The man made it hard to want to do anything else. He gave her a final kiss on the forehead before standing upright again.

She stood reluctantly. "I'd better head on back. It'll give me time to shower and rest up before our dinner at Jackie's tonight."

"Our what?" Liam squinted.

"Don't even joke. I told you about it like ten times. My mom is coming in from Spokane."

"I know, I know." He put up a hand. "I didn't forget. I'll be here about another hour or so."

"Great." She kissed him, expecting a peck but getting a heart-racing, blood-pumping, soft, wet kiss that curled the hair on the nape of her neck.

It was almost harder to leave Liam after that than when she left for the fishing trip. The taste of his mouth lingered as she walked, heading south along Pearl Avenue before turning left up the hill.

Bea hadn't made it to Nick's proposal, which meant Cynthia had to make a special trip to discuss her departure. Of course Bea expected it, but it still wasn't easy. She was like a mother figure—well, not a mother figure, but a quirky controlling aunt who helped out even if she didn't like to.

The front display of Bea's Bouquets showcased brilliant yellow lilies, with a cornsilk table cloth and bulkier green potted plants below. Cynthia finally stood on the other side of the glass. She was the one returning on *Harpeth Rose* while everyone else carried on about their day in town.

She was finally doing what she loved, while she was with the man she loved. It couldn't get any better.